TRICKS

RENAUD CAMUS

PREFACE BY ROLAND BARTHES
TRANSLATED & WITH A NOTE BY RICHARD HOWARD

ACE CHARTER BOOKS, NEW YORK

To Philippe St.,
without whom this book . . .

Published by arrangement with St. Martin's Press

ISBN: 0-441-82425-0

First Ace Charter Printing: September 1982
Published simultaneously in Canada

Manufactured in the United States of America

2 4 6 8 0 9 7 5 3 1

Cover photo taken at: The Ice Palace, N.Y.C.

CONTENTS

Figures of love, as my poetry desired them . . .
furtively encountered in the nights
when I was young

CAVAFY

PREFACE

Why have you agreed to write a preface to this book by Renaud Camus?

Because Renaud Camus is a writer, because his text belongs to literature, because he cannot say so himself, and because someone else, therefore, must say so in his place.

If it is literary, the text must show as much for itself.

It shows as much, or you can hear as much, from the first turn of phrase, from a certain way of saying "I," of conducting the narrative. But since this book seems to speak, and bluntly, about homosexuality, some readers may forget about literature.

Then for you, asserting the literary nature of a text is a way of taking it out of quarantine, sublimating or purifying it, giving it a kind of dignity which, according to you, sex doesn't have?

Not in the least. Literature is here to afford more pleasure, not more propriety.

Get on with it then, but make it short.

Homosexuality shocks less, but continues to be interesting; it is still at that stage of excitation where it provokes what might be called feats of discourse. Speaking of homosexuality permits those who "aren't" to show how open, liberal and modern they are; and those who "are" to bear witness, to assume responsibility, to militate. Everyone gets busy, in different ways, whipping it up.

Yet to proclaim yourself something is always to speak at the behest of a vengeful Other, to enter into his discourse, to argue with him, to seek from him a scrap of identity: "You are . . ." "Yes, I am . . ." Ultimately, the attribute is of no importance; what society will not tolerate is that I should be . . . *nothing*, or to be more exact, that the *something* that I am should be openly expressed as provisional, revocable, insignificant, inessential, in a word: irrelevant. Just say "I am," and you will be socially saved.

To reject the social injunction can be accomplished by means of that form of silence which consists in saying things *simply*. Speaking *simply* belongs to a higher art: writing. Take the spontaneous utterances, the spoken testimony then transcribed, as increasingly utilized by the press and by publishers. Whatever their "human" interest, something rings false in them (at least to my ears): perhaps, paradoxically, an excess of style (trying to sound "spontaneous," "lively," "spoken"). What happens, in fact, is a double impasse: the accurate transcription sounds made up; for it to seem true, it has to become a text, to pass through the cultural artifices of writing. Testimony runs away with itself, calling nature, men and justice to witness; the text goes slowly, silently, stubbornly—and arrives faster. Reality is fiction, writing is truth: such is the ruse of language.

Renaud Camus's *Tricks* are simple. This means that they speak homosexuality, but never speak about it: at no moment do they invoke it (that is simplicity: never to invoke, not to let Names into language—Names, the source of dispute, of arrogance and of moralizing).

Our period interprets a great deal, but Renaud Camus's narratives are neutral, they do not participate in the game of interpretation. They are surfaces without shadows, *without ulterior motives*. And once again, only writing allows this purity, this priority of utterance, unknown to speech, which is always a cunning tangle of concealed intentions. If it weren't for their extent and their subject, these *Tricks* might suggest haikus; for the haiku combines an asceticism of form (which cuts short the desire to interpret) and a hedonism so serene that all we can say about pleasure is that *it is there* (which is also the contrary of Interpretation).

Sexual practices are banal, impoverished, doomed to repetition, and this impoverishment is disproportionate to the wonder of the pleasure they afford. Now, since this wonder cannot be said (being of an ecstatic order), all that remains for language to do is to figure, or better still, to cipher, as economically as possible, a series of actions which, in any case, elude it. Erotic scenes must be described sparingly. The economy here is that of the sentence. The good writer is the one who utilizes the syntax so as to link several actions within the briefest linguistic space (we find, in Sade, a whole art of subordinate clauses); the sentence's function is somehow to scour the carnal operation of its tediums and its efforts, of its noises and its adventitious thoughts. In this regard, the final scenes of the various *Tricks* remain entirely within the domain of *writing*.

But what I like best of all in *Tricks* are the preparations: the cruising, the alert, the signals, the approach, the conversation, the departure for the bedroom, the household order (or disorder) of the place. Realism finds a new site; it is not the *love scene* which is realistic (or at least its realism is not pertinent), it is the *social scene*. Two young men who do not know each other but know that they are about to become partners in a specific act, risk between them that fragment of language to which they are compelled by the trajectory which they must cover together in order to reach their goal. The *trick* then abandons pornography (before having really approached it) and joins the novel. The suspense (for these *Tricks*, I believe, will be read eagerly) affects not behavior (which is anticipated, to say the least) but the characters: who are they? how do they differ from each other? What delights me, in *Tricks*, is this juxtaposition: the scenes, certainly, are anything but chaste, yet the remarks are just that: they say *sotto voce* that the real object of such modesty is not the Thing (*"La Chose, toujours la Chose,"* Charcot used to say, as quoted by Freud), but the person. It is this *passage* from sex to discourse that I find so successfully achieved in *Tricks*.

This is a form of subtlety quite unknown to the pornographic product, which plays on desires, not on fantasies. For what excites fantasy is not only sex, it is sex plus "the soul." Impossible to account for falling in love or even for infatuations, simple attractions or Wertherian raptures, without admitting that what is sought in the other is something we shall call, for lack of a better word, and at the cost of great ambiguity, the person. To the person is attached a kind of homing device that causes this particular image, among thousands of others, to seek out and capture me. Bodies can be classified into a finite number of types ("That's just my type"), but the person is absolutely individual. Renaud Camus's *Tricks* always begin with an encounter with the longed-for type (perfectly encoded; the type could figure in a catalogue or in a page of personal want-ads); but once language appears, the type is transformed into a person, and the relation becomes inimitable, whatever the banality of the first remarks. The person is gradually revealed, and lightly, without psychologizing, in clothing, in discourse, in accent, in setting, in what might be called the individual's "domesticity," which transcends his anatomy yet over which he has control. All of which gradually enriches or retards desire. The *trick* is therefore homogeneous to the amorous progression; it is a virtual love, deliberately stopped short on each side, by contract; a submission to the cultural code which identifies cruising with Don Juanism.

The *Tricks* repeat themselves; the subject is on a treadmill. Repetition is an ambiguous form; sometimes it denotes failure, impotence; sometimes it can be read as an aspiration, the stubborn movement of a quest which is not to be discouraged; we might very well take the cruising narrative as the metaphor of a mystical experience (perhaps this has even been done; for in literature everything exists: the problem is to know *where*). Neither one of these interpretations, apparently, suits *Tricks*: neither alienation nor sublimation; yet something like the methodical conquest of happiness (specifically designated, carefully boundaried: discontinuous). The flesh is not sad (but it is quite an art to convey as much).

Renaud Camus's *Tricks* have an inimitable tone. It derives from the fact that the writing here initiates an ethic of dialogue. This ethic is that of good will, which is surely the virtue most contrary to the amorous pursuit, and hence the rarest. Whereas ordinarily a kind of harpy presides over the erotic contract, leaving each party within a chilly solitude, here it is the goddess Eunoia, the Eumenid, the Kindly One, who accompanies the two partners; certainly, literally speaking, it must be very agreeable to be "tricked" by Renaud Camus, even if his companions do not always seem aware of this privilege (but we, the readers, are the third ear in these dialogues: thanks to us, this bit of good will has not been given in vain). Moreover this goddess has her retinue: politeness, kindness, humor, generous impulse, like the one which seizes the narrator (while tricking with an American) and causes his wits to wander so amiably with regard to the author of this preface.

Trick—the encounter which takes place only once: more than cruising, less than love: an intensity, which passes without regret. Consequently, for me, *Trick* becomes the metaphor for many adventures which are not sexual; the encounter of a glance, a gaze, an idea, an image, ephemeral and forceful association, which consents to dissolve so lightly, a faithless benevolence: a way of not getting stuck in desire, though without evading it; all in all, a kind of wisdom.

Roland Barthes

FOREWORD

THIS IS NOT a pornographic book. Nor a commercial exploitation of sex, nor an attempt to titillate the reader: failures and demi-fiascos, contingencies and absurdities are reported equally with those pleasures most thoroughly shared. No prowess is registered here.

This is not an erotic book. The narrator's art, if there is an art, does not consist in an effort to make the narrative more poetic, more cultural, more dignified, or, consequently, more socially acceptable. No estheticism.

This is not a scientific book, in any case, not even a sociological document. The episodes reported owe their arrangement only to chance, or to the most subjective determination.

This book attempts to utter sexuality, in this instance *homosexuality,* as if the battle were already won and the problems which such a project raises already solved: *calmly.* Or, as the writer Duvert would say: *innocently.*

*

This book is not—is anything but—a panorama of homosexual life. It would be a mistake to extend its application. Illustrated here is merely a particular aspect of a specific existence. If a certain image appears, nonetheless, through these encounters—the image of a certain kind of life, it is that of no more than a minority of homosexuals. The majority, most likely, frequent neither bars nor baths, neither parks nor "specialized" movie houses. Many meet only accidentally, as the occasion arises, recognizing each other wherever they happen to be. Some live as couples, according to a scheme which is not specifically homosexual. Others refuse to grant their tastes expression and satisfaction. Still others, and doubtless they are even today the majority, are unaware of such tastes because they live in such circumstances, in such circles, that their desires are not only for themselves inadmissible, but inconceivable, unspeakable. They possess no discourse of accommodation with which assume such desires and could change lives only by changing words.

*

This is not the chronicle of a life during a given period: there is no question here of work, friendships, love, intellectual interests, or only marginally, in the idle course of conversation.

This is not even the chronicle of a sexual life in its entirety.

A great deal happens that is *less* than a trick: contacts, inconclusive cruising, complete fiascos. Such episodes are not in question here. For the trick to exist, something must emerge; specifically: come, as Sade would say. To this degree, and to this degree alone, these chapters are a list of *successes*. It will be seen, however, if they are read, that there is not always much to boast about in them.

Furthermore, there is a good deal that is *more* than a trick: passing fancies, sexual friendships and camaraderies, brief and extended affairs, marriage. The trick then constitutes the minimal degree of relationship in this domain. It is to be understood that such categories are open, and that we can shift from one to another; but when the narrative devoted to him was written, or envisaged, the eponym was as yet only a trick.

*

The word itself has nothing pejorative in it, of course. And if one or another of the tricks collected here might have inspired, or experienced, a certain amount of irritation on the occasion, almost all were the object of much affection, sometimes of more, and of gratitude.

*

A trick must be unknown, or almost so. Only first encounters are related here. This is why each *trick* presents itself from the start as a *narrative*.

*

It is hardly necessary to say that names, and everything which might, by identifying persons, infringe upon the dominant morality or the law, have been changed. But an effort has been made to preserve the connotations of these various elements.

*

Exhibitionism is an obvious charge. The word implies the abusive revelation of what, by its nature, should remain hidden. But why is sex accorded this special status, except by the obsession of twenty centuries? Which is to grant it too much importance. Sex has its joys, certainly, which are among the finest: but none which deserves to make it the secret *par excellence*. If this book helps to make its subject banal *as subject*, it will not have been written in vain. Once we know where the obsessions are, then we can talk about something else.

I should hope that at least there will be no question, with regard to this book, of immorality, or of amorality. Neither the book nor the phenomena it relates, with a few exceptions (symptoms of egoism, indifference, vanity, culpable alienation), offend what I persist in calling, despite the present fashions, *morality*. It is precisely a *moral* rage that is inspired in me by those who persist in repressing sex.

*

Perhaps—as I hope—several paragraphs of this foreword, however necessary in France, are irrelevant to the American reader. At least they will remind him that these narratives by a Frenchman, however factual and without commentary, derive from and attest to—even when they describe, as in the final chapters, episodes which occurred in the States—a social, intellectual and moral context somewhat different from his own. Homosexuality, before having a (very hypothetical) *nature*, has a history and, of course, a geography; or in the words of three decades ago, is an *experience* before being an *essence*.

Renaud Camus

Paris, December 16, 1978

❧ I ❧

WALTHÈRE DUMAS

Friday, March 3, 1978

It was nearly two in the morning, the *Manhattan* was about to close. I had already collected my things at the coat-check and I was looking for a quieter place to put on my sweater and leather jacket. He was sitting on a bench upstairs, that is, on the main floor. Apparently he had been there a long time; in any case, I don't remember having seen him downstairs. (Yes, I do.)

It was his wrists and hands that excited me right away: covered with silky black hairs, even on the fingers. His hair was short; he had a very thick moustache, a slightly yellowish complexion, and he seemed to squint a little. He was wearing beige corduroys, a greenish beige herringbone shirt, a V-necked sweater that was also beige, and a black or very dark brown windbreaker.

I put on my clothes beside him, then I leaned over the rail, as if I were waiting for someone downstairs. Our elbows were touching. He didn't move away, but he wasn't looking at me, or at least I couldn't tell if he was, and then he yawned. The lights were turned on, everyone was leaving. He stood up, he went out. I followed him. He turned right into the Rue des Anglais, and so did I, behind him, though my previous intention had been to take a turn around the Square Jean-XXIII. He was walking slowly, and I slower still. When he reached the Boulevard Saint-Germain, he stopped and turned around, but not toward me; he remained motionless at the corner, looking toward the bar we had both just left. I took a few steps toward the Rue Saint-Jacques and I stopped too, opposite a bench on which I put one foot. Slowly, as if he were waiting for someone or something, he started back toward the door of the *Manhattan*, so that I couldn't see him any more. A

1

fairly good-looking guy, a little too thin, with whom I had once gone to bed and whose name I've forgotten—he works in fashion, I think, and often goes to Milan—came over to speak to me:

"What would the *Manhattan* be without you?"

"Oh, it's not that bad. I don't go there every night. I haven't set foot in the place for almost a week."

"What'd you think of the thing at the *Palace* the other night?"

"Not bad. In fact I liked it a lot. Except for Grace Jones, the usual disaster."

"You're telling me! She managed to turn the whole place against her in five minutes. Of course she was completely wrecked, but that's no excuse for fucking over the public like that."

"I saw her last New Year's Eve in New York, at *Studio 54*, and she was a monumental flop. No one clapped, people were hissing all over the place."

Meanwhile the other one had come back to the corner, but except for a quick glance, he wasn't paying any attention to me. I wondered what to do. X, the designer, seemed to be cruising me; he wasn't bad, I didn't feel like going home alone and he seemed a sure thing. The other one, not at all. What made me take a chance was a hostile remark of X's that pissed me off:

"It's funny, you're a writer but you spend all your time in these dumb places."

"What's that got to do with it?"

And I went over to the stranger. By then he had crossed the Rue des Anglais and stopped on the boulevard sidewalk, toward the Place Maubert. Two or three yards away from him, a boy whom I had vaguely cruised earlier, without any encouragement from him, suddenly spoke to me:

"We danced together one night."

"We did—when was that?"

"One Wednesday."

"That's right, I remember."

But I went on toward the stranger. This time his eyes didn't avoid mine, he even smiled. So I went up to him:

"Funny, leaving that way."

"What way?"

"Leaving the *Manhattan*. Before, people used to stand in the street for a while, in front of the door; now they scatter all around. No one really leaves. They come back, everyone makes a few last attempts, people stare at each other—I think it's funny . . . You look like you're falling asleep on your feet."

"I haven't slept much in the last two weeks."

"Living it up?"

"No. It was too hot."

"The tropics?"

"Yeah."

"Where in the tropics?"

"Equatorial Africa."

"Where in Equatorial Africa?"

"Nigeria."

"Where in Nigeria?"

"Lagos."

"I see."

"What are you doing?"

"When?"

"Now."

"I don't know."

"It all depends?"

I laugh.

"Exactly."

"You want to come home with me?"

"Sure."

He laughs.

"We could go to this maid's room a friend of mine lets me use. But it's not very inspiring. We can't go to my place."

"No, I'd rather go to my place."

"So would I."

"Do you have a car?"

"No, I was going to bring my bike, but I walked. Where do you live?"

"Dupleix. We'll take a taxi."

3

"OK."

We walk toward the taxi stand, at the foot of the statue in the Place Maubert. I discover his name is Walthère, t-h-è-r-e- I'm humming.

"*You're* in a good mood . . ."

"More than good."

"What about?"

"That we're going to the Fifteenth Arrondissement."

"Yes, the Fifteenth is nice."

Several people are waiting for taxis ahead of us, including the fashion designer, who leaves with a smile. The drivers ask everyone where they're going, and turn most of us down:

"Oh no, not the Trocadéro, no I'm going toward Vincennes, I'm off duty now." We agree that it's a pain in the ass. Moreover, Walthère isn't one for smiling, on the whole. Once we get a cab, he doesn't open his mouth the whole way. He directs the driver very carefully, and we pull up in front of a huge modern apartment house with curving balconies, behind the Front de Seine. All he has is a hundred-franc note, no change, so I pay for the cab, after which, despite my protests, he sticks a few coins in my pocket:

"It's not enough, anyway."

According to the plate over the bell, his name is Walthère Dumas.

He lives in a studio, but a very big one. One whole wall is windows opening, as I would see in the morning, onto a long and quite wide balcony. Very little furniture, modern. Nothing actively ugly. Hanging on the wall, a piece of weaving, probably Indian, and a little primitive painting of a Latin American village with an enormous white baroque church under a uniformly blue sky.

There's also a kitchen, not too small, a bathroom—very comfortable, very bare, and an enormous closet, almost a room.

"You want something to drink?"

"Just some water, or a Perrier. Yes."

"Tonic? Coke?"

"Tonic would be fine."

"With some gin?"

"No thanks, nothing."

"You don't smoke, you don't drink—"

"Yes I do. Sometimes. May I take the liberty of removing my shoes?"

"Of course. You like music?"

"Yes."

"Classical?"

"Fine."

"What?"

"I don't know. You choose."

"I have mostly Requiems."

"Oh no, no Requiems, if you can help it."

"The Lully *Te Deum?*"

"Sure. Fine."

"You know it?"

"No, not especially, but I'd guess it's a lot like the rest of his work."

"I wouldn't know, it's the only thing by him I've ever heard."

"What's this thing with Requiems?"

"I decided to get into opera. So I thought this would be a good way to start."

"Funny place to start . . ."

I sit cross-legged on the bed. He comes over and lies down beside me. We kiss, on the neck, then on the mouth. I run my hand under his shirt. He's a little less hairy than his wrists might suggest, but still pretty much so. I undo his sleeve buttons in order to caress his forearms, which are splendid. We both get erections. We're lying against each other. His shirt doesn't unbutton all the way down the front, he can only take it off over his head, but I've pushed it up enough to lick his chest. He takes off my shirt. When

5

the record is over, we're both completely naked. His legs and especially his ass are covered with an incredible mat of hair, long and black, that gets me wildly excited.

"I'm going to put on something I really like."

"What's that?"

"You'll see. It's electronic."

As he changes the record, I can see his completely erect cock right beside the amplifier. He has turned out all the lamps, with my consent, but arranged a lot of little construction lanterns around the room, about a dozen in all.

"It looks like a racetrack."

"Or a Christmas tree."

So now we're naked, stretched out together, me on top of him, my hands under his buttocks, caressing them and his thighs. We kiss each other, but quite superficially (nothing comparable to David the day before yesterday). My obsession is to lick his buttocks, to thrust my face between them and to stick my tongue as deep in there as I can. He lets me do what I want, but without any special enthusiasm. Yet he offers no resistance. Once more, kissing him, I thrust my cock under his balls and gradually raise his legs. (The other morning, David: "I see what you're up to, you're about as subtle as a sledge hammer." "I'm not doing a thing!" "Too bad.") A first attempt to put my cock inside him, with no more help than the saliva left there a moment before, gets nowhere. I put on more with my hand, also on my cock. Then I manage to get halfway in, but he winces. I pull back out, and he winces even more. His bent legs against my chest, my forearms under his back, my hands behind his neck, I have my head down against his balls, deep in the incredible forest of hair at his crotch. This seems to excite him, and me as well, so much so that I decide to try fucking him again. Another attempt succeeds a little better, but judging from his expression, he still seems to be in pain. I withdraw and stretch out beside him. We kiss a little while, arms around each other's shoulders, side by side. He plays with himself. So do I. But since I don't get much out of that, I put some saliva in my ass this time, straddle him, and stick his cock, which isn't so

6

big, up my ass without much difficulty. With one hand, I caress his thighs or press his buttocks against me, and with the other I play with myself. Leaning forward, I kiss his neck. This position excites me a lot. I come on his belly. He doesn't seem to want to fuck me any more. I stretch out beside him again. He plays with himself. I have one arm under his back, and with one hand I caress his thighs, his balls. He comes just when one of my fingers is against his asshole.

He puts on another record, but asks me if I want to go to sleep.

"Yes, I'd like to; that's nice of you—I don't have the energy to get up and go home."

"No, of course not, that's not what I meant."

I caress him a little, but he barely responds, and we fall asleep practically without touching, each of us on his own side of the bed.

When I wake up, his eyes are wide open.

"I can't sleep any more. I'd like some music. Do you mind?"

"No. What time is it?"

"Ten o'clock."

"Oh, that late?"

The Mozart *Requiem*.

"Which recording is that?"

"I don't know. Is there more than one?"

"Yes. Almost everyone has Karajan's."

Which is what it was.

We lie together for a minute, but I'm a little restless. My advances get nowhere.

"Want some tea?"

"Yes, thanks."

He gets up. As do I, and put on my shirt.

"Why are you getting dressed?"

"I don't know. It's time to, isn't it?"

He has pulled on a soccer shirt with a big number on the front and back, and white socks with colored stripes at the top, which reach to his knees; this way, all I see of his body are his muscular thighs, tanned, and hairy, and his ass. We have our breakfast sitting opposite each other at a big table.

"What do you do?"

"I write."

"What?"

"Novels."

"What's your name?"

"Camus."

"You can see there aren't any books here. They wear me out . . . Have you been doing it long?"

"The first one was published about three years ago . . ."

"Do you make a living from it?"

"If you can call it a living."

"What do *you* call it?"

"A pittance."

"How old are you?"

"Thirty-one. I'm a little tired of this bohemian kind of life. After thirty, you know . . ."

"But couldn't you write things that would make you some money?"

"I don't know. Maybe. I've never tried."

"You should. What do I know? Anyway, I could never live like that. I've gotten used to certain things."

"What do *you* do?"

"I'm a corporate lawyer."

"Yeah? I'm a lawyer too—I mean, I studied law."

"You got your degree?"

"Two, in fact."

"In what?"

"Oh, odd things, whatever seemed least boring to me at the time, just to get the degree—History of Law, Political Science."

"I went to the Institute of Political Studies, too."

"So did I. How old are you?"

"Twenty-nine. What was your field?"

"I began in Political Science but I wasn't any good in economics. I had to change. So then I took the gut subject, I don't remember what it was called."

"International Relations?"

"No."

"Social Studies?"

"Yes, that's it."

He gets two telephone calls. The first one is a girl, to whom he talks about his trip to Lagos. Interesting enough professionally, but the climate is impossible. The water and electricity go off four hours a day. The traffic is crazy, the main roads have fallen to pieces, most of them are dirt roads anyway, you know, the cars and trucks are all wrecks put together with string and chewing gum, rattling around in all directions. It takes six hours to get from the airport. But he was lucky, and it took him only four and a half. Kano, oh yes, Kano is much better. She wants to go to the movies with him, but he doesn't feel like it, he hasn't gone to the movies for over a month, he doesn't feel like movies these days. Tomorrow they'll have lunch together, out in the country with some friends.

Then someone he was supposed to go out with the night before. But his dinner lasted longer than expected, he had decided it was too late to call. Yes, he went to the *Manhattan,* yes, yes, he had a good time, thanks a lot, yes, still here, exactly, and so what did you do last night? When are we going to begin our exercises? At the *Samurai,* yes, or at the *Porte Maillot.* Yes, it's expensive, but they all are. He saw Alain and Tony last night, they go to the *Vitatop,* in Montparnasse (Tony? *My* Tony? He was at the *Manhattan* last night, as a matter of fact, and there can't be so many Tony's in circulation. And is Alain that very good-looking boy I had noticed, the one who was talking to him later? Does Tony go to the *Vitatop?* But I say nothing.) No, he doesn't know what he's going to do today, nothing at all, lie around the house, probably. In any case, he'll call back tonight, around seven.

He's lying on his bed, still wearing the same things. I suck his cock while he's talking on the phone, but he barely gets hard. Later he's on his back, his arms behind his head, and he's smoking. I caress him.

9

"I turn you on, huh?"

I laugh at this and answer:

"I guess *so!*"

"Funny . . ."

A moment of silence. Then:

"What are you thinking about?"

"About that phrase you used just now—'I turn you on?' "

"Something strange about it?"

"No, just a little surprising."

"Probably says a lot about me, doesn't it?"

"Oh, plenty of other things say a lot about you. Tell me about this operatic interest of yours."

"Oh, I have a friend who knows all about opera. I just like the noise it makes (he has spoken of music several times now as *noise*). I got interested. So I decided to start with what was easiest—with things I like. But I haven't really gotten into it yet. I bought this set-up, which is pretty good, and a few records, but that's all, up to now. You know, I'm just starting. It's like everything else. Before, I didn't have any kind of life. I've only been really alive for a little more than a year . . . Do you go to the *Manhattan* a lot?"

"On and off. But these days, yeah, I go there quite a lot. Do you?"

"Oh, maybe every weekend. It's new. A friend took me there a month ago. I'd never gone to places like that in France."

"But abroad?"

"Yes, in Costa Rica, in Colombia . . . but they were just bars."

"What kind of company do you work for?"

"Engineering. Why? Are you interested?"

"Yes, of course."

"Because they happen to be recruiting right now."

"No, that's not what I meant. Besides, I know less law than a first-year student."

"Oh, that doesn't matter. I didn't know anything either when I started. Look, I studied international relations, and all I handle now is labor contracts."

"What's the Métro stop nearest here?"

"Dupleix, or Charles-Michels."

"Right. Charles-Michels is good for me, I don't have to transfer."

"You know where it is?"

"No, but I'll find it."

"I'll go out with you. I have some shopping to do. You want to come with me?"

"No, I don't like markets—they're too picturesque."

"Not this one."

Since he's suggested I wait for him and still hasn't moved, I stay where I am, lying stretched out beside him. He smokes, then he says:

"God, this is just what I like: nothing to do, some good noise . . ."

I look at the painting over the bed, the South American village.

"Do you like that?"

"I like the place it represents. It looks like a nice place. Is it in Colombia?"

"No, Honduras. It's exactly like it looks. There's no road. You have to walk three hours to get there. The painter lives there, in that village. An old guy, amazing . . . I met him there. He's the one who sold me the picture."

"Is it really as white as that?"

"Yes. The only difference is that the women don't wear Indian costumes so much any more."

"Were you in Latin America for a long time?"

"A year and a half."

"And in Honduras?"

"A year, being sort of a technical adviser."

"It's very poor there, isn't it?"

"Yes, the poorest country in America, after Haiti."

He gets dressed, putting on the same clothes he was wearing the night before. No doubt he plans to change later, after his bath. We leave together. Good weather. An old tiny Fiat 500, rusty and dented, with diplomatic plates, is parked in front of an annex building of some international organization. He looks at it pityingly:

"UNESCO doesn't pay so well, it seems."

11

"I almost worked for them, one time, for their French publication."

"Where are you from?"

"Chamalières."

He laughs.

We're at the Métro entrance. It's noon, a Saturday.

"Thanks for your hospitality, Monsieur."

"See you later."

He crosses the street, heading toward the market.

[*Seen again several times, but for five minutes, and always by accident. I interest him, he says, but not for the reasons which make him interesting to me. He'd like to have* discussions *with me. He gave me his telephone number. One night, when I called him, he was obviously making love. He declined the offer of my telephone number ("I know I won't use it, that's how I am"), but urged me to telephone him again, which I won't do.*]

❧ II ❧
PHILIPPE OF THE COMMANDOS

Saturday, March 4, 1978

At the *Manhattan* around midnight on a Saturday; in other words, in a crowd so dense you can barely move; I was standing upstairs, looking down, cruising someone, I think, but without conviction, and suddenly I saw this boy staring at me, tall, brown hair, a moustache, wearing a black corduroy shirt and black jeans. His face, like his body, was too thin for my usual tastes, and his chin bore an unfortunate family resemblance to those of certain kings of Spain, Philip III or Alphonse XIII. But his shirtsleeves, rolled up to his elbows, revealed forearms that were muscular and very hairy, as was his chest, judging from what his wide-open collar allowed

12

me to see. As a matter of fact, I had trouble looking at him because he didn't take his eyes off me.

Walthère from the night before, whom I hadn't seen until then, came over to talk to me, and described his day. After two or three minutes of conversation, I sat down facing him on a kind of ledge jutting out from the wall, where there was room enough for two, though just barely. The boy in black was sitting opposite me, beside Walthère, both leaning back against a partition that forms a little artificial corridor there. Hearing and talking in this dense crowd became increasingly difficult because of the distance, a yard or two between Walthère and me. The boy in black kept staring at me, and so insistently, though shyly too, that I couldn't let my eyes catch his without immediately having to smile at him or say something. Moreover we exchanged a friendly nod. Then he said something to me which I couldn't make out at all. I imagined he wanted to sit with me, on the back of an upholstered bench which looks solid enough, but which happens to be quite soft, so that once you set your backside on it, you collapse onto the people who happen to be sitting on the bench itself. So I said to him, and this was my first sentence:

"I don't think that's a very good idea."

As it happened, he was telling me that he was going downstairs, and suggesting that I join him there. When I managed to reconstruct what he had said, he was already far away. I decided he was a foreigner.

Walthère was still there which I found a little surprising, and he even asked me if that was all right. But now that we had stopped talking I thought I'd go downstairs and see what had become of the boy in black, when he reappeared, after an absence of about three minutes. I explained the misunderstanding that had just occurred. He spoke French like a Frenchman, though with a regional accent I couldn't identify. He wanted to know if I was a Parisian.

"Uh-huh. At least I've lived in Paris a long time. And you?"

"Clermont-Ferrand."

"I don't believe it. So am I!"

"Really?"

13

"Well, from Chamalières, to be exact."

"I know—where Giscard comes from."

"Right! He's simplified life for me a hell of a lot. Because believe me, before that, no one had ever heard of Chamalières. You always had to explain—how do you spell it? There was no end to it. But now, everyone knows. . . . You live in Paris now, or are you here on vacation?"

"No, I'm here for a couple of days. I'm at the base at Aulnat. Know where that is?"

"Sure. You're in the air force?"

"Right, cargo planes. I had two days to spend so I decided to try Paris. It's the first time I've ever been here. This bar was one fucking hard place to find, believe me. Someone told me it was near the Boulevard Saint-Michel, so I did the whole fucking boulevard. I asked everyone. No one ever heard of it. Finally some guy told me it's actually nearer the Boulevard Saint-Germain. But, hell, I'd already walked . . . God only knows."

Between one sentence and the next he leaned toward me and kissed me on the mouth, very gently and timidly. I responded more eagerly after having caressed his forearms, his chest, and discovering, once I slid a finger between two buttons of his shirt, that his belly was as hairy as his pectorals, and very hard.

"You know where Saint-Rambaud is?"

"Saint-Rambaud . . . Wait a minute. That's near Lezoux, isn't it?"

"Right, well, near—about fifteen kilometers."

"A village on top of a hill?"

"No, that's not it. It's down on the plain, near Pont-de-Dôre. You know Pont-de-Dôre?"

"Yes, sure. I'm mixing it up with Beauregard-l'Evêque, for some reason: you know the place I mean, a pretty little village to the left of the main road between Pont-de-Château and Lezoux."

"No, never heard of it, even though I went to school in Lezoux."

Before his military service, he worked for a year in Thiers, at the wire mill:

14

"Ever heard of it?"

"I know Thiers, of course, but not the wire mill."

"No, lots of people don't. It's not on the main road."

He was to be discharged in a month, and planned to get his old job back:

"My buddies tell me they've hired a lot of people since I left. That's a good sign. It means business is good. They'll take me back too. At least that's what I think."

"You want to look around downstairs?"

"Oh sure, if you want to."

We went downstairs, pushing our way through the crowd as best we could, and danced a little, five minutes, maybe less, facing each other. He had the impression that I knew everybody and he found it was hard to breathe.

"Want to go back upstairs?"

"Sure, at least it can't be this hot up there."

"Wait, I'll get my things at the coat-check, because later it's a mob scene, people line up after one-thirty."

We stopped for a moment at the turn of the stairs, where it was relatively cool. I discovered he had no room, no luggage either. He had arrived by train this morning, about eleven, at the Gare de Lyon:

"I wanted to take a bus, but I didn't know where they went, so I walked. The first thing I came to was the Place de la Bastille. And then I saw the cathedral, a lot higher than the one in Clermont, huh?"

After that, he started looking for the *Manhattan* in the middle of the afternoon, because you never know. He managed to find it a little after ten. Of course no one was there.

"And then, it was getting later, still no one, you know, maybe ten guys, fifteen, and since I knew the place was closing at two, I thought I was out of luck, just today no one would be here, unless they were coming around one, one-thirty. I asked at the bar if there was usually more of a crowd."

"They must have had a good laugh at that."

"No, not especially. They explained that people came around eleven-thirty, twelve, and that's what happened, everyone got here at the same time."

"Well, if you want to see people, you came to the right place."

"All right, but enough is enough, huh?"

"You want to leave?"

"Sure, if you do."

He put on a wool jacket, a thick one with big checks. I got my windbreaker, and we left. We turned down the Boulevard Saint-Germain and walked west.

"Funny, this summer, on the Coast, it worked just the same way as here. Real fast. I was at Roquebrune. You know, there's a base there. But I could get off almost every night. The Coast, I really know my way around; Cannes, Antibes, Nice . . . In Cannes there's a lot of guys, huh?"

"You know, I was down there too, just then, in August, near Antibes. But we went over to Cannes all the time. We could have run into each other."

"Sure. That would've been great, huh?"

"But I don't remember seeing a base at Roquebrune. Where could they find room for one in such a little place? Down below— or up on the cliff?"

"No, there's no airfield at Roquebrune, just barracks—both places, up on top, and down below too. One day I was coming back from Cannes. There was this guy in a car, about twenty-five or thirty, pulls up beside me, asks me if I'm going toward Nice. Yes. I get in with him, I could tell right away you know, he was just like me, I mean, like us, well, and that he wanted it, and so did I. I liked the way he looked. I saw him a few times more, during the summer. In fact, I think he's the one who told me about the *Manhattan,* and isn't there something on the Avenue Saint-Anne?"

"Yes, the Rue Saint-Anne, that's on the other side of the Seine. There are a couple of places over there, but I like the *Manhattan* better; you would too, probably. Listen, there's a slight technical problem. We can't go to my apartment. There's someone there. I have use of a kind of maid's room. We can go there, but it's not very comfortable."

"Whatever you say."

"Oh, look, I'd be very pleased to take you to my attic. But it's up to you."

"Hell, what do I care about the room!"

On the way I showed him the *Apollinaire*, the *Deux Magots*, the *Flore*.

"You're in the air force. Do you fly?"

"No, not much, I'm really in the commandos. I flew a little at the start; in Nîmes. We did some parachute jumping and all that, but not now. Not any more. My brother did his military service in the air force too and he didn't fly once. Not once. He was real pissed off . . ."

"What's it feel like when you jump? I mean right at the start, when you leave the plane. Do you really feel you're falling free?"

"The first time's all right. You're not afraid then, you don't know what's happening. It's after, for me. The second time was when I started to get scared."

"I'd be scared the first time, I'm sure of that. Just the thought of jumping out of a plane . . ."

"Yeah, but the second time, you know everything that could happen to you. You see how you could easily break a leg, or who knows what . . ."

"You don't jump any more?"

"No, now I don't do anything. I'm waiting for my discharge. I'm sick of the army. You don't know how sick I am."

"Don't you have any friends?"

"Sure I have friends. They're sick of it too. Anyway, it's over soon."

We walked through the lobby of the building in the Rue Saint-Simon, the courtyard, and started to climb the service stairs.

"I'm sorry, it's always like this with maid's rooms. There's a long way to climb."

"Oh, that's OK. With all the walking I've done today, a little more doesn't make any difference. Where I come from, this is

17

something they don't have, stairs like this . . . How many floors is it, seven, eight?"

"Seven. Seven's enough, too. Don't worry, there are only three more."

As soon as we reached the room, he wanted to take a piss. I showed him the way, down the hallway, and I followed him when he was through. When we were back in the room I explained that since no one lived here and the heat wasn't turned on, the sheets would be very cold, and it would be grim for a minute or so. I took off my clothes and got into bed first. I could tell he was looking at me to get some idea of what he was supposed to do. I discovered he was the way I thought he would be, thin but very solid, muscular and very hairy—on his chest, belly, buttocks, thighs, and forearms. He turned out the light before joining me in bed. We pressed together hard, giggling and shivering, even exaggerating the effects of the cold. He was turned on by kissing. "I've always liked hair," he said, "but this time I'm really getting my money's worth!"

"I could say the same thing."

Most of the time I was on top of him; sometimes we were both on our sides, but as soon as he was lying on top of me, his forearms behind my back, he came without a sound, without even any particular movement. I remarked with a laugh that he might have warned me.

"I couldn't wait any more. All this hair drives me crazy."

I made him roll over on his back, and, my mouth in the hollow of his shoulder, I came almost immediately, on top of him. We lay there a few moments without moving while the come dripped over the sheets.

"Is everyone like you at the *Manhattan?*"

"I don't know. Why? You want to go back?"

"In any case, you know, in Clermont, there aren't many like you."

"What do you mean?"

"So hairy."

"Well, there's you, for starters . . ."

18

Five minutes later, we were kissing each other again, licking and caressing. We pressed our bodies together, moving from left to right, very excited by the sound and sensation of hair rubbing together. The come, still warm, and the sweat made this contact softer, lubricated. Our cocks were one beside the other, or on top of the other. We both came again, exactly together, me lying on top of him, and not noiselessly this time. Not ten minutes had passed since the first time.

"We must have broken the speed record."

"Mmm. Real athletes . . ."

"Too bad no one's going to be able to sleep on this side of the bed. There's a real little lake over here. And it's cold."

I was thirsty. I went to get a drink of water, kept in a row of little Coca-Cola bottles lined up in the refrigerator. I took advantage of being up to wash myself off, sponging away the come that had stuck to my belly. He got up too and did the same. Then we stretched out again on the other side of the bed, my arm under his neck. He murmured:

"I like touching you. I could feel you for hours, it feels so good."

"So do I. If hairy guys turn you on, it's better to be hairy yourself, then the contact is really exciting."

Another five minutes and we came again, still in the same way, face to face, and again at the same time.

"I never did all that so quick before."

It couldn't have been twenty minutes since we had gone to bed.

We both slept very soundly, each of us in one of the two little beds which, pushed together, seemed to be one big double bed. We woke up around ten in the morning. And a moment later, new ejaculations, as simply and rapidly achieved as before, and as perfectly simultaneous.

"Sorry not to be able to make you breakfast—there's nothing here, as you see."

"Oh, it doesn't matter. I'm not hungry."

"You're not? I sure am, after all that exercise. . . . What are you going to do today? Are you going to play tourist?"

"Oh, I'll go for a little walk, maybe, I don't know, over by the Champs-Elysées."

"If you want to see the Louvre, or the Tuileries, that's right near here."

"Oh yeah?"

"Sure. Wait a minute, I'll draw you a map."

I drew him a rough map showing where we were, the Rue du Bac, Boulevard Saint-Germain, the *Apollinaire* and the *Manhattan*, Notre-Dame, the Châtelet, the Louvre, the Tuileries, the Champs-Elysées, the Arc de Triomphe, the Trocadéro and the Eiffel Tower, which he wanted to see close-up. I showed him the top of it through the window. I advised him to start at the Louvre and walk down the Tuileries and up the Champs-Elysées to the Arc de Triomphe, then across to the Trocadéro and the Eiffel Tower. Since he wanted to take the Métro, he could take it from the Étoile to the Trocadéro. The view was good from there; you could see all of Paris, and then it wasn't far from the Tower, you just had to walk down past the fountains. I also offered him my bicycle, but he refused:

"No, I'll be fine walking and taking the Métro. I'll manage fine."

"You can telephone me at my place if there is a problem. I'll be home all afternoon. And later you could come and take a bath if you wanted to—no one will be there."

"No, I'll wash up here. Maybe I can shave too. That'll be fine."

In a tiny zippered pouch, he had an electric razor ("You need one, in the army. At first, I didn't like it, I never felt I was shaved. Now I'm used to it.") but no toothbrush.

We left together and walked as far as the Rue du Bac.

"Telephone me. I'll be home all afternoon, except late, when I may go out. I'll probably look in at the *Apollinaire*—you know, the café I showed you yesterday. You can go there if you want.

There's always a crowd there on Sunday around six or seven. You might like it. And if you want to sleep in the room tonight, you're welcome to it."

"Thanks a lot. I'll call you later. I'll be walking around most of the afternoon."

"OK. Have a good time. Ciao!"

"Ciao!"

[*He did not telephone that evening, unless it was before nine-thirty, while I was having dinner with friends. He was leaving the next morning for the Auvergne.*

I saw him again six months later, at the Manhattan. *Like the first time, he had just got to Paris and he hadn't been here in the meantime. I was with Tony. We took him back to the house, and the three of us went to bed together. In the morning, he also made love with an American friend of ours who was staying with us for two or three days, and who didn't speak a word of French.*

He was fed up with Thiers, and even with Clermont-Ferrand. He was thinking of moving to Paris soon, or perhaps to Nice, if he could manage to find work there.]

᚛ III ᚜

DANIEL X.

Sunday, March 12, 1978

At the *Manhattan* on a Sunday, the eve of the legislative elections: I was attracted by a boy who didn't seem at all interested in me, but whose glances in my direction from time to time kept me from giving up altogether. Another possibility was developing; another boy, more or less the same type as the first, but who turned me on much less. This one, without actually cruising me, did not look away when our eyes met, and gave the impression of being more or less available.

We were in the biggest room downstairs, not far from the bar; I was standing on the two or three steps which lead to the check-room and the stairs, the first boy to my left in a dark corner, talking to friends of his, the second to my right, near the banquette along the bare stone wall. The boy on the left went away toward the dance floor. The one to my right sat down on the banquette. I went over to him, and sat on the top of the banquette, with my feet on the wooden felt-covered seat. My left knee was then level with his shoulder. Occasionally, he glanced at me; to do so, he had to turn around and lift his head. I kept time to the music with my left leg, which brushed against his right arm. After a minute or two, he rested his elbow on my thigh. I put my hand on his forearm and caressed it. Almost immediately he turned toward me:

"Can we get together this week?"
I laughed:
"Yes, of course."
"Why are you laughing?"
"I don't know, it just sounds funny."

To tell the truth, I couldn't see him very well. He had short hair, a rather long moustache drooping down either side of his mouth, and he was wearing a plaid shirt with rolled-up sleeves, open over a rather hairy chest, and blue jeans. His face was slightly heavy and nothing special, and as for his body, I couldn't tell much, wondering only if he wasn't quite as thin as he should be. On the other hand, I hadn't entirely given up on the first object of my interest, and so I was hesitating over whether to commit my-self. It was only twelve-thirty; I would have liked to make a few further explorations. When he asked me if I wanted to leave, I said no, not yet.

I stood up and danced a little where I was standing, right in front of him, ready to leave, if only for a moment. But, still sitting, he drew me against him. I kissed him in the hollow of his neck, and stuck my hand down the front of his shirt. He brushed his mouth against my crotch. Then, after these first gropings, he repeated his question, putting it a little differently:

"Would you like to go?"

"Go where?"

"To your place, or mine."

"Sure, if you do." ·

"Now?"

"Now? Why not, if you want."

While we were getting our things out of the checkroom, I learned that his name was Daniel. We went up to the street floor. At the top of the stairs stood the boy who had interested me first, and now he was staring at me. I stopped beside him, on the pretext of putting on my windbreaker, without taking my eyes off him. But Daniel was already at the door, and I couldn't make him wait. So I followed him out, annoyed at having to leave so quickly.

We walked toward the Seine. He asked me questions:

"Did you listen to the election returns?"

"Yes."

"How did they turn out?"

"Not very clear. The Left is ahead, but nowhere near so much as was expected. The socialists have a much lower percentage than the polls predicted, 23%, I think. The Gaullists have 22%, the communists 21%, and the liberals 20%, more or less. Anything can happen, they say."

"Did you vote?"

"Yes. You?"

"No, I didn't vote. I don't vote in Paris. I'd have to travel over 200 kilometers if I wanted to vote. It's a ways, you know. I'll go next Sunday. Once is enough."

"Where do you vote?"

"In the Orne. That's where I'm from. I don't have a Paris residence yet."

"The Orne's a nice place. Which part are you from?"

"The eastern end, toward Nogent-le-Rotrou, you know where that is?"

"Sure I do. In other words, you're from Le Perche."

"Yes, that's it, exactly. How do you know? You from there too?"

"No, not at all, but I like that part of the country."

I followed him without asking any questions about our destination. We had almost reached the quai and his car, a dark blue Renault 5. Where were we going? I explained my situation, that I couldn't take him to my apartment, the maid's room I could use, etc. In any case, he preferred going to his place on Boulevard Voltaire.

"OK, but how will I get home?"

"I'll drive you home tomorrow morning if you want."

"That's nice of you. But tomorrow morning I can take the Métro."

"The station's just outside my building."

"OK."

We drove past the Hôtel de Ville. All of the windows on the Seine side were lit up. He leaned forward over the steering wheel:

"Look. Chirac must be counting his votes."

And except for that, the ride continued in virtual silence. I was in a bad mood, annoyed that I had let myself be dragged into this affair without particularly caring one way or the other, and regretting the other boy, whom I had given up on too quickly.

We turned into the underground garage of a very big modern apartment building. The door worked automatically by the insertion of a plastic card into a special slot. From the basement, we got into the elevator, and walked out into a very long hallway.

"I have to apologize for the way my place looks. Everything is a terrible mess; I really haven't moved in yet."

The narrow vestibule was in fact crowded with crates, boxes, open suitcases. Through the bathroom doorway to my left, I could see a lot of sheets and towels drying over the tub. We walked straight ahead into a very disorderly bedroom. The folding bed was open but not made up, and fit into an extremely rococo Louis

XV headboard. The bare wood, which seemed to have been carved very recently, was neither painted nor varnished. Over the woodwork had been hung—the day before, I was told—a huge modern tapestry copied from an old original, representing a staghunt: a stag with enormous antlers was trapped in the dark depths of a pool, surrounded by a pack of fierce hounds. The hunters' clothes were from the period of Henri III, who may indeed have been depicted among them wearing a big round strawberry colored hat, a close-fitting slashed tunic, a short cape, slashed culottes and high boots.

"If I promise to be good, can I have a glass of water? I'm very thirsty."

"Yes, of course. Would you rather have a beer?"

"No, thanks. Tap water would be fine."

The bed reached almost to the opposite wall; a chest or little table against the wall was almost invisible under the blankets and clothes piled everywhere.

Daniel brought me some water in a stemmed glass, also Louis XV, and drank his own beer out of the bottle. Then he undressed completely:

"I'm going to take a shower—I got all sweaty dancing."

While he was gone, I looked at his records and his books. Most of the records, except for a complete recording of *The Merry Widow,* were LP's of French music hall stars, ranging from Yvette Horner to Patrick Juvet, including Jacques Brel, Claude François and William Scheller. The books, arranged on three short shelves with interior lighting, were almost all hardcover editions, some very old, seventeenth- or eighteenth-century works of piety and pharmaceutical treatises, in quite good condition, and some more recent works, collector's editions. One volume of Jules Verne, *Les Cinq Cents Millions de la Begum,* a reproduction of the Hetzel edition, was displayed sideways. Among the other hardbacks were a novel and an essay by Roger Peyrefitte, four novels by Yves Navarre, and one by Françoise Mallet-Joris. I opened a leather-bound edition of Baudelaire and was reading the pages on hashish when Daniel came back from the bathroom. He stretched out on the bed.

I undressed and lay down beside him. We kissed (he had also brushed his teeth) and began playing with each other until we both had erections. I ran my tongue through the hair on his chest. He was anything but thin. At first I was on top but he turned me over on my back and lay down on top of me. He put one hand under my balls and stuck his fingers into my ass.

"You want me to fuck you?"

"Mmm . . . not especially."

"You don't like that?"

" . . . "

Without insisting, he slid off me. We had both lost our erections. Two or three minutes later I was playing with him again, he got hard again, and so did I. Now it was my turn to run my hand over his ass, between his buttocks, and to lift up his thighs, but he did nothing to make matters easier in this direction. Finally, lying against him, one arm under the back of his neck, I played with his cock while I nibbled one of his tits, and he came very quickly. Then he began to play with me too, but I stopped him. He got up to find a towel and wipe himself off. When he came back, we played with each other a little more, and then I said I would let him get some sleep.

"You're leaving?"

"Yes, it's not very late, I'll go home now."

I got dressed quickly. He went to the door with me, naked. I kissed him, on the shoulder. And I walked home, by way of the Rue Saint-Sebastien, the Boulevard Beaumarchais, the Place des Vosges, the quais of the Île Saint-Louis, and the Square Jean-XXIII.

[*Never saw him again, I don't think. Occasionally I see someone who looks like him, but who doesn't seem to recognize me.*]

❧ IV ❧

DANIEL WITH THE HELMET

Friday, March 17, 1978

Around two-fifteen in the morning (of the 18th) I climbed over the fence into the Square Jean-XXIII, behind Notre-Dame. As I walked toward the river, on my right were the bushes that are planted along the fence of the parish garden, and to my left the flower-beds, the lawns and the fountain. On this left side were two men in motorcycle outfits, holding their helmets and standing with their legs wide apart. One had a beard, the other very short hair and a moustache; the short-haired one was staring at me as I passed in front of them, and I stared back. Having gotten almost as far as the gardener's shed, I stepped into the bushes. There were two guys there, neither of whom interested me. Through the branches, I watched the two motorcyclists. They hadn't moved, and seemed to be paying no further attention to me. So I came out of the bushes again. But then the one who had stared at me, and who turned me on, came toward the bushes, straight toward the opening where I was standing. He brushed past me, and I immediately followed him. He headed between the bushes toward the wooden fence that marks out the gardener's yard. I went over to him. He was standing at the foot of a tall tree with his legs wide apart, his helmet in one hand. He was wearing a white T-shirt under a black leather jacket with the collar up, very faded jeans torn and mended over one thigh, a broad belt with a round metal buckle, and heavy leather boots that came up almost to his knees. He must have been between thirty and thirty-five. I came up to him and put my hand on his fly. He did the same thing, immediately. With my other hand, I caressed his pectorals, which were very solid and highly developed. He opened his jacket so I could get my hand under his T-shirt. His stomach muscles were very hard and very articulated. He opened my fly and took out my cock, which he began playing

27

with. We began kissing. Then he put his helmet on one of the fenceposts and undid his belt and pulled down the zipper of his fly. I played with his cock, which was rather small, and then took it in my mouth. He sucked mine, too, right afterward. We pressed against each other, kissing, our hands on the back of each other's neck or else holding each other's ass. He was kneading mine quite hard, and ran one finger into my asshole. I stuck my hand under his balls and caressed his buttocks, which were big, hairy, and very hard. Pushing up his T-shirt, I licked his chest and bit his right nipple, which seemed to excite him a lot:

"Yeah, oh God, do that!"

Meanwhile, an Arab of about forty had approached us, and I suddenly felt his completely stiff cock against my ass. I pushed it away with one hand. Furthermore, about a foot and a half away stood a potbellied man of about fifty who kept staring while we were kissing or sucking each other's cocks. The man with the helmet and I looked at each other, sighed, and I asked him if he wanted to go somewhere else. He answered *yes,* pointing toward the gardener's yard.

"You don't want to come to my place?"

"No, I can't. I'm with a friend. He's waiting for me."

We more or less readjusted our clothes.

"Over here?"

"No, come with me."

I followed him. In fact, he wasn't heading toward the shed, but farther on, walking around it. So we came out onto the path again and reached the part of the gardens that runs down from the cathedral to the river. He was walking along the parish fence, and he stopped about halfway, at a very brightly lit place.

"Here?"

"Yes. There's a lot of light, but no one can see."

He started undressing me again, and he took my cock out of my pants. On the way I had pulled off my sweater, tying the sleeves around the collar of my windbreaker, setting the whole thing on the fence of a flower-bed. We sucked each other's cock some more. I caressed the muscles of his stomach and chest, which were exceptionally well developed and hard as an anvil. Then he moved to my right, his cock against my hip, one arm around my shoulders, and played with my cock with his right hand. When he felt I was about to come, he leaned over and took my cock in his mouth. But at the last moment he straightened up again, went on playing with me, and my sperm spattered over the ivy and the sand.

Immediately afterward, I began sucking him again. He was speaking almost in a whisper:

"Do my tits, yes, that's it, both at the same time, while you're blowing me."

"That's going to be a little complicated. Wait a second."

My pants were down around my knees. I pulled them up, zipped my fly and buckled my belt. Then I crouched down in front of him, took his cock in my mouth, and squeezed his nipples between the thumb and forefinger of each hand.

"Yeah—shit!—that's good. Squeeze hard, yeaaah!"

He came very quickly. I stood up smiling, and I turned around to spit out his come. He was smiling too. Shadowy figures were coming toward us. He laid one hand on my forearm.

"Do you always come that much?"

"I don't know. Why? Was there a lot?"

"I'll say. It never stopped."

"Well, no, I'm surprised. I must have been really hot."

"You get that way a lot?"

"Well, yes, it happens, thanks very much."

We walked together toward the back of the cathedral, laughing. He was still holding his huge helmet in one hand.

"What's your name?"

"Renaud. What's yours?"

"Daniel. I haven't been here in a long time. You from Paris?"

"Yes. You?"

"I'm from Lille . . . we'll separate here, OK?"

"OK. So long!"

"So long."

An exchange of slaps on the back. He walked faster ahead of me, and rejoined the friend he had been standing with earlier, as well as another boy, very big on the bike and leather scene and whom I've known for ten years. I waved to him in passing.

"All right, chief?"

"Hey, Renaud, you whore! What are you doing here?"

"Me? Nothing. I'm just on my way home to bed."

[*Never saw him again.*]

V
JACQUES'S BROTHER

Thursday, March 23, 1978

To speak here of Jacques's brother is to juggle the criteria I have established as to what constitutes a trick, since he was not entirely a stranger to me. But then again, we didn't know each other very well. Jacques had introduced me to him a few weeks earlier, we always said *hello* to each other with a smile, and *how are you?* and not much more. I knew his name was Pierre, that he was a little older than his brother, and that he lived in Paris, unlike the rest of his family, Gypsies all, who were at Gonesse, a veritable tribe, as I understand it. They are not French citizens, the children don't go to school, none of them can read or write, not even numbers, although they seem to be shrewd businessmen. Both brothers were married by their parents, but they hardly know their wives, and never see them. Pierre looks very much the classical Gypsy: very black curly hair, moustache, gold earring, sometimes a red scarf around the throat. But he's very short; just over five feet, maybe.

30

That evening at the *Manhattan,* he was much more communicative than usual. Not that he made any advances, but I kept finding him in my path. Once, when I was sitting down, he came over and stood beside me. He said nothing to me, however, and after a moment or so I gave up my seat to him. Later, upstairs near the top of the stairs, he approached me again. We were both standing. I was leaning against the wall, but I kept my feet as far apart as possible, in order to make myself closer to his height. Then, fearing that this position would seem too artificial and too obvious, I straightened up, taller by head and shoulders than he, which was no less embarrassing.

I knew he had a *friend* (his expression), and he couldn't get out as much as he liked:

"So you managed to escape tonight?"

"Yeah. Is it always as crowded as this during the week?"

"No, not this early in the week. Do you only come here on weekends?"

"Only Saturdays."

"And where's your brother? In Gonesse?"

"I don't know. I don't know what he's up to. He may be out tonight—he goes somewhere else."

"Where's that?"

"Oh, he goes to the *César,* or the *Scaramouche,* or *18 . . .*"

He remarked that there was a boy over on the banquette who wasn't bad, and I pointed out another whom I found attractive. A Spaniard, he told me. But we remained side by side, without saying anything more. My arm behind him, I stuck a thumb into his belt, once or twice, but there was no reaction on his part. I told him I was sleepy.

"You should dance a little."

"No, I don't have the energy. But I'll go watch the others."

So I left him where he was and went back downstairs. I circled the dance floor slowly. Ten minutes later I felt two arms around me, embracing me from behind. It was Pierre again. I put my hands in his pants pockets—which were wide-wale corduroy—then

I caressed his forearms, which he had crossed over my stomach. Then, when I got behind him in turn, I stuck my hands in his pockets again or else I crossed my arms over his chest, squeezing now, my legs wide apart, my chin on his shoulder. He went to sit down in a corner. A moment later, since I was staring at him, he signalled me to come over and sit down next to him, which I did. Putting my arm around his shoulders, I kissed him in the hollow of the neck. Then I caressed his back through his shirt. He began to laugh:

"You in love?"

"Why? In love with who? No."

"The way you're handling me."

"I'm not handling you, I'm caressing you."

But I stopped.

"Are you mad at me?"

"No. Why? Not at all."

Now it was he who was running his hand over my tennis shirt, down my back, caressing my forearms and hands.

"You sure you're not mad?"

"Yes, I'm sure."

With both hands, he turned my head toward him, and kissed me on the mouth. All the same, I watched the dancers a moment longer, without paying him much attention. It was only when he drew me toward him a second time that I gradually leaned back, or rather to one side, on the corner banquette where we were sitting alone. My cock was getting hard against his hip. I stuck a couple of fingers between two buttons of his shirt, under his tiny necktie. His pectorals were round, solid, covered with hair. We stayed there about fifteen minutes kissing like that, half reclining. He had an erection too.

It was almost closing time. The music was shut off and all the lights turned on. We headed for the coat checkroom. He told me to give him my ticket, and cutting into the line, he picked up my things along with his and refused the two francs I owed him. We walked back up to the street floor. At the door, he asked me what I was going to do.

"Go home to bed. And you?"

"I'm going over to *Pim's*. Don't you want to come to *Pim's* with me?"

"No, I'm bushed."

"Too bad."

"You could come with me, if you want to."

"No, I have a friend."

"Oh, in that case . . ."

Just then I glanced around us a bit and we were separated by all the men leaving at the same time we were. But out in the street, from the opposite sidewalk, he signalled me to join him.

"You're going home now?"

"Yes."

"Which way do you go?"

"Down the Boulevard Saint-Germain."

"I'll walk with you a little."

So we set out side by side.

"I'll tell you what I want to do. I'll come home with you, but I won't stay."

"All right. But we can't go to my apartment. There's someone there. We can go to a maid's room I have, around the corner from it."

"It doesn't matter to me. You have a friend too?"

"No, but I live with someone."

"You know, this is the first time I've cheated on my friend. It doesn't feel so good."

"Then you shouldn't do it."

"But you turn me on. Let's stop here and have some coffee."

"Coffee? No, you don't need coffee, you won't be able to sleep if you drink coffee now."

"It doesn't keep me awake. You order what you want. I'd smoke a cigarette over the body."

"What?"

"I said I need a cigarette. I have to buy some."

He started to go into the café at the corner of the Boulevard Saint-Germain and the Rue de l'Ancienne-Comédie.

33

"No, not there. They don't sell cigarettes. There's a place farther down."

So he went into the *Navy.*

"You want something to drink?"

"No, thanks."

I waited outside. He didn't get any coffee.

"Is it much farther?"

"Seven, maybe eight minutes."

"If I had known, we could have taken a taxi. You walk this distance every time?"

"Yes, I'm used to it. And I'm warning you now, you'll have to climb six flights, too."

Not much was said the rest of the way, except for admonitions on his part not to mention what was happening between us to his brother.

"All the same, when I think of it, who would have believed it?"

"What?"

"That we would leave that place together, you and me."

"I don't see what's so extraordinary about that."

"Still, if my friend knew! You won't say anything about it, will you?"

As soon as we get into the room, he takes off his clothes. His body is very well proportioned, rather dark-skinned, very muscular, especially the arms and thighs, which are exceptionally developed.

I tell him I have to go take a piss. When I come back, he wants to go too, and puts on his underwear to walk down the hall. I get between the icy sheets. When he comes back, he asks if there is hot water here. Yes? Really? Then he very carefully washes himself off, from the waist down. I explain that there is neither a candle nor a bed lamp, and that we can have either the big light on or no light at all. He suggests that I put a towel over it, but that doesn't make much difference. Then, under the sink, he discovers a little lamp I never knew was there.

"You're not going to wash up?"
"I already did."
"So did I."

When his ablutions are completed, he comes and stretches out beside me in the bed, which is still just as cold, despite my solitary efforts. We press against each other, kissing, and warm up that way for quite a while. He seems to be very interested in my ass. He sucks my cock. I run my tongue through the hair on his chest, over his right nipple, his belly, and then I take his cock in my mouth too. This provokes so much agitation that he is now lying completely across the bed. Continuing my descent, I take his balls between my teeth, then I stop at his asshole, which I lick while continuing to caress his torso. He plays with himself, breathing hard. Then I turn him around so he's lying full length on the bed again, and lying on top of him, with his legs spread and my cock under his ass, I kiss him on the mouth again, on the chest, on the belly, suck him some more, and again suck his ass, leaving as much saliva in it as possible. Then, taking his legs in my arms and having moistened my cock, I start pushing it between his buttocks, where it goes in quite easily. "Easy, Renaud," he says, "easy."

Then I stop and it is he who, by his movements, gets me deeper inside him.

My hands under his shoulder blades, I kiss him on the mouth, in the hollow of his neck, on the chest. He chants my name like a nostalgic wail. Sometime I fuck him very slowly, then, just about to come, very fast and hard and always with enthusiasm. He plays with himself. I burst out laughing.

"Why are you laughing?"
"Because I'm happy. This is great."
"I like you a lot, you laugh all the time . . ."

This lasts about ten minutes. Then he tells me he's about to come.

"Now?"

"Yes, now, now, yes . . ."

"Me too, me too . . ."

We come at exactly the same instant, as if it were my own sperm that was spurting out of his cock onto his belly, up to his chest and even onto his shoulders. I fall back beside him, releasing his legs from my arms. He looks at me, smiling:

"You're a little bastard."

"Why?"

"You're a real bastard. Usually I don't get fucked—on principle. . . Now why are you laughing? You don't believe me?"

"Sure. But why do what's usual?"

"I don't say it never happens. It's happened a few times . . . but not usually, that's what I mean. Is that all you like to do?"

"No, I like to do everything. I do whatever anyone wants."

"Let me wipe myself off, I'm completely covered . . ."

"I'll say. What a range! Wait, I'll get you a towel."

I get up and hand him a towel, and wash myself off.

"What time is it?"

"Three."

"At four, I'll go."

"All right. I'll close the curtains, that way I won't have to get up again."

Then back in each other's arms again, his head on my shoulder. I caress him.

"What is *Renaud,* anyway, is that your family name?"

"No, my first name."

"People call you that? Renaud? It sounds strange."

"My other Christian name is Jean."

"Ah, your real name is Jean. You decided on *Renaud* for yourself?"

"No, my name is actually Jean-Renaud, but Jean-Renaud's a little too long."

"Still, Renaud sounds funny. Like the name of a car."

36

"You don't like it?"

"No, wait . . . I'm going to call you . . . *Rocky*. Yes, *Rocky's* good. You like the way it sounds, Rocky?"

"It sounds all right to me, if you like it."

"OK, Rocky, that's what it is: Rocky. What do you have to say for yourself, Rock?"

"There you go, getting familiar right off—you could make it *Rock*. I like that, I like that even better."

"OK, Rock . . . anything you say, Rock. . . . I'm thinking about my friend. About the scene he's going to make when I come in."

"Maybe he'll be asleep."

"Dream on. I know him, the bastard, you can be sure he hasn't slept a wink. I know him. He's waiting up for me, wondering where I've gone. It bothers me a lot."

"Then you should leave now."

"I wonder what I'll tell him . . . Maybe that I went to the *Sept.*"

"Suppose that's where *he* went?"

"No, he never goes out. That's why we argue all the time."

"You like to go out a lot?"

"Sure, I'd like to go out every night. Not to cruise, you know. Just to be somewhere, you know, where there are people, dance, have some fun, go to the movies, even to the theater, *do* something. But he just comes home from work, he watches television, and bang! right into bed. He doesn't even wait for the late show. I watch the late show alone—some life!"

"Where did you meet him?"

"At the *Scara* . . . The *Scaramouche,* you know the place?"

"So he used to go out, then?"

"Yes, before, he went out all the time, but not now, now he won't set foot outside the door."

"It's because you're all he needs."

"Yes, that's exactly what he says. He says: I have you, why should I look for anything else? Tonight I wanted to go to the movies, that's why we argued. He said we'd go next Saturday. I said no, not Saturday. I don't want to go Saturday, I want to go tonight. He said he wasn't going, I said I was. So I went, and then afterward I went to the *Manhattan,* and then there you were first thing, and so here I am."

Again he begins caressing my ass. Then he starts sucking my cock. I get hard. He kneels between my legs and with his hand puts some saliva between my buttocks. I add some of my own. Then he raises my legs, and gets inside me right away. His cock is rather small and doesn't reach very far. His body is perpendicular to mine, and I pull him toward me, to kiss him, and cross my legs behind his back. I direct his mouth toward my right nipple, so that he can suck it. He does this a little, then straightens up again. My erection goes down, which he notices. Then he pulls his cock out of my ass and begins sucking me again. I get hard again almost immediately, and begin playing with myself, my hand against his mouth. He sticks his cock back inside me, but after two or three minutes I lose my erection again. The same thing has happened to him, apparently.

"You tired?"

"A little."

"You want to stop?"

"If you do."

And again side by side: I think he talked some more about his friend's worrying about him, asked me again what time it was, and about taxis, then about where we were.

"I don't know why I can't get it up any more."

"I could come in a minute."

I am lying on top of him.

"You can come like that?"

"Sure can!"

I kiss him, but he keeps changing position, and I find myself, although still on my stomach, lying on the mattress. I play with him, and he gets a little hard. Then I pass my hand behind his balls and caress his buttocks, one finger just barely thrust between them. My cock is hard against his hip.

"You get it up better when you're on top, huh?"

38

I laugh. The pressure of my hand against his ass apparently gets him more and more excited, and his cock is now perfectly stiff.

"Oh, you turn me on!"

I kneel between his thighs, then I lick his ass again, keeping it up in the air with my forearms. He plays with himself and moans a lot. His chin is against his chest. Our eyes meet down the length of his torso, we keep staring at each other while my tongue thrusts between his buttocks.

Then I fuck him again, very excited this time. I have a big erection now and so does he. I try to slow down his right hand's movement around his cock, so that the pleasure will last longer. But he pushes me away with his left hand:

"No, Renaud, I'm going to come, no, no, I'm coming now, yes, now, yes!"

He comes about five seconds before I do.

Afterward he gets up to wipe himself off, and hands me the towel. Then he climbs back into bed and lies in my arms:

"I don't know what I should do, go home or not . . . It must be four by now, isn't it?"

"Yes."

"He gets up at six."

"I'm not surprised he doesn't like going out nights."

"What time are you getting up today?"

"Oh, around one."

"So what should I do?"

"I don't know what you *should* do. Of course I'd rather you stay. But it's up to you to decide, you know the situation better than I do."

"God, he gives me a pain. It's his fault anyway. I suppose it has to end some day . . . I wish I could find someone like me, who likes to go out all the time. I think I'll sleep here, since you don't want me to leave."

"Hey, wait a minute. Don't get any ideas. I never said I didn't want you to leave. I said I'd rather you stay, personally. But that I understood perfectly well that you might want to go home, especially if you think your friend is upset."

"You're not kidding, he'll be upset . . . all right, I'll leave, then . . ."

But he doesn't move. I put my arms around him, his back against my chest, our legs bent and parallel. After about ten minutes:

"Look out, you're going to fall asleep."

"Oh, so what. He pisses me off. I'll tell him I spent the night in a hotel."

"He'll never believe that."

"He can believe whatever he wants."

After which I fall asleep, this time with my back to him.

He wakes me up getting out of bed, beginning to put on his clothes. It is just getting light.

"What are you doing?"

"I'm going home."

"What time is it?"

"Where's your watch?"

"In the drawer. It was too loud."

"Monsieur has very delicate ears . . . it's seven. Or maybe eight, I don't know. Look for yourself."

He does not know how to read a watch.

It was eight o'clock.

He comes back to bed.

"Now what are you doing?"

"I'm going to stay, since you don't want me to leave."

"You can leave if you want. Only it seems like a funny time to get up, since we went to sleep around four."

"I didn't sleep the whole night."

"Hmmm . . . Do you have to go to work?"

"Usually. But I'm too tired."

"All right, but make up your mind. I want to get some sleep."

He had turned on the light, although the room is light enough for him to get dressed. And he's humming. I groan.

"What?"

"I'm trying to sleep!"

"You mean you're not even going to get up to say good-bye?"

"What a pain in the ass you are! Come and say good-bye yourself."

"You'll have to close the door!"

"No, just shut it behind you."

But I get up all the same, to kiss him good-bye. He leaves. And I sleep until noon.

[*Saw him again very often, though we never slept together again. After this episode, he broke off with his friend, for which, he says, he's very grateful to me: it had to end someday, and it's much better this way. He's always very pleasant, very sweet and invariably in a good mood. When he found out that I was a writer, he said he hoped I'd write something about him.*]

VI

ETIENNE POMMIER-CARO

Wednesday, March 29, 1978

I first caught sight of him near the checkroom at the *Manhattan*, probably when he was coming in: almost my height, very dark, thin, with rather long hair, black eyes, fine features and a huge moustache which curved down each side of his mouth to the bottom of his chin. In his open shirt collar you could see a lot of thick hair at the base of his neck. I immediately decided that he turned me on and that I would cruise him.

He passed in front of me without paying me the slightest attention. I made the circuit of the rooms downstairs in the opposite direction from the one he had taken, but I did not meet him. I supposed he had turned back and had gone upstairs. I went upstairs as well, but did not see him. When I managed to track him down, he was on the lowest of the three steps of the narrow, vaulted passageway that leads from the dance floor to a sort of little annex, and was watching the dancers. I stood just behind him, actually touching him. He did not move forward to avoid me, but did not step back either. Besides, he probably had no notion of who was standing behind him. Then I moved alongside him, staring at him with some insistence, and his eyes met mine once or twice, but very rapidly and without stopping. He left to put his glass on the bar, but came back to stand in exactly the same place. Again, I moved behind him. When either of us happened to move, we touched each other, but he displayed no active interest. He did not push me aside or move away, and exerted no pressure against me.

Then someone came over and spoke to him: a heavy, moustached man of about thirty-three or thirty-four who is always interested in the same boys that interest me, and with whom I must have shared more lovers than with anyone else. I once knew his brother slightly, and I believe his name is Regis, or Rémy, or Jean-Rémy. Jean-Rémy was saying to my mystery man that he should take off his sweater, that he would be too hot in here; there were other remarks I couldn't hear. I imagined they already knew each other, but when Jean-Rémy asked: "We've met before, haven't we?" the other fellow didn't seem at all convinced. Then Jean-Rémy went away.

Then I noticed that Tony was standing quite close to us, talking to Pascal, a friend of ours. He nodded to me, and I thought he understood the situation. I also thought that it would be irritating to get shot down in front of him, and even more irritating if he should happen to cruise my man and succeed. In any case, it was unpleasant that Tony was there, and I had almost made up my mind to clear out. But I offered a kind of prayer to Providence, pointing out that I had not been presented with many satisfactions recently, and pleading that I might be granted one boy who pleased me, and a successful outcome as well.

He, meanwhile, had gone away to dance. I hesitated to follow him and to dance in front of Tony, especially while I was obviously cruising. So I satisfied myself by going over and standing against the back wall, beyond the dancers. Then I noticed that I could no longer see Tony, who had probably gone back upstairs. I began dancing, closer and closer to the mystery man, who, to my absolute astonishment, suddenly flashed me a big smile. We danced face-to-face for a moment, sometimes so close as to be almost touching, sometimes moving away. Our mouths must have been half an inch apart for an instant, but we didn't kiss. All the same I got rid of my chewing gum. Later on, we put our hands on each other's hips. I noticed and touched a rhinestone star attached to his sweater, on the right side of his stomach.

"I use that to snag guys wearing sweaters."

"I'll go get mine."

"Your what?"

"My sweater. So you can snag me."

"Ahh!"

Then we kissed for quite a long while, still dancing. He said he was tired, stopped dancing in the middle of a number, and went over to sit down on a banquette in a corner, where I joined him. He set one hand on my thigh and again we kissed.

"You must be dying of the heat in that sweater."

"I am!"

"Take it off!"

"I can't, my shirt is all ragged."

"You must be completely nuts!"

"Completely."

"People here don't give a shit about ragged shirts."

"I know. But I do."

"Well, in that case . . ."

Tony had come back to the edge of the dance floor and noticed us, as had Jean-Rémy. My companion—I had just learned his name was Etienne—indicated him to me with a glance:

"I'm afraid I've pissed him off."

I smiled:

"No, I suspect I'm the one who's pissed him off. As for you, I had the impression he was practically in love."

"Yes, he is. He's a pain in the ass. Well, that'll teach him a lesson. Shall we dance?"

"Now? Sure, if you want to. What did you say?"

"I said: shall we leave?"

"Oh, I thought you said, shall we dance . . . Yes, absolutely, let's get out of here."

The coat-check boy, to whom I handed my ticket, thought it necessary to comment on the situation:

"What, leaving already? You must be crazy, it's hardly one . . ."

"It's an emergency."

"I see. Monsieur's made a connection."

I turned to Etienne:

"He's pretty wild, your friend there."

"I don't even know who he is. You're the one who's such good friends with everyone in here."

We immediately started down the Rue des Anglais toward the Boulevard Saint-Germain.

"Your place or mine? I live on the Place de la Contrescarpe. Do you know where that is?"

"Absolutely."

" 'Absolutely!' So where do you live?"

"Rue du Bac. But we can't go to my place, there's someone there, and tonight there's a friend from out of town staying in the maid's room. So . . ."

"So we'll go to my place. All right if we walk?"

"I'd like to."

We were on the Boulevard, walking toward the Place Maubert. Etienne touched my elbow to signal we were crossing:

"It's on the right."

"And up the hill, yes, I know."

"Are you really French?"

"Absolutely."

"You have an accent. Where are you from?"

"From Chamalières, sir!"

"Chamalières? Where's that? Somewhere in the north, isn't it—no, the east?"

"You don't know Chamalières? Everyone knows Chamalières!"

"Oh yes, of course. Giscard with his accordion. So you're from the Auvergne?"

"Well, they don't make them like me any more, but yes. And you? Where are you from?"

"Lots of places. From Morocco, from the Lot-et-Garonne . . ."

"I've always liked the Lot-et-Garonne."

"You know it?"

"No, but I've always thought it must be really nice."

"Well, it's not. Oh, the Lot is very pretty, the valley of the Tarn, the Gers, the Garonne. All that's very pretty, but not the Lot-et-Garonne."

"Too bad. Still, there's a sort of old-time Third Republic tinge to the place."

"That's right, there sure is. You have a weakness for the Third Republic?"

"Absolutely. I would have loved being a big fat senator with a big red nose at the end of every political dinner. You know, the kind who has his finger in every pie and gives out favors with a free hand—tobacco licenses and army retirements, so he can say to everyone: 'After all I've done for you!' I like saying, 'After all I've done for you!' Unfortunately, the opportunity doesn't come up very often."

"Too bad. Anyway, I can't stand the Lot-et-Garonne, and I never go there if I can help it. I lived there for seven years. That was enough."

"Where were you born?"

"Morocco."

"Shit, it's raining. Look—that's my favorite house in Paris— it's the parish-house of Saint-Etienne-du-Mont. Over there, on the corner."

But he didn't seem much interested in architecture, nor to know much about his own neighborhood:

"What street is this?"

"The Rue Clovis, no?"

"No."

"Sure it is. This was where we used to come and register for school, when I was young. Look, you can see the house perfectly now, isn't it splendid? Why couldn't you live there?"

"Nice idea. Especially when you see where I do live. It's disgusting . . . no, that's not true, it's fine. I like the Contrescarpe. The trouble is, people make a lot of noise all night long. Easter weekend was terrible; there were hordes of tourists until four in the morning."

"Shit, it's raining buckets now. Lucky I have my little hat."

I took out of my windbreaker pocket a beige canvas hat which I unfolded and put on. Etienne stared at it, laughing:

"We're here anyway."

"Oh well . . ."

"Surprise. I live with a woman. But don't worry, she's not there tonight."

"No surprise at all. And I'm not worrying. If we couldn't go to your place, I was going to suggest visiting a friend of mine, a woman who has an extra room."

"You really have a funny voice, a funny way of speaking. You don't happen to be an actor?"

"No, for God's sake, spare me that. Why an actor?"

"I don't know, something about the way you talk, down in your throat—it's hard to understand you. I see theater everywhere, I suppose."

"Oh no, I've committed yet another *faux pas!*"

"No, not at all, I know what you mean. I don't like the theatre very much any more, myself. Not the way I used to. But I'll explain it to you later.

The stairs were very narrow, rickety, and unpainted. Etienne lives on the fourth floor, overlooking the Place itself. You come into a very messy room. On a table to the right, in front of a window, are a lot of papers, scraps of writing, some crumpled up, unfolded letters, notes, memoranda, pencils, blotters, books lying open and face down, an ashtray overflowing with butts. At the far end, to the left, is a kitchen, the door ajar. On the opposite wall, what looks from a distance like colored drawings or watercolors, tacked up.

"Go straight through, this room is really unbearable."

But the second room is just as chaotic. It's bigger, deeper. To the right, another window. Opposite the door, another table on trestles, bigger than the first and also entirely covered with papers, press cuttings, books, piles of magazines, and another heaping ashtray. Above it are children's drawings that cover the whole wall and even overlap. Clothes are strewn over all the chairs. Somewhere at the other end, to the left, is a broad bed covered with a rumpled brown spread that looks as if it had seen better days. To the right of the bed, shelves of books.

"If I'm very good, do you think I might have a glass of water?"

"That's all you want? Nothing but water?"

"Exactly what I want. I don't know why I'm so thirsty—"

"Wait, I'll go get you a glass."

While he's in the kitchen, I look at his books. I pull out one, whose title is unknown to me, *Les Antipodes,* by Pierre Lepère. There's a dedication from the author, *affectionately,* to Etienne and Corinne. I'm leafing through it when my host returns.

"What have you found? Oh that—someone I know. He's an ass. You like that book?"

"I don't know, I've just opened it. On the whole, poetry . . . you know . . . Still, there are one or two lines which sound pretty. There, look . . . Where's Corinne?"

"How do you know about Corinne?"

"There's a dedication in the book. As I knew there would be."

"How did you know?"

"Because I'd never heard of it. It was a little . . . eccentric in relation to the others."

"You mean it's the kind of book no one would buy."

"No, I didn't mean that . . . or maybe I did."

"I don't like the man."

I put the book back. Etienne watches me:

"What do you do?"

"In *life?*"

"Yes."

"I write."

"You do? How terrific! What?"

"Novels. And you, what do you do?"

"I write too."

"You do? Interesting. So now we can talk about the miseries of the writer's lot."

"I have a manuscript that's been rejected by Gallimard, by Seuil—"

"You should send it to my publisher."

"Who's that?"

"I've just changed. I used to be with Flammarion, but the guy who runs the series I was published in—I don't know if you've ever heard of it, *Textes?*"

"No."

"Well, he's gone to Hachette, so I followed him. Now I'm published by Hachette."

"Hachette's deadly, isn't it?"

"No, it's not so bad, there's a new series. Only three or four books have come out so far. The series is a little different from the rest of the house—it's more literary."

"How many books have you published?"

"Two. Actually, I wrote one novel, and then a character in that novel has written another. And then there's a third novel that will be coming out in the fall."

"What are they?"

"One's called *Passage,* and the other *Echange.* The next one will be called *Travers.*"

"I'd like to read one."

"It's a little too late to pick up one for you tonight. Even the Saint-Germain Drugstore is closed by now."

"No, not tonight, tomorrow. No, not tomorrow. Some

48

women are coming here to work with me on the *Lux* festival. You know what that is?"

"No, what is it?"

"Everyone's talking about it. You really don't know much about what's happening, do you? It's a festival of fantasy films."

"Oh, right. The *Lux* is a theater, the big one with a bare front, nothing on it but a rectangle and the name."

"Yes, that's the one, nothing on it but a rectangle, like you said. I have to write something about the festival."

Still talking we stretch out on the bed. We begin making love very slowly and gradually. At first we touch each other only at arm's length. He opens my shirt.

"God you're hairy!"

So is he, on his chest, to the pit of his throat, but oddly enough, almost nowhere else. His belly is white and smooth, flat, his cock not very big.

He opens the bed, we finish taking off our clothes and get in. We kiss each other, he sucks my cock, I suck his cock, we press close together. He still hasn't got an erection, and sometimes he stops moving altogether. Then we start talking again, I don't remember what about exactly. [*I started writing this chronicle after a long delay, it is now four days later, Monday, April 3. And, before going on, I must take into account an episode that occurred last night and that colors Etienne's character differently.*

I met him again at the Manhattan, and asked him how his performance of Bacchus went. He asked me how my trip to Milan went, and immediately added that a lot had happened during my absence:

"*First of all, I read your book.*"

"*You did! How did you find it?*"

"*I don't know yet, I haven't finished it.*"

"*No, that's not what I mean. I mean find—it's not so easy, the book isn't in every drugstore.*"

"*I went into a bookstore, I asked for the book by Monsieur Camus, they said, 'Of course, Monsieur, no problem.'*"

"Beats me."

Whereupon he walked away. A little later, I was in the little room where the pinball machines are, and he joined me there.

"Now tell me about all those extraordinary things you said have happened to you."

"It's too embarrassing."

"What's happened?"

"I met someone you know, and I talked to him about you."

"You did? Who?"

"I can't tell you."

"Terrific!"

"He said terrible things about you."

"Better still. Like what?"

"I can't repeat them."

"Now listen, buddy. Your little story pisses me off. I don't think you understand what you're saying. I don't know who told you what, and I can't defend myself. You don't do that to people. If you want to be mysterious, then just keep your mouth shut. Besides, I'm completely paranoid. You chose the right victim."

"That's just what he said. He said you were paranoid, completely crazy."

"If that's all, it's not so serious. Doubtless I'm a little crazy, but not much more than anyone else. Average crazy."

"He said I should be very careful around you, that you're a kind of praying mantis, very dangerous."

"What does that mean, a praying mantis?"

"I don't know exactly."

"Doesn't add up to much."

"No. And besides, he's really an ass, I think. I mean . . . I'm in an impossible position. I can't stay here talking to you. You won't be mad if I leave now?"

"Mad isn't the word."

"What is?"

"I don't know, the whole thing pisses me off."

"But it's all right if I leave now?"

"What a funny question! Of course you can leave. What right do I have to keep you from leaving?"

"Oh Christ! I'll call you tomorrow."

"Fine."

"Or else I'll stop by."

"Monday's not such a good day. It's the one day when I'm not always at home. And besides, there's someone staying there now."

"The Italian?"

"No, the Italian was a friend who stayed for three days in the maid's room. He's gone. No, in my apartment. But that'll be over too, by the end of the week."

"Good. So I'll call you, OK? I have to go now."

"OK. So long."

"So long."

To tell the truth, during the first few seconds of this conversation, I had suspected that the mysterious third party must have been Tony, which bothered me a lot and in fact would have put all three of us into a delicate situation. But even in the present state of our relations, Tony, of course, wouldn't have badmouthed me. Besides, he wasn't at the Manhattan that evening, whereas the unknown slanderer had to have been there, since Etienne was so nervous.

The fact remains that this more recent episode somewhat overshadows that Wednesday night.

[Tuesday, April 4, five-thirty in the afternoon: there's a growing gap in this attempt at a chronicle. I should now be recording what concerns Trick VII (Calogero) and Trick VIII (Didier), and I can't manage to finish what concerns Etienne. He telephoned me this morning, but I was still asleep, and I wasn't even the one who answered the phone.

To get back to last Wednesday:]]

I licked his ass and tried to fuck him, raising his legs. But he stopped me:

"Wait, we need some of my magic cream."

I stretched out beside him, he didn't move, and there was another of those singular interruptions I have already mentioned.

Then we went back to kissing and hugging. Later he got up and put some sort of cream on my cock and in his ass. I fucked him without any real difficulty, and for quite a long time, either kissing him on the mouth or licking the hair at the pit of his throat or around the right nipple, or playing with his cock: this was how I made him come and how I came immediately afterward.

We fell asleep lying together very comfortably, and slept until one in the afternoon. When we awoke, we started making love again. This time I put some more cream in his asshole and on my own cock. The "magic" was surprisingly solid cream which I later found out was pure vaseline. I didn't like the way it felt, and it wasn't very effective, for when I was fucking him, Etienne told me that I was hurting him. So I withdrew and lay down on top of him, both arms around his torso, my mouth in the hollow of his neck. In this position I came once again, quite rapidly.

Then he got up to make some tea. He also went out, hardly dressed at all, to buy croissants. The bakery must have been two steps away, for he couldn't have been gone five minutes. When he came back, he caught me reading a little note in English on the table in the first room: the signer, David, thanked him for letting him spend a very pleasant afternoon alone at his place, reading and dreaming, after which he had *happily dissolved into the evening mist.*

Another note, this one from Etienne himself, indicated that he had to go out but that he was leaving the keys, and that the addressee, probably still asleep, could stay as long as he liked.

"Hmm, going through my papers?"

"Yes, I found the sweetest little note here. Besides, it was right on top, face up, in the middle of your desk."

"Well, I just got a letter from my mother."

He arranged some cups on the kitchen table and sat down on a stool to read his letter.

"She sends you her best."

"Very kind of her."

"She says: Give my best to your friends."

I sat down on another stool in the doorway, and drank a cup of tea and ate a croissant.

"You think it's disgusting here?"

"Absolutely."

"Corinne is even worse than I am. You saw her drawings?"

"No . . . oh, those are hers?"

I pointed at the sheets tacked up in the first room, behind me.

"No, those are things by Wols. You know who that was?"

"Sure."

"Anyway, there aren't many of her things left here. Here's one, though, this is hers."

He referred to a huge drawing more or less in the manner of Hans Bellmer, which I looked at for a moment:

"And your writing—when are you going to show me some of that?"

"You really want to see it?"

"Yes, I'd like to. I don't mean I want to read a whole novel right away, but I'd like to see a few pages."

He handed me several typed pages. The first pages of the story were missing. The action seemed to take place in China during the thirties (there was some question of the northern communists), but questioned on this point, the author said that he hadn't intended anything so specific. The central character was called Françoise-Joseph (Etienne had told me the night before that his huge moustache had until very recently been connected to equally long sideburns, à la Franz-Josef, the emperor): sometimes she was a girl, Françoise, sometimes a boy, Joseph. Other doublings occurred. It was all happening during a war, apparently.

"It looks very interesting . . . funny, that double character. Our minds seem to work along the same lines."

"You want to see the other one?"

"Sure."

"Here it is."

This time it was all boys, lovers, bulging cocks, straining muscles, tattoos, "fierce penetrations." The tone was a little provocative and shrill. Various beaches in Morocco were mentioned, and someone was called Etienne, and here again it wasn't very clear who was looking at whom, who was talking about whom, and if the desire he expressed wasn't for himself.

"I like the other one better. But your obsession with this theme is amazing."

"What theme?"

"The . . . the separation from the self."

"Wow, how well put . . ."

"OK. It's two o'clock and I have to leave."

"But you said you didn't do anything but write."

"Yes. That's exactly why I have to go."

"You can write whenever you want."

"No, I work on a schedule."

"You mean you start writing every day at the same time, and write until the same time, and it works?"

"Sometimes it works, sometimes it doesn't. There's always something you can do. In any case, that's the only way *I* can work; I'm like a petty civil servant."

He seemed equally surprised that it took me two years to write a book. If that was all I did, two or three months seemed more than enough to him.

I told him I'd like a photograph of him, one that was on the table, and he asked me if I wanted to see others. He had two huge albums of them. Photographs of other people were scattered between the pages; only those where he himself was represented were pasted in. In most, he was very handsome. One in particular I really liked: he was wearing turn-of-the-century clothes, he seemed to be making a film, one eye close to the viewfinder of a camera on a tripod, standing in the middle of a country lane. Sometimes he had neither moustache nor sideburns, and the fine contours of his face, very clearly drawn, showed up better. In certain shots with friends, he seemed to be participating in a tumbling show in the street.

I repeated that I had to leave. He told me he was going to the country that evening, rehearsing the next day, and that Saturday night he was acting in Cocteau's *Bacchus*.

"You know the play?"

"No, I don't think so. It hasn't been performed in a long time, has it?"

"Probably not."

"I'm leaving the day after tomorrow, until Sunday."

"Where are you going?"

"Italy. Milan."

"Wow, are you ever lucky!"

"Yes, I like Milan a lot. All right, so long, I'm leaving."

He was sitting cross-legged on his bed, and didn't move. I went over and kissed him in the hollow of his neck and walked out the door, which I closed behind me.

[*Saw him frequently. He certainly no longer belongs in the category of tricks. But we never managed to come to much of an understanding. I am embarrassed by his frequent aggressiveness, his student-like mannerisms, a bohemianism a little too carefully codified for my taste, his extreme self-satisfaction. Moreover, he has no telephone but refuses to call, except on extraordinary occasions, and wants people to stop by his place instead. He feels I am a snob and Lord knows what else. When I got back together with Tony, I more or less lost sight of him. But we're still friendly enough.*]

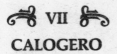

VII

CALOGERO

Saturday, April 1, 1978

That Friday evening I had gone to the *Rosamunda*, in a suburb of Milan, with Philippe, to whom I had talked at length about this enormous *locale di ballo*. We had had a splendid dinner at *Giannino's*, and I was still wearing white ducks, a checked vest and gray jacket, a wing collar and a black bow tie.

As soon as we came into the *Rosamunda*, I noticed a very dark boy with a moustache, wearing a white turtleneck shirt, whom Philippe instantly nicknamed "The Lebanese." I stared at him, he stared back, and we found ourselves quite close to each other, dancing on the huge floor. But each time I danced closer to him he turned his head in another direction. In any event—he was very thin, and even his wrists were of a delicacy which bordered on the sickly.

At this moment I noticed another boy, also very dark, with a moustache and rather long curly hair, wearing a brown plaid shirt open wide at the neck, the sleeves rolled up, and dark brown corduroy pants. He was short, stocky, almost plump. His chest and heavy forearms were covered with thick black hair. He was part of a very animated little group of girls and boys sitting at a table on the edge of the dance floor.

I no longer remember clearly our first exchange of glances. But there were quite a lot of them, I remember that—several accompanied by a faint smile.

He went over to sit down on the steps to the emergency exit. I followed him to this retreat, where he sat completely alone, and looked at him. But as soon as my glance fell on him, he turned away. After a few minutes of this little game, I went for a stroll, rejoining Philippe, who asked me how things were going with the Lebanese. When I turned back toward the steps, the boy in the plaid shirt was still sitting there, still alone. I went over to him, leaned on the railing, and bent over it toward him. He looked up at me. I smiled at him. He made no response. So I walked away again, stopping only at the other end of the room, where I stood leaning one shoulder against the wall. Three or four minutes later, he came over to the same end of the room and took up a position exactly symmetrical to mine, about ten feet away. He looked at me only when I wasn't looking at him, and when I turned toward him, he turned his head in another direction. Tired of this, I walked around the dance floor. From a distance, I saw him climb the stairs toward the exit. I decided he must be going to the toilet, or else outside for some air. I sat down just about where he had been earlier, to watch for his return. It was twenty-five after twelve, and I decided to wait until twelve-thirty. Five minutes passed without his reappearance. So I went back toward the dance floor and did not see him again that evening. Philippe wanted to try *La Divina,* and we went there at one.

At *La Divina,* Philippe pointed out that a certain boy was cruising me. And indeed, the one he indicated had come over to stand right next to me, where I was leaning on the bar. But each time I looked at him, he looked away. He was reasonably appealing, but I didn't like the way he wore his jacket sleeves pushed up to the elbow, according to the season's fashion, nor his turned-up shirt collar, nor the two moles on his face that looked like beauty marks. So I paid no more attention to him and, a little before two, Philippe and I left. Our car was parked just opposite the entrance. I was already behind the wheel, leaning over to open the door for Philippe, when the man with the moles appeared. Changing strategy, he had run after us, and now was asking if Philippe and I would like to come and have a drink with him at a friend's house. Philippe answered that he would have to ask me. We looked at each other, and I accepted the invitation. The friend arrived and sat in the back with Philippe, while the man with the moles sat beside me in front. We drove to an apartment house, quite far away, but just off the expressway we had immediately turned onto. The apartment was absurd, fussy, entirely covered in cut-velvet, with life-size reproductions of Claude Lorrain on the walls, framed in huge gold hoops. The host was quite nice, rather withdrawn, but the boy who had invited us was altogether infuriating, both snobbish and clumsy. We decided to titillate him a little, mostly on my initiative. Now that it was acknowledged that he was turned on by me, I was retrospectively exasperated by his attitude at *La Divina.* And I was tempted to project onto him my growing irritation that evening with certain Italian ways of cruising, or of reacting to being cruised. So we talked about the *Rosamunda,* which of course more or less horrified all these middle-class Milanese boys:

"You didn't go there! It's an impossible place! Besides, you never see any real Milanese there, only little workers who come up here from the *Mezzogiorno.* What an image you must have of Milan!"

Having imagined from the way we were dressed that we were glamorous foreigners from whom they could find out if we knew this or that Parisian couturier, or at least his lover, *who moreover is not at all faithful to him, as I am particularly qualified to say, etc.,* they were bitterly disappointed. Nonetheless, since Philippe, swept on by my enthusiasm, ruthlessly insisted on grilling them about all the cruising places in the city—parks, men's rooms, bus stations, specialized movie theaters—they began to suspect, I think, that the attitude implied by such remarks was perhaps very elegant in Paris: after all, we had dined at *Giannino's:* that point had been established. And although they had at first claimed to know nothing of this, they soon began egging each other on to supply us with all kinds of precious information. This was how we learned of the existence of the *Alce* movie theater in the Piazzale Martini, whose "extreme vulgarity" seemed to us a very good omen.

And we went there the next afternoon, on Saturday.

At the *Alce* there were no ushers, any more than at the *Dal Verme* or at the *Argentina,* other local movie houses. To get into the theater itself you have to shove aside two sets of heavy velvet curtains about five feet apart. The film was Italian, but its action seemed to be set in Chicago in the thirties. There were a lot of big black limousines and lots of shooting. Most of the rows were empty. On the other hand, many figures were grouped behind the last row of seats, or were hovering to the right or left. Most of these were older men, and as far as could be judged in the semi-darkness, quite ugly. One of the scenes of the film, in which some *padrone* or other had gone to identify one of his killers in the livid light of the morgue, allowed us to get a clearer notion of the premises, their layout and their occupants. The right-side aisle between the seats and the wall led to a rather big, high-ceilinged men's room. In the hallway leading into it, two men of about thirty, both emphatically macho, were groping each other's pectorals, biceps, and crotches. Further on, others were waiting without looking at each other, leaning against the damp, leprous wall. The women's room, whose door was ajar, was deserted. In the

58

men's room, two bald forty-year-olds, each holding a cigarette butt between thumb and forefinger, were positioned meditatively in front of the closed doors of one of the toilets.

Returning to the theater after this inspection, I thought I recognized, sitting in one of the rows, the boy who had disappeared from the *Rosamunda* the night before. He was in the last seat of one row, hence right on the aisle. There was someone immediately to his left. I stopped against the wall opposite him and looked at him. He turned his head toward me once or twice, but mostly he seemed to be absorbed by the film, and paid me little or no attention. After having stayed beside him for more than five minutes, I returned to the back of the house. Philippe, whom I rejoined, was rather turned on by two very young boys who were vigorously fucking, standing up between the two rows of curtains, but I didn't have the nerve to go see what was happening. When I came back toward the right-hand aisle, the boy from the *Rosamunda* (for it was indeed he: on the screen, the *Mafioso*'s funeral was taking place in the blinding light of his native Sicily) got up and headed for the toilets. I followed him, but slowly. When I went into the part reserved for men, I saw him waiting in front of a closed door. Then he came out and went into the women's toilets. [*Sequel, Wednesday, April 5: I have to write this faster: we have to give the manuscript of* Travers *to the publisher before the end of the month.*] I followed him in. He was leaning against the tile wall, his eyes on the ground. I went over to him. He smiled. He turned toward me. We were very close to each other. I closed the door behind me. Then I touched his body, through his open shirt. He drew closer. We then touched each other's chest, crotch. Then kissed. Someone came in, a man who went into one of the toilets, leaving the door open, and who watched us while playing with himself. At which point my companion seemed uneasy and hesitant, as if he wanted to leave. I hugged him close, pushed aside his shirt, which was almost completely unbuttoned, and passed first my mouth, then my tongue over his right nipple, which seemed to please him a good deal. His chest, belly, and forearms were absolutely covered with long, thick black hair. He was not slender, but not heavy either; rather hard and solid.

I decided it was time to try out my Italian on him:
"Vuoi andare qualche parte d'altre?"

He seemed to understand, and nodded what I took for agreement. He left and I followed him out, but failed to find him in the darkness of the theater. He was in the lobby, beyond the double curtains, sitting on a banquette covered with velours. I sat down beside him, smiling. He smiled back. Then he asked me if I was in Milan for long, when I had come, and where I was from. I launched into a long speech:

"Sono in un' albergo. Vuoi venire con me? Non sono certo che è possibile di entrare in la camera, ma probabilmente si. Hanno una camera con un'amico, le gente dell'albergo non sai quel è l'amico, sai che hanno una camera per due, so sei tu e io entrara insiemo, erai probabilmente no problema."

Again he seemed to get the gist of what I was trying to explain, and in any case was willing to go with me to my hotel room. He asked me what hotel we were staying in, he knew the hotel *Del Duomo,* which is a large one, and according to him we would have no difficulties. I told him that I would have to tell my friend who had come to the theater with me that we were leaving. So I went back into the darkness. Philippe gave me the keys to the car, and I found my little Italian waiting for me where I had left him. We left the place together, but he had a car too, so I went back inside to return the keys to Philippe.

His car was a Fiat 500, dark blue and considerably banged up. During the ride the driver spoke very little, probably supposing I would not understand anything he said. All the same, I learned that his name was Calogero and that he was from Naples, or more precisely, from Caserte, and that he had lived in Milan for eight years. He went to Caserte every year at Christmas and at Easter and spent his Easter vacation on Capri. Did I know Capri? Yes, and I knew Caserte too, and I liked it a lot. He seemed surprised at that, and failed to share my enthusiasm. I wondered if I had made a mistake and if Caserte, of which I had seen only the palace and the park, was not in fact a miserable industrial city. In any case, Calogero felt that the palace looked like a barracks.

The night before, after leaving the *Rosamunda*, he had gone to the *H.D.*

He parked his car in one of the little streets near the Archbishop's Palace, to the right of the Duomo. It was drizzling. We walked around the cathedral, across the square, and he said something about how crowded it usually was on Saturdays.

As we entered the hotel lobby, I saw two friends of mine, Giancarlo and Gianni, who were leaving me a note at the registration desk. I introduced them to Calogero, but could not introduce him, for I had forgotten his first name. I had been a little nervous, fearing some difficulty with the concierge, but their presence, which confused the situation, facilitated matters. They walked with us, chatting, over to the elevators. Rudolf Nureyev, wearing a long double-breasted leather overcoat which came down to his ankles and a huge cap, walked out of the elevator we were about to take, and this managed to distract attention from us completely.

Once we were in the room, I asked Calogero to excuse me for a second, and went to take a piss. Then he did the same. During his absence, I took off my shoes and socks and stretched out on the bed. When he returned I was leafing through a picture-magazine Philippe had bought. He took off his shoes too and lay down on Philippe's bed, which had been about a foot and a half from mine, but which I had pushed next to it. I explained that he was on my friend's bed, and that we had better not mess it up, and drew him over onto mine. We immediately began kissing. Then I opened his shirt, or rather the last two buttons still left to unbutton, and ran my fingers over the hair on his torso. He also unbuttoned my shirt. We pressed together, kissing, with a certain frenzy. Then we took off each other's trousers, and fell on each other again, one of my legs between his, our cocks together, my arms under his body, my tongue in his mouth. Each time I took one of his nipples

61

between my lips, raising his torso with my right hand, he uttered a moan of pleasure and repeated *"si, si, si."* With my tongue I spread saliva all over the hair on his belly and his chest, and we pressed together in the combined moisture of saliva and sweat. His enthusiasm seemed equal to mine, which was thereby doubled.

I sucked his cock, moved on to his balls, to his perineum, to the crack between his buttocks, in a dense forest of long black hair. He raised his legs to allow my tongue to get in deeper.

Again I kissed him, again I bit his left tit lightly, my forearms under his shoulders. My cock was between his thighs, its tip between his buttocks. Then I raised his legs with both arms and very slowly pushed my way into his ass. He attempted to make me go even slower, but without too much insistence. My hands in his curls, I raised his head to kiss him. Or else I licked the hollow of his throat or the tips of his nipples, and sometimes I bit them a little without interrupting the movement of my cock between his buttocks: this double sensation was what excited both of us the most. Sometimes I barely moved, sometimes the oscillation of my pelvis became very fast and almost violent. Then I began playing with his cock. He came and so did I, immediately after him.

We lay still for a moment in each other's arms, bathed in sweat, saliva and sperm, our mouths full of each other's hair. Then I went to find a towel. I asked Calogero if he wanted something to drink, and said I was going to order some tea for myself. He said he would have the same, and when the waiter brought the tray, I asked him through the closed door to leave it in the vestibule. It seemed to me he agreed very drily.

Between cups we talked as much as my Italian permitted. Apparently, I did fairly well according to Calogero, especially in comparison with another Frenchman whom he had encountered last January and who had not been able to say even one word. Calogero intended to visit Paris at the end of this month; he would be staying in the Rue Racine for four days. I gave him my address and telephone number. He asked me what I did—he himself was a mechanic.

"Qualle sorte di mecanico? Lavora per le automobile?"

No, he made office furniture, chairs and tables, in a big factory near the airport. But he didn't expect to stay much longer in Milan. One of his friends was going to leave, either for Palermo or for Geneva, and he himself was hesitating between these two cities.

"Penso che Palermo è molto migliore . . ."

"Si," perhaps, but Palermo didn't offer much in the way of diversion.

"Ma Ginevra non ha alcune distrassione. Ginevra è bella, ricca, si, ma le gente sono molto seriosi, austeri, protestante. Si tu vuoi molti distrassionni, non penso che Ginevra è una buona idea, no . . . E è necessario di parlare francese, a Ginevra."

Yes, he knew that, and he was prepared to learn French, eventually. He lived out in Linate with his mother. He had a brother and four sisters. Two of his sisters were married, they lived in town. The brother was younger than Calogero, but he was married, and his wife, their baby and he lived with Calogero and his mother, because he would soon have to do his military service. He, Calogero, had finished his service in December. He had been stationed in Verona and had had an affair there with another soldier, the first boy he had made love with, but that was over now.

The night before he had left the *Rosamunda* because there wasn't a big enough crowd for his taste. It was never really full except on Saturday. He went out with the same friends most of the time, a boy and a girl from Palermo.

I didn't look thirty-one, in his opinion: he would have said twenty-three or twenty-four; he, on the other hand, looked much older, he said, but was only twenty-two.

It had grown dark, but we had not turned on any lights. The lights from the square outside and from the cathedral came into the room—some of the statues, which looked more pagan than Christian, were just outside our window.

He was lying on the bed, I was sitting cross-legged on the floor, and we were both naked. I took his completely limp cock, with its one bead of sperm on the tip, into my mouth. He got an erection almost immediately. I stretched out beside him again, we kissed some more, and then I went back to sucking his cock.

The telephone rang. It was Philippe. Someone at the *Alce* had told him about another movie house, the *Argentina*, did I want to try it with him? No, thanks, I was in no condition for cruising or anything else, and very happy with my lot. He would return to the hotel at eight.

I went back to sucking Calogero's cock, which was now entirely erect. With one hand I accompanied the movements of my mouth, and with the other I caressed his chest. He kept sighing with pleasure, and when he came, I swallowed all his sperm. I immediately stretched out beside him. I wanted to kiss him and transfer from my mouth to his what sperm remained between my lips, but he turned his head away. So I kissed him in the hollow of his throat, one hand on his chest, the other between his buttocks, and very soon I came again on his belly.

Then, I think, we slept for a while. As we changed position, we caressed, licked, kissed each other. I suggested that he have dinner with us. Where were we going? I didn't know yet. Yes, he would like to, but he had a financial problem: when he left home this afternoon he had taken only enough money to go to the movie theater, and now he had virtually nothing left. I told him this didn't matter at all, that he was our guest. He then accepted and telephoned his house to say he wouldn't be home for dinner.

We would have to get dressed to be ready for Philippe's return. We took a shower together. At eight, Philippe telephoned. He was in the hotel, downstairs, with a boy he had met at the *Argentina*, could I let him have the room and leave the key for him at the bar, where he would wait for me? This was what I did, and Calogero and I went for a drink in the *Galleria,* where we both had a vermouth. I spend a great deal of time telephoning the restaurant *Solferino* with no luck. The line was constantly busy; then it turned out to be impossible to reserve a table there. I asked Calogero where all the soldiers were in the *Galleria,* was there anything going on? No, he thought it was because the soldiers preferred to go out in civilian clothes, look, all those boys, the ones with short hair, are soldiers. He pointed out some who according to him were "selling their wares," or something like that: I wasn't sure of what he meant; certainly the word *mercato* had something to do with it. He had done that too, at the beginning of his service in Verona. Did the phrase mean to do it for money? I still don't know—he quickly broke off; in any case, the subject embarrassed him.

We met Philippe at nine in the hotel lobby. His trick wasn't having dinner with us, he was expected by his fiancée, whom he had telephoned to say he would be late. Calogero knew a restaurant near the Duomo, *Il Dollaro,* with a lively clientele, he said. But despite what I had been told on the telephone, Philippe was determined to try the *Solferino,* which had been highly recommended. The restaurant was in the Via Solferino, at the end of the Via Brera, and we had some difficulty getting there, finally abandoning the car and taking a taxi. Philippe managed very skillfully to get us a table, despite the crowd and our lack of reservations, claiming that we had come all the way from Paris just to eat here. The patrons were more or less middle-class, many families with children, and anything but gay; the atmosphere was quite pleasant, and the food very good.

During dinner, Philippe talked about his trick, Emmanuele, a young gymnast very proud of his muscles and of the photographs that had been taken of him in the shower. He also asked Calogero a lot of questions—as many as his Spanish-inspired Italian permitted—about gay life in Milan. Calogero thought that the best bar was *La Divina.* Philippe agreed, though it seemed to me the *Rosamunda* was superior. As for the movie theaters, Philippe preferred the *Argentina,* but Calogero was faithful to the *Alce* because at the *Argentina* you couldn't move much. You had to stay seated, and although you might change places from time to time, you couldn't really walk around. I described the movie theater in Rome, the *Nuovo Olimpico,* of which I had fond memories.

Philippe joined me in trying to dissuade Calogero from going to live in Geneva, about which he seemed to have very distorted ideas. Calogero recommended that we order the *maccheroni al basilico,* which was in fact excellent. We communicated with the help of a pocket dictionary I had had the foresight to bring along.

Philippe told Calogero that despite all our efforts, we hadn't been able to get seats for La Scala. But Calogero had no use for the opera. A popular singer named Mina stayed at our hotel, he said, when she was in town; she lived in Lugano but didn't sing in public any more. He also liked Patti Pravo, and *basta!* so much for the Italians. Though he liked a lot of foreign singers.

After leaving the restaurant, we walked to the Brera, where I had parked the car. All three of us were going to the *Rosamunda.* We dropped Calogero at his own car and agreed to follow him, for the night before I had lost the way. But we quickly lost him in traffic and had to get there as best we could by ourselves. We saw him coming toward us down the street as we were parking, and he reproached us for not following him closely enough.

At the *Rosamunda* there was a huge crowd, and Calogero had a lot of friends there. I left him to speak to Gianni and his friend Vittorio. We ran into each other once more and stood together a moment in the uproar, without speaking.

When Philippe wanted to go to *La Divina,* Calogero was nowhere to be seen. Philippe thought he had already left. So we had no chance to say good-bye to each other.

[Saw him again a few weeks later, in Paris. He had not been able to find his friend in the Rue Racine. We made love together one afternoon, but his tastes or his inspiration had changed in this realm, and he no longer wanted to do anything but fuck me. I offered him my

maid's room for the two or three nights of his stay. He was to telephone me about this, after a visit to the Continental-Opéra baths. No
doubt something better turned up, for he did not call back.

A few months later, I received a postcard from him. He apologized,
gave me his address, and asked me to write him. I did not write.]

~❧ VIII ❧~
DIDIER

Sunday, April 2, 1978

With Didier, the problem of the definition of a *trick* recurs, a
problem already encountered with regard to Jacques' brother,
whom I knew before beginning this journal, but only slightly, and
therefore decided to introduce here. I met Didier on Sunday evening, had dinner with him yesterday, slept with him a second time
last night, and am to see him again tonight. Perhaps he will be
more than a trick. But at the moment of writing, Wednesday, he
can still be considered as such.

I met him at the *Manhattan,* just after my unsatisfactory encounters with Etienne, which I have already related. He was sitting in
the little room that has banquettes all around the walls, and I
noticed that he was looking at me. He was certainly not my type,
nor was he the type generally encountered at the *Manhattan;* but
rather very young, with smooth, straight, rather long, very light
brown hair that fell over his forehead in a huge shock, regular
features, no moustache. He seemed very solidly built, with broad
shoulders and very muscular thighs, their curves well defined by
his jeans. Our eyes met several times, with increasing insistence. I
thought he was cute, was flattered by his attention; he looked nice,
lively and smiling. I was in a bad mood, and I wanted to talk to
someone agreeable and friendly. I also thought that he would
doubtlessly please Philippe. But another boy, who was sitting opposite him, had gone over to sit beside him, offering him a ciga-

rette, or a light. They talked for a moment, but each time I passed, or turned my head toward him, he looked up at me, and finally we exchanged a broad smile before bursting out laughing. Nevertheless, since he wasn't alone, I stayed where I was.

A little later, when I was standing on the steps separating the little room with the banquettes from the dance floor, he stood up, put on his windbreaker, which he had kept with him, and stood at the entrance to the other corridor that leads to the checkroom and the stairs. Since he was still smiling when I passed close by, I spoke to him:

"Are you French?"

"Yes, why?"

"I don't know. You look a little like a foreigner. I don't know exactly why."

"Funny. Everyone always says that. It must be true."

"If your admirer sees us together, I'm going to get myself killed."

"What admirer?"

"The boy you were talking to just now."

"Oh, him . . . no. We just discovered we have the same first name."

"What's his?"

"Didier."

It was almost two, everyone was leaving, a line was forming in front of the checkroom, and I moved with it to keep my place. Didier stayed where he was. When I got my leather jacket, though, he went up the stairs at the same time I did, but then immediately went out into the street. I stayed inside for a few seconds to put on my things. When I came out, I saw him waiting on the sidewalk, opposite the door. I went over to him and asked if he was going to *Pim's.* No, he didn't have any money.

"Almost everyone here is going to *Pim's,* I think."

"What about you?"

"No, not me. I never go there. Besides, I don't have any money either."

I went to get my bicycle, which was chained to a post a little farther down the street. He walked off alone, toward the Seine, then stopped. I caught up with him. We were then on a street whose name I didn't know, at the other end of the Rue des Anglais from the Boulevard Saint-Germain [*The Rue Lagrange*]. I didn't want to proposition him, first of all because I was turned on by his cruising me, and also because his declaration about having no money made me suspect that he was some sort of hustler. Clearly he corresponded in no way to the typical image of the *Manhattan* habitué. We walked toward the river, then slanted off to the left, and reached the Boulevard Saint-Germain.

[*Thursday, April 6, after a third night spent with him. Is there still any question of a trick here? Yesterday he referred to Monday evening* ("No, it was Sunday." "Oh, right, there was a gap—we didn't see each other on Monday . . ."), *remarking that it was amazing we had met at all:* "Because even granting that you were looking for someone at the Manhattan, you weren't looking for someone like me. I'm nothing at all like the local product. And besides I never go to the Manhattan, I go to the Keller when I go out at all. But I'm glad it happened."

Last night we dropped in at the Manhattan together (which allowed me to see Etienne again; but that is another story) and something rather funny happened. Didier was playing the pinball machine, and I was watching him; a boy whom I know slightly came over to me and, following my eyes, said: "Cute kid, hmm? I've tried cruising him, but no luck."]

Between the Rue Saint-Jacques and Saint-Germain-des-Près, I learned that he lived out in Meudon, that he was in an agricultural lycée near Reims, that he was on his Easter vacation, that he was leaving Friday for the Île de Ré, and that usually he went to the *Keller*.

"I've only been there once, and didn't have a particularly exciting time. What's it like?"

"Oh, it's nothing special. I don't know why I go there."

"Is it much more seriously leather than the *Manhattan*?"

"A little. About half the guys there are really into leather. The others aren't."

At the start of our conversation, I learned that he had only dollars with him, which his father had given him. He had thought he could change them for francs at the Invalides air terminal exchange booth which had been open the preceding Sunday, but which was closed today. To his repeated insistence that he did not have one *sou* of ready money on him, I answered correspondingly that as a matter of fact all I had with *me* was *lire.* I am now ashamed to admit that this raised in me a certain suspicion about him, and when he offered to walk my bicycle for me, since I had complained about having to drag it along, it suddenly occurred to me that he might jump onto it and ride away. It was only when he began speaking in great detail about his lycée, about the agricultural *bac* and his program, that I was finally convinced he wasn't just stringing me along.

The nature of our encounter and our respective intentions and destinations were still vague. I even asked him where he was going:

"I don't know. It doesn't matter. I like walking."

"Just anywhere?"

"Sure. The other night I walked all the way home."

"To Meudon? That's a long way."

"Not all the way. But I didn't take the shortest route. I walked to the Étoile, through the Bois de Boulogne, and Saint-Cloud. At Saint-Cloud I took a bus."

"That's a pretty long walk all right, especially starting from the *Keller.* But isn't it dangerous, walking through the Bois de Boulogne at night?"

"Hell, it takes more than that to scare me."

When we crossed the Place Saint-Germain-des-Près, I decided it was better to bring matters to a head, so as not to take him ultimately too far out of his way:

"I can't ask you back to my place, there's someone there. But I also have a maid's room, in another building. It's not so terrific . . ."

To which he made no reply, and we walked on to the Rue du Bac, talking about other things. I learned that the agricultural lycée nearest Paris was at Saint-Germain-en-Laye, and that fifty percent of the students in his school were from the city.

"Fifty per cent! I wouldn't have thought that. I imagined almost all of the guys who went to agricultural lycées were people who would be inheriting land. What makes a boy brought up in town want to go to an agricultural lycée? A yearning to get back to the land?"

"No, no, at least not for me. You know, you can do all kinds of things with an agricultural degree. You don't have to become a farmer."

"But it's very specialized, isn't it?"

"No, not really. There's a lot of math, for instance. And we have a rotten teacher on top of it, who thinks the regular manuals are lousy, so we have to do the specialized math programs. And then, of course, we also have to do (but here came words I'm not sure of, starting with zoology and even one I never heard of, which I've forgotten, ending in *-ology*)."

"*What* -ology?"

"Something-ology, it's plants."

"Yes, of course."

We had reached the corner of the Boulevard and the Rue du Bac, in front of the *Escurial*.

"So what are we doing? I've got to know, because if I'm alone, I'm going home, over there, to the left, and if not, we'll go straight ahead."

"Whatever you like. I don't want to hassle you."

"You aren't hassling me. I'm just sorry I can't take you to my place. The maid's room is kind of grim. There aren't any records, no books, nothing."

"Oh, I don't care about that. What would you like?"

"I'd like you to come with me. Of course."

"So let's go."

"Fine. I should also warn you—there's a lot of stairs to climb."

When we got to the room, he said it wasn't as bad as all that.

71

"I know. I always make it sound worse than it is, so then it's a pleasant surprise."

He wanted to use the toilet, and he found on top of the refrigerator a roll of toilet paper that I had never noticed, and which he took away with him. When he came back, I was lying on the bed, my shoes and socks off. He sat down beside me. I was leafing through an issue of *Egoïste*, and I showed him an interview with Yvette Horner, whose name he had mentioned much earlier at the *Manhattan*. (I: "Judging from the music, they're really trying to tell us we have to clear out." He: "Yes, next they'll be playing Yvette Horner.")

"Poor thing, the interviewer isn't very kind to her."

"I know—even the title!" ("Vulgarity is something I don't really understand.")

He asked me what I do.

"I write."

"What?"

"Novels."

"What kind of novels?"

"Oh, the boring kind. You know, the kind that gets printed in an edition of three thousand."

"No, I mean, what *type* of novel? Tell me—I read everything."

"Something to do with the *nouveau roman*, I guess you could say."

"Back at the lycée, they can't believe the kind of books I read. Artaud, for instance—and not just any Artaud. I've read *Heliogabale*, for instance. You know what that is?"

"Yes."

"Day before yesterday a girl friend of mine saw me reading that and she was blown away."

"There are girls there too?"

"Oh sure, more and more of them. In our lycée, there are more than thirty now, out of two hundred and sixty. And one day in study hall (I never work in study hall, anyway. My grades are good, I don't need to), a proctor caught me reading an issue of *Opéra*, a thing about *Das Rheingold*, you know *Das Rheingold?*"

"Yes."

"It turns me on, because I'm something of a mystic myself."

"But isn't it *Parsifal* that has more to do with mysticism?"

"They all do. God, all those stories of gods and heroes! They're so tangled."

"Yes, nobody's ever really figured it all out. But some of the librettos are better than others, in Wagner. *Tristan,* for instance . . ."

I was caressing his forearm, which was resting on one of my hips or on my stomach. We must have jabbered on like that for a good hour, almost entirely about his school. There are no dormitories, but rooms shared by four boarders. This year the doors were taken off to make it easier to keep the residents under surveillance, because all kinds of things were going on.

"They were? I should think if you were four to a room, that would limit the possibilities, wouldn't it?"

"What do you mean?"

"I don't know: there's always at least one who doesn't fit in or who won't cooperate, isn't there? Someone you have to watch out for—"

"Oh, it's not what you think. Mostly it's about bringing food back to the rooms."

"Sorry: I have a dirty mind. Bringing back food?"

"Sure, there's never anything to eat at school. I lost five pounds right away. So I began bringing in a few cans of stuff, sardines, paté, everything. Then everyone did it, and there were real banquets all night long. You should have seen us. Cassoulets and everything. We really started cooking."

"There's a farm attached to the lycée, isn't there?"

"Sure, there's a sort of château, and a little farm. And a whole flock of chickens disappeared. We cooked every one of them."

"But how did you kill them?"

"It's not very complicated, you know—especially chickens!"

"No? It always seemed such an elaborate business to me. But I guess it's harder with rabbits. And ducks—don't they run around for an hour after you've cut their heads off?"

"Yes, but nowadays, you know, it's different. You have them all lined up in a row, the chickens or the ducks, and there's this

73

little needle that comes down, click—in fact, it's like that with everything now. It's all automated. It used to be the horses that were really hard to kill."

"I don't think I really want to talk about that. I once had a horse I was very fond of, and he had an accident and broke something, and they sent him to the slaughterhouse."

"Yes, with horses, there's only one place you can be sure of getting them. If you miss . . . it's like the steers: if you mess up a steer, he gets away. He can break out of anything. Just break bars as big as this. You really have to know what you're doing. The guys who do that are not real sociable to begin with, you know. But after a while, living in all that blood all the time, it drives them completely nuts . . ."

"Uh-huh. Why don't we talk about something else?"

So we went back to talking about the rooms, where plants of all kinds were cultivated.

"But the school authorities must know how to recognize marijuana plants, don't they?"

"They do, but the women who take care of the rooms, they just ask us what this one is, it's so pretty . . . Before, there used to be really decent supervisors. They used to come into the rooms and there'd be the smell of grass, or hash, even, strong enough to knock you down, but they'd close the door and say, I'll come back some other time. But now that's all different. They really hunt us down now."

Except for vacations, the students could get out only on Wednesday afternoons. Sometimes they went to Reims, but there's nothing much to do there. "I don't exactly fit in there, with all the peasants. God, what dolts they are. Just my dog collar gets them all upset."

In fact, I forgot to note that he was wearing around his neck, quite tightly, a simple iron chain with rather large links.

"Is that a real dog collar?"

"Sure, guaranteed: seven francs twenty. You thought it came from Cartier's, didn't you? I went into a pet shop and made them show me all the collars they had: isn't there one a little bigger than

74

this, a little smaller than that? Finally the girl said: 'But what kind of dog is it for?' I told her: 'It's not for a dog, it's for me.' You should have seen her face."

"But how do you get it open, is there a clasp?"

"No, just one link that isn't completely closed. But it never comes open. It's really well designed. Of course, you don't want your puppy to get away."

Didier walks through Reims with his schoolmates. They know his tastes. The other day they went into a record store, and immediately saw their opportunity, there were nudgings, whisperings. "They said, 'Just your meat,' and of course it was some poor queen, not at all my type, I told them they'd have to find me something else."

"Straights are all like that, they think fags will sleep with anything in pants between fifteen and eighty-five."

"But I'll tell you, the old record salesman would have loved a young student from the lycée. I could have gotten *Rheingold* and all the others for the price of just one forty-five."

He's glad to be going to Île de Ré. It's great there now, there's even a new disco. "It's my grandfather who sent me there. He saw I was going crazy at home. And as soon as I came in I saw the kind of place it was, all right, I told myself, this changes everything."

"But the clientele must get pretty stale, doesn't it?"

"Oh, you know, there are guys from all over, guys I've seen again here in Paris, in the bars. Besides, I never stay long—I'm the one who keeps it from getting stale."

"Yes, I see. That's always a nice feeling."

I don't know at which moment in the conversation the silence fell. We looked into each other's eyes, he smiled, leaned over toward me; I put one arm around his neck and we kissed. The next moment, I was lying on top of him. His body was solid, muscular, with a few traces of baby fat. Five minutes later, I suggested that we get on the other side of the bed, which is to say, on the other bed, which is a little wider and more comfortable. Then came the problem of the lamp—too strong but which we didn't want to turn off. He was the one who covered the shade with an assortment of towels and rags. Meanwhile I had got between the sheets. He joined me there, showing—as did I—a good deal of enthusiasm. We kissed frantically, we squeezed our arms and legs around each other. He also liked licking the hair on my chest, or at the pit of my throat, which turned me on a lot. In five minutes we had pulled the bed completely apart. I sucked his cock, which was quite large, though the head was slightly out of proportion to the shaft, which was thick and rather long. Then I licked his ass for a long time.

I have forgotten to note that while we were undressing, he asked me whether or not I wanted him to keep his dog collar on. Yes, why not. This along with the reference to the *Keller*, suggested that he was probably a masochist to some degree, and I was very eager to turn him on as much as possible. But I wasn't sure what to do. His erections were irregular. Biting his nipples had no special effect on his cock, nor did several ventures in the directions of (very light) slaps, which provoked no reaction either way. What gave him the biggest hard-on was for me to hug him as hard as possible, and to wiggle around on top of him very energetically.

After having covered his asshole with saliva, I noticed that the insides of his thighs and the back of his balls showed signs of an irritation, which worried me a little. That I was about to start fucking him had no effect on his cock, but he did nothing to prevent me; anything but. Still my first attempt got nowhere.

I got up to look for a tube of Hyalomiel. When I stretched out beside him again, my cock against his and he licking my neck, I hugged him very hard, until he got a complete erection. Then I rubbed some cream into his asshole, and followed it with my cock. I raised his legs and penetrated him without difficulty. The noises he made could have come from pain as well as pleasure, but he did not push me away. The backs of his knees against the insides of my elbows, my hands under his shoulder blades, I fucked him for a long time. He hugged my head against his. Or else he licked the pit of my throat, which I encouraged him to do, repeating "Yes, yes, lick me," not without thinking of the dog collar. Once or twice I ran a finger inside the collar and, by slightly twisting my hand, tightened it around his neck. But I received no special indication that I should continue doing it.

Sometimes I straightened up, letting his legs down, and played with his cock, which was still not very hard. Or, my legs extended, supported on my arms, I fucked him harder and harder, hoping that his muffled cries were of pleasure. While I was doing this he caressed my chest.

A little tired after spending what must have been a good half hour inside his ass, I knelt down and pulled him up and over me. We were then face to face, my cock still inside him, he squatting so as to straddle my thighs, his arms around my shoulders. When I started playing with his cock again in this position, my hand between his belly and mine, he managed to get very hard. His moans, shorter and closer together, became very specific, less subject to interpretation. And that was how he came, very copiously. Then I tipped him over onto his back, raised his legs again, and in the same position as before, I came a moment or two later. Then, my cock still inside him, I slid over to his left, his thighs against my belly, his legs still around my arms. We lay that way for a long moment, smiling, kissing, and finally sleeping a little.

His dried come was sticking to my belly and my chest. I got up to wash a little, as did he. Back in bed, I watched him standing in front of the sink, as he moved a washcloth over his torso:

"Nice pair of legs you have there, kid."

"They look good with my boots. That's another thing that drives them crazy in Reims. I have these boots that come up to here, to my knees, and I wear them with very tight jeans. You should see their faces."

"Yes, I can imagine. Do you want to sleep here?"

"I don't know. What do you think?"

"Do whatever you want. If you go, I'll leave with you. I'm not about to sleep up here alone, believe me."

"I have to go to the dentist tomorrow morning. My appointment's at eleven."

"What time do you have to be up?"

"What's the nearest Métro stop?"

"Bac."

"That goes straight to Montparnasse, right?"

"Right."

"Oh, nine-thirty, then."

"Well, there's an alarm clock here. But I don't know how it works. Try to set it yourself."

He set the alarm, and came back to bed. We slept very well, lying pressed together, he with his back to me, our legs bent and parallel, my arms around his chest.

When the alarm went off, he didn't get up:

"How many stops to Montparnasse?"

"Four."

"Then I can stay here another minute."

And he fell back to sleep. But I didn't. Fifteen minutes later, I shook him and asked if he still wanted to go to the dentist:

"I don't know."

Nevertheless, he got up and dressed quite rapidly. The night before, just before we fell asleep, I had offered him my telephone number. He had said he was about to ask me for it. He now wrote it on a Métro ticket. Then he kissed me and closed the door behind him.

[*Thursday, April 6, eight o'clock: two phone calls from him this afternoon, the first at five-thirty. I was with Etienne and Jean-Christophe. I still didn't know what I was doing in the evening, and I asked him to call back between seven and eight. The second at seven-thirty. I had made an appointment with Etienne for dinner. So I told Didier I couldn't see him this evening. He leaves tomorrow for Île de Ré, and then returns directly to school. I feel a certain remorse, because he's extremely nice (as only making love with him can fully testify), and I enjoyed his company. Regret, too, because Etienne, who is physically much more my type, is of an aggressiveness which augurs badly for our future relations.*]

78

[*Saw him again very frequently. I even had a kind of little affair with him, interrupted by my reconciliation with Tony. Once I went to bed with him and Etienne together, and he would not have been adverse, I think, to a reprise of this kind with Tony. But Tony is not at all interested in him.*

The specialization of his sexuality appears to be intensifying: he functions in a milieu about which I know nothing. But I see him quite often, and we are very good friends.]

❦ IX ❦
MAURICE

Friday, April 14, 1978

I had already seen him several times, and vaguely cruised him. As so often, my attraction had focused on his forearms, covered with thick, very light brown, almost blond hair. But he had not paid me the slightest attention. Yet he told me the day before yesterday that he had "spotted me" (his expression) a long time ago, but that he had always been with his *"friend."* Each time he mentions his *"friend,"* he makes the same gesture—he holds his hand out flat, palm down, about four feet from the floor, doubtless to indicate, *"you know, the short one."* And in fact I remember the friend in question, who is not much shorter than he, and equally muscular.

Friday night, then, at the *Manhattan*, he walked past me, quite close, and for the first time I had the impression that our eyes met. He was going to dance. I went over and started dancing near him. But his eyes were invariably looking somewhere else, and he even moved away a little. After five minutes, I gave up. Then I saw him two more times upstairs, and I thought I noticed, again, that he was looking at me a little. Yet when I glanced at him, he turned away. He went right by me again, his eyes meeting mine. He was

79

on his way downstairs. At first I did not follow him, but about ten minutes later, I went downstairs too. He was dancing at the edge of the floor. I danced beside him, as before. Our glances met again, two or three times. But he came no closer. Suddenly he turned his back to me, so that now I was dancing behind him. My hands brushed his. He pulled away. My fly was touching his ass, I began to get a hard-on. And when our hands touched again, he grabbed mine. I then pressed against him, and we danced like that, together. Then he turned around and faced me, smiling. But when I made as if to touch him, he stopped me with a gesture. He said something I couldn't hear. I even thought he was speaking a foreign language. But he added:

"They're all so uptight here!"

"Less here than anywhere else, though."

I decided he must be pretty uptight himself, since it had been weeks now that we knew each other by sight, and since he didn't want us to touch while dancing, except when his back was turned.

He took me by the arm:

"Let's go somewhere where it's quieter."

At first he stopped in the vaulted corridor leading from the checkroom. But just standing there, face-to-face, was enough to block traffic. Then he suggested we go back to the street floor:

"It's incredible, you can't even find a place to stand!"

"What kind of an accent is that?"

"I've lived in Paris for over seven years."

"Still, that's not a Paris accent! Just now I thought you were talking a foreign language."

"I'm from Béziers. You know it?"

"No, but I know where it is. I know a place near there, though, Bédarieux."

"How come?"

"I had a friend from Bédarieux, a long time ago."

"Was he gay?"

"Mmm . . . yes, more or less."

"That's really funny."

"Why?"

"Because I'm from Bédarieux too. I said Béziers because it's simpler—most people have heard of Béziers. But I'm from Bédarieux."

"You're right, that *is* funny."

"What's your friend's name?"

"Oh, I don't remember any more . . . Pierre."

"No, his last name."

"That I don't remember at all."

"How did you meet?"

"We were in school together."

"What were you studying?"

"Political science."

"But you . . . did you do anything with him?"

"Sure. A little, vaguely. But we were just kids. He's probably married with a family by now."

"When I go back there, I spot them right off. It's easy. But I never get involved with them. It's such a little place."

"I think he lives in Paris now. I see him every now and then."

"That's really funny . . . No one ever knows Bédarieux. The other day someone told me Peyrefitte was from there, but I don't know which Peyrefitte—there are two brothers, aren't there?"

"No, I don't think so, there's the writer and then there's a politician but they're not brothers. I don't think they're even related. In any case, the politician is not from the Hérault, he's from Provins. But I don't know much about him: he's the mayor of Provins, but maybe he does come from the Hérault, after all."

"I don't know anything, I never read. And you're a Parisian—or no, where are you from?"

"I'm from the Auvergne."

"The Auvergne! That's funny."

"Why?"

"I don't know. I think it's funny, coming from the Auvergne."

"Why is it so funny?"

"Because it means you're from the country—you're a country boy!"

"You know, there are towns, even in the Auvergne. And I'm not really from the country. I'm from Chamalières."

"Chamalières. Wait a minute, I've heard of that."

"Sure. It's the town Giscard was mayor of. It's near Clermont—really one of the suburbs."

"In any case, you don't have an accent."

"No, they don't have much of an accent in the Auvergne."

We sat down at the back of the room upstairs, near the door to the corridor leading to the toilets. He was watching the lineup for these:

"What are they doing in there—cruising, groping, or what?"

"Oh, some of them are even trying to take a piss."

"It's pretty funny. You come here often? I spotted you a long time ago."

"You did?"

"Sure, but I was with my friend, so—you know. What's your name?"

"Renaud."

"Renaud? That's an easy one. There are thousands of *Renaults* all over the world."

"What's yours?"

"My name is Maurice. Yes, there are still some of them around. You live far from here?"

"No, not very far. Rue du Bac."

At this moment, Walthère (Trick I) passed by. He came over to talk to me. Then, recognizing Maurice, he began chatting with him:

"All alone? What have you done with Roger?"

"He's at Le Touquet, with his family."

"His family?"

"Well, you know, with his other half."

"Oh."

They seemed to know each other well. I didn't follow the rest of the conversation. Since it went on, and since I wasn't participating, I got up and someone immediately took my place. I went to get a drink of water from the tap in the toilet. When I came back, Maurice stood up, left Walthère, and came toward me:

"Sorry, we got to talking. He's a friend of Roger's—my friend. He comes from the Midi too. You know him?"

"Yes. He's from the Aude."

"He's a good guy."

We were standing against a wall. I had one finger in his belt, in the hollow of his back. He turned toward me and we kissed. But just as I was beginning to get turned on, he pulled away:

"You live alone?"

"Yes. Well, no, but right now there's no one else at my place."

"You have a friend?"

"No, but usually I live with someone."

"He's away."

"Yes."

"You plan on staying here long?"

"No, not much longer."

"Me neither. I'm leaving soon. Maybe we could leave together?"

"Good idea! It never would have occurred to me."

"But I want to dance a little first."

"OK."

But he didn't move. I caressed his chest through the opening of his shirt. But he stopped my hand:

"You like hair, don't you?"

"I do? Whatever makes you say that?"

"I can tell. It's psychological."

After a while, I started downstairs, perhaps a little abruptly. He didn't follow, and I waited at the foot of the stairs. Three or four minutes later, he joined me:

"Why did you leave?"

"Leave? You're a little gaga, buddy. You're the one who said you wanted to dance. So I come downstairs, and you don't move."

We danced for about ten minutes, without touching each other. After three numbers, I stopped, exhausted. He went on for two or three minutes, then came over and joined me at the edge of the floor:

"Ready to leave?"

"Sure."

I headed for the checkroom through the crowd, which was very thick now. But once there I realized he wasn't behind me. I waited for him a moment. When he arrived, he was completely out of breath:

"Wait a minute, I met a friend, I want to talk to him for a second, OK?"

"OK."

I walked around the rooms downstairs, once more.

[*Tuesday, April 18*] I forgot to note that while we were sitting side by side upstairs, near the door to the toilets, he had one arm around my waist. Pinching a piece of flesh just above my hip, he made some remark—I have forgotten the exact words (something like: "A nice little love-handle here!"), to which I made no answer, but which turned me off a little, especially since he himself seemed to be made out of reinforced concrete. At another moment, I don't remember when, as he touched my thighs he remarked that I was much more muscular than I seemed.

"I don't want to disappoint you, but no one's ever loved me for my muscles."

"You go in for sports?"

"Not much. You?"

"Sure, I do a lot of sports, and exercise, swimming, even [*I've forgotten the name for the kind of flying that's done with big canvas wings*]."

"It seems to produce great results."

For he was covered with muscles just about everywhere. His biceps and his back were especially impressive.

We found each other again and left together. I no longer remember clearly what we talked about on the way. About Walthère, among other things: that they were at all acquainted sur-

84

prised me somewhat. He, Maurice, lived near the Place d'Italie. It seemed to him that everyone knew everyone else at the *Manhattan*, and for this reason one shouldn't go there too often:

"And the guy you live with is your friend?"

"He was. Not now."

"But you've lived together a long time?"

"Yes, a very long time."

"How long?"

"Nine years."

"And now it's over?"

"Yes."

"That must be hard for you, isn't it?"

"Yes. But it's not so bad right now, because he's not there. When he's there, it's quite painful. The apartment is really too small for two people."

He caught sight of my bicycle on the landing, and wanted to know if it was mine:

"I thought so. You look like the kind of guy who rides a bike."

"I do? How does that kind of guy look?"

He made no answer.

"You must pay a lot of rent in this neighborhood."

"No, actually it's almost nothing. Before I used to pay fifteen hundred francs a month, but they revised the rates—the ceilings are too low—and now we pay only two hundred francs a month, almost nothing."

"Shit, I pay over a thousand, in the Thirteenth Arondissement, and it's smaller than this."

"Of course, it's falling to pieces. The landlord isn't much inclined to make repairs."

"How high do standard ceilings have to be?"

"Eight feet."

"And how high are the ceilings here?"

"Not quite seven, at this end."

I pushed the button for France-Musique, but it was almost two, and the programs were ending. We heard the *Marseillaise*, which seemed both to surprise and please him. Then I put on a tape, almost at random: Glenn Miller. Maurice was lying across the little mattress, which is set directly on the floor:

"But when he's here—when your friend's here, you both sleep on this little bed?"

"No, most of the time no one sleeps here. There's a big bed in the other room. If both of us are here, the one who comes in last sleeps here. But usually when just one of us is here, the other isn't, and so it works out."

He studied the pictures and drawings on the walls, especially a drawing by Twombly:

"Did you do this?"

"No."

"Some kid?"

"No."

"But it's graffiti, isn't it—like graffiti?"

"Yes, a little."

"But who did this? Someone you know?"

"No, it's by an American named Twombly. He lives in Rome."

He also looked a long time at *Dollar Bill* by Warhol and wanted to know if I had painted that. He asked if a framed text by Gilbert and George was some kind of diploma.

"No, my diplomas don't look that good, unfortunately."

I stretched out across the bed, parallel to him, but not against him. He sniffed at his own shirt:

"Stinks of tobacco, when you come out of that place!"

"Yes, I know, mine does too. There's nothing you can do about it. You don't smoke?"

"No."

"Neither do I."

We caressed each other's chests between our shirt buttons. Then we moved closer and kissed. I was lying on top of him. Gradually we got our shirts off:

"You're good and hairy."

He seemed to like rubbing his body against mine:

"But your beard is so prickly!"

"So's yours."

His belly was very hairy, more than his chest, and extremely solid, articulated with little round muscles. When he sat up to take off his shoes, I suggested we go to the bed in the other room. He followed me in. We took off our clothes and got between the sheets. His ass was very beautiful, round, small, very hard, and covered with a light down. His cock was rather small. We rubbed our bodies together again, and his powerful arms pulled me to him while we continued kissing.

"My face is going to be all broken out tomorrow."

We remained like that, both with erections now, for ten minutes, maybe longer. Most of the time I was on top of him, but sometimes it was the other way around. Then my mouth moved down his body, across the hair on his belly, down to his cock, which I sucked for a minute, before going on to his balls and his buttocks. Then he made me turn around so I was lying against him, and he sucked my cock too, then my balls. Legs curled around each other's necks, we both thrust our tongues into each other's assholes. Then we kissed each other some more. Lying on top of him, I placed my hands under his ass, while he wrapped his arms around my neck. He talked into my ear:

"You turn me on so much, I think I'm going to come."

"No, wait, it's too good. Make it last longer."

Then he turned me over on my back and knelt between my legs, which he lifted up. He seemed determined to fuck me. He spent quite a while licking my ass. Then he tried to get into me.

"Wait a minute."

I managed to find the tube of Hyalomiel that was under the mattress, and put some of the cream in my ass, some on his cock. He then got into me without difficulty. He slung my knees over his shoulders. But that was too high for me, and I wasn't very comfortable in this position. I slipped my legs under his arms and crossed them behind his back. Leaning forward, he kissed me, while I played with myself. Again he said he was going to come, and again I persuaded him not to. All the same, when at a certain moment it seemed imminent, I pushed him back, his cock came out of my ass and came up against mine. We were kissing each other, clasped together by our legs and our arms. I grabbed the tube of cream, which was lying on the sheet. This didn't escape his notice:

"That's for me?"

"Yes, why not?"

"No, I don't get fucked."

"Oh, come on, just this once."

"No."

"That's not fair! I guess they've never heard of fair play in Béziers . . ."

My tongue in his mouth, I played with his ass. When, two or three minutes later, I picked up the tube again, he protested further:

"Bastard! Stop!"

I dropped the tube.

"You didn't put the top back. Now there's going to be stuff all over the sheets."

"Exactly. So why shouldn't I put a little of it up your ass?"

He didn't answer, but pushed the tube away so that I fell off the bed. This time I was the one who pretended to be angry:

"Bitch! I'm going to rape you right now."

"Promise?"

I took this as encouragement and pulled him across the bed, with his ass at the edge. I knelt on the floor between his thighs, and sucked his cock. I managed to pick up the tube of Hyalomiel and put some cream between his buttocks, completely ignoring his protests:

"You bastard! You're disgusting!"

I moved him back to the center of the bed, raised his legs, and pushed my cock up to the crack between his buttocks. But I couldn't get in. No doubt he was squeezing his ass together. I gave up.

A moment later, he was fucking me again. I was on my back, legs up, ankles crossed around his hips. I caressed his torso with one hand and played with myself with the other. He was breathing hard:

"God, you turn me on. I'm going to come now!"

"No, not yet. It's too good. Wait. Kiss me some more."

But he couldn't hold back any longer.

"All right, come now! I'm coming too!"

So he came in my ass, and I shot my sperm over my shoulder, all over the pillow.

I got up to find a towel and he followed me into the bathroom. In passing, I put another cassette into the tape deck, Vivaldi oboe concertoes that happened to be lying on the machine. We washed up, one after the other. He went on talking, though hardly convincingly:

"It's pretty nasty. What we just did."

"What?"

"What we did—for a guy to put his cock up another guy's ass . . . you don't think so?"

"Come on!"

We lay down on the bed again.

"OK. I should leave now."

"You don't want to sleep here?"

"I can?"

"Of course, idiot."

"What time do you get up?"

"When I wake up."

"I have to be on the job by noon. I work at the post office, Rue du Louvre. We'll get up in time, won't we?"

"Sure."

We slept very well, and woke up around ten-thirty. Sitting cross-legged on the floor, we drank tea and ate some Patterson's biscuits. I asked if he wanted a bath.

"No, I'd rather take a shower."

"The shower doesn't work right. It's either boiling hot or ice cold, and it switches from one to the other right in the middle. Whenever someone tries to use it, I hear these terrible screams. I think you'd better run yourself a bath."

"I've taken maybe three baths in my life."

But apparently he had developed a taste for them, and he remained in the tub quite a long time without moving. He also shaved. As he had feared, the skin of his face was red and irritated. He also complained about the dirtiness of his shirt, but refused to let me lend him one.

Afterward, while getting dressed—very slowly—he told me about his job. He had worked for the post office for about seven years, but had just changed departments. He had had to take an exam to reach a new level and now was in the telegram service, with a lot more work. But he preferred this, because if you don't do anything, you get bored. He worked every other day from noon to eight, and the alternate days from eight in the morning till noon. That way he had lots of free time. Right now he was fixing up his studio, which he had just moved into. They had put in a telephone for him, an orange one he liked a lot, but the line wasn't in service yet. Each time he went home, he rushed to the phone to see if those bastards at the office had finally turned it on. They had promised him it would be ready today.

I couldn't possibly imagine the stupid things people put in their telegrams.

"All the same, it must be interesting, what people say, isn't it?"

"Yes, especially for me—I'm very nosy. But we don't let just anything go through, you know. I mean, I don't care, personally. But often they refuse to send messages, obscene stuff. And then some people send things in code, incomprehensible sentences, doesn't mean a thing, but you can bet your ass it means something to the people who get it. Sometimes we call the sender for explanations. The other day there was someone who said he had found a pile of guns in his cellar. When it's suspicious like that, we ask questions, or else we notify the police . . . What's not so much fun is all the death notices, you can't believe how many. Sometimes there are days when people have nothing else to send to each other. It gets depressing. But I'm moving up to the Telex soon. First I have to learn how to operate it."

90

The night before, he had said he never took anyone's phone number, just went home with guys, like this, and then *ciao*.

"Do you want my number, or is it against your principles?"

"No, not at all. Give it to me. That was when I had my friend, but now . . ."

So I gave it to him and he left. He was very pleased to be able to walk to work, even though it was almost noon.

"You won't be late?"

"Oh, the hell with it. They'll wait for me. They've kept me waiting long enough for my telephone."

[*Seen him often, though we've never slept together again, even if both of us claim we want to. He is always very friendly and smiling.*]

ALAIN

Wednesday, April 26, 1978

At the *Bronx*, Rue Saint-Anne, there's a little recess at the back, very dark and irregularly shaped, with its own toilet at one end. People tend to crowd in here, even if the outer room is far from being full. I was near the corridor that leads to it when I noticed a boy whom I have known by sight for a long time, who frequently cruises me, and who claims—someone told me, I don't remember who, someone who's also a friend of his—that I turn him on. He, on the other hand, doesn't attract me much physically: a short boy with a brown moustache, medium-length hair, and something about the shape of his chin or his nose which gives him a vaguely bulldog look that's not exactly becoming. But there was no one around who interested me more, and the determination of his attention turned me on somewhat.

Since we were both in the doorway, very close to each other, I waited without encouraging him, without even looking at him, until he touched me on the crotch. I was already getting hard. I touched him on the same place. Then he stood right beside me, and in another minute we were kissing. He smelled good. Someone who was standing near us unzipped my fly and took out my cock. He took it in his hand and began playing with it. He put his other arm behind my head and pressed my mouth against his. But I was too hot. We were jammed into a crowd that was jostling us on all sides, those who wanted to get to the toilet, and those who were struggling to get out. I moved away, got to a quieter corner, took off my windbreaker, my sweater and my tie, then put my windbreaker back on. He had followed me and was standing about a yard away.

I went into the outer room, the one you come into from the street, and left my sweater under a velours cushion facing the bar. When I came back into the little room, I passed right beside him, sitting now on a high stool against the wall, near a corner. He held out his arm and drew me against him. We went back to kissing each other. He unbuttoned my shirt to caress my chest, and bit my left nipple hard enough to hurt.

In the same corner, to his right and also sitting on a stool, was an older man, who, in the darkness, looked quite attractive: thirty-five maybe, not shaved, with a huge moustache. His thigh was against mine, and I brushed against it with one hand, which I finally rested on it. It was impossible for him to tell, squeezed in as we were, if my gestures in his direction were deliberate or not.

Meanwhile the younger one had opened my fly and taken out my cock. Later he took out his too, which was quite large. My left hand was against that of our neighbor's, which it finally squeezed, and which squeezed it back. He had very muscular thighs, as well as torso and belly, which I touched successively. From time to time I glanced over at him, trying to see him better, and he seemed to me very attractive indeed. I don't know when it was that the younger one, whom I was still kissing, realized that I was also in

92

contact with someone else, but it was just afterward that he suggested I come home with him. I hesitated before replying:

"Oh, I don't think I have enough energy, really, to go anywhere."

"It seems to me you have a lot of energy."

The man to my left had opened his own fly now and taken out his cock, which was more or less hard, and rather small. I went on kissing the younger one, whose cock I also sucked for a few seconds. I was trying to get them together, but they didn't seem at all interested in each other. I kissed the second one in the hollow of his neck, then on one cheek, but after that I didn't pay any more attention to him. A little later, he adjusted himself and went away. I then got up on the stool he had abandoned. The first boy stood up and came over in front of me. Again, he ran his tongue over my chest, but he had a tendency to bite rather than to lick. He sucked my cock in turn for two or three minutes. Then he asked me if I had made up my mind.

"About what?"

"My proposition?"

"No, I don't think so, I'm really completely wrecked. I'll look around a little, to pull myself together. And I'd like to piss, but it's not easy here."

"No, they're all jammed up around the doorway."

"Even so, I'm going to try."

To tell the truth, I wasn't at all sure I wanted to go home with him, there wasn't much about him that turned me on except the desire he seemed to have for me, which he seemed to have had for a long time. I wanted to look around the place once more in order to see if there wasn't someone who inspired me with a more direct or less perverse desire, especially around the recess in which a lot of men were seriously interested in doing something. So I did up my trousers, if not my shirt, and went away. The toilet was just about inaccessible, but when, despite the mob, I finally managed to get the door open, I found that two men had entrenched themselves in there in total darkness. I touched several bodies, virtually at random. But no one really interested me.

My suitor kept his eye on me over the heads of the crowd. For a moment, thrust on by the movement of the crowd, I found myself beside him again:

"You're right, it isn't easy."

But just at that moment I thought I saw the toilet door open and the two men come out:

"Ah, now I think I have a chance. I'm going to try again."

This time I was able to take a piss. Then I explored as best I could the tiny vestibule outside the toilet, and ran my hand over several bodies, all dripping with sweat. Emerging from this recess, I glimpsed him sitting on a stool again, looking quite melancholy. I walked around the inner room, then the outer one, and came back to him:

"They close at two here?"

"Yes."

"Oh, then it's time to be going: I don't like being around when they suddenly turn on all the lights, I really hate that."

"My offer still stands."

But for him to succeed, he would have had to renew that proposition, and more specifically. Which he did not do. We remained side by side a while longer, occasionally exchanging a kiss. I looked at my watch. Finally the people behind the bar began turning on the lights. He looked at me:

"All right, I'm leaving."

"Me too."

He left. I went to get my sweater. When I came outside, he was in front of the door. We walked together to the Avenue de l'Opéra. I turned toward him:

"Well, you're not mussed up at all."

"Mussed up?"

"Yes. I mean, usually when you leave the *Bronx*, you're completely wrecked, your hair's sticking to your forehead, you're sweating, soaked through, your shirt's torn, all that. *You* look fresh as a daisy."

"So do you."

"I do? I don't feel fresh, not one bit. You want to go to the *Sept?*"

"No."

We stopped at the Avenue de l'Opéra, standing motionless on the curb, not speaking. As I said, only his desire to go home with me would have turned me on. Therefore he should have expressed this as much as possible, even insisted a little. But he said nothing more. I was the one who had to speak:

"Are you going somewhere now?"

"No, I have to get up tomorrow morning. I work. Not very early, but still . . ."

"What time do you have to be at work?"

"Eleven."

"Oh, that's not so bad."

"And what are you going to do?"

"I don't know."

I began thinking that I should go see what *Pim's* was like, since I was close by.

"You still don't want to come home with me?"

"Suppose we went to my place?"

"Fine. It doesn't matter to me where we go. Where is it?"

"Rue du Bac."

"Fine. Wherever you like."

"I'd prefer to go to my place."

"All right. I have a car."

"One more reason then. If I went home with you, how would I get back?"

"You might have had a car too. And there are always taxis."

"Taxis—I'm afraid I'm more of a proletarian than that, sir. I don't have a car, and taxis cost too much for me."

We turned back into the Rue Saint-Anne, where his car was parked. I think it was a little Renault, an R5. The seats were covered with a kind of plush, rather worn.

"Which way do I go?"

"It's complicated from here. There are a lot of one-way

95

streets, so you have to go a roundabout way. You turn right here."

We headed toward the Rue de Richelieu and turned into it.

"What's your name?"

"Renaud."

"Hmm, good."

"And yours?"

"Alain. And what do you do in life?"

"I write. Where do you live?"

"In the Thirteenth Arondissement."

"And what do you do *in life,* as you say?"

"I'm a hairdresser."

I don't know if I'm imagining this, but there are so many jokes about hairdressers in Parisian homosexual circles—their number, their supposed tastes in interior decoration, or in dogs, or in clothes—that it may be a little difficult to say that that's what you are. I have known more than one, in any case, who postponed as long as possible what then figures as a confession. To say nothing of those who proclaim a little aggressively, in the first seconds of a conversation, their *you know, I'm a hairdresser,* as if to defy you to raise an eyebrow. Anyway, on these occasions, I become a little nervous by a kind of inverse paranoia. Probably because I imagine, no doubt wrongly in almost all cases, that my reactions are being studied and that I am being watched to see if I smile or if I have cooled off. So I immediately go on talking without any particular change in tone, but not without wondering if, by doing so, I don't pigeonhole myself from the start as one of those people who go on talking too quickly when you tell them you're a hairdresser, thereby revealing that in their opinion there might be something embarrassing about such an admission, etc., etc.

"And you don't go to work until eleven?"

"*I* don't have to. The others start at nine."

"Shitty for them."

"No, I work much later than they do. Now what do I do?"

"Go through the Louvre, cross the Seine, and then take the Rue des Saints-Pères."

"What do you write—articles?"

"No, novels."

"In magazines?"

"No, books. You know, there aren't many novels in magazines nowadays. Unfortunately."

As soon as it had been decided we would go home together, I regretted this choice. He was not really my type, to say the least; I didn't really want to go to bed with him, and I was even afraid I wouldn't be able to get it up. It was for this reason that, as we were crossing the Seine, I uttered a sentence I had been working up for two or three minutes, but which came out all wrong:

"You know, Alain, you're not exactly getting a present."

"I'm not?"

From his tone—very serious, patient, controlled, the tone of someone ready to discuss any proposition, almost thanking you for being so good as to warn him ahead of time—I decided he was expecting me to ask him for money. I hastily tried to correct my error, or his:

"I mean, I'm not good for much tonight."

"Why not?"

"Oh, I've had too much to drink, smoked too much—I'm completely used up."

"You should take better care of yourself."

"Oh, it's nothing that a good eight hours' sleep can't fix."

At the corner of the Rue des Saints-Pères and the Boulevard Saint-Germain, he started to turn left.

"No, straight ahead. You don't know where the Rue du Bac is?"

"I'm not sure."

"I thought everyone knew the Rue du Bac!"

"I know it's around here, but not exactly where—"

"It's a pain in the ass to find. You have to keep going around these one-way streets."

I told him to turn right into the Rue de Grenelle, but I was a little late and he had to put on the brakes abruptly.

"Wow! Lucky there was no one behind us! I have another confession to make—there are a lot of stairs to climb."

"I do very well with stairs. I have eight flights at home. But there's an elevator."

"Where I live there's no elevator, as you'll soon see . . . Turn right here and then left up there. Yes, you can park it here. I don't think I'll ever be able to make the stairs tonight."

"It's all right, I'll push you."

When we got to the apartment, we went directly into the kitchen.

"Wouldn't you know I'd have only a half bottle of Perrier and a half bottle of Vittel. Which do you want, they're both probably flat . . ."

"I don't care. I'm not really thirsty."

"Here."

"Thanks."

We went into the larger room.

"Nice. You have a terrace."

"Yes. It's falling to pieces, but still, it's nice, especially from now on."

"You can lie out in the sun when it gets hot?"

"Yes."

We were standing face to face. I took him in my arms. I lifted him up under the buttocks. I led him into the bedroom, stretched him out on the bed, and lay down on top of him and kissed him.

"It's a rape!"

His cock was hard already. Not mine. He began undressing me, beginning with my shirt. He kissed my shoulders, my chest.

"Wait a minute. Excuse me a second, I'll be right back."

I went to piss. When I came back, he hadn't moved.

"May I take off my shoes?"

"Please, take off whatever you want."

"Thanks. But in that case, maybe we could get into bed, under the blanket—it's a little prickly on top."

"Sure."

As I had much less to take off, I was undressed first, and got into bed.

"Nice shorts."

"Don't be silly."

"I'm not being silly. They're blue?"

"You never wear shorts?"

"Sure, but not with jeans."

When he joined me he had a full erection; I had nothing of the kind. He wasn't thin or fat, but a little shapeless, especially around the chest, which showed no division from the stomach. His ass was low, round and solid, his balls were thick and heavy, like his cock.

We started kissing, and I began to tell myself a little story, a variant of several others that had served in analogous circumstances. We're on a big sailing ship in the eighteenth century. The first lieutenant looks like Captain Troy in the television serials of my childhood, with something of Clark Gable in his attitude (I had recently seen *Mutiny on the Bounty* again). All the cabin boys sleep with him, but he's in love with the captain's nephew, a very young officer who's there because of his family connections, very innocent and cute. Or else it's the nephew who's in love with the first lieutenant. Who, in any case, fucks everyone on board. Then the action shifts to London, around 1880. A young telegraph operator delivers a message to a dandy slightly older than he, twenty-five or thirty, and who has the same physique as the second mate on the ship. It is the telegraph boy who makes advances. The dandy receives him in his dressing gown. The telegraph boy wants to be fucked more than anything.

Same scene, but this time in a contemporary American prep school. A rather sulky boy, sixteen or seventeen. The other is twenty, but has a man's body: moreover, he's a letterman in every sport, the most virile kid in the school. He's lying on his bed, bare-chested, the top button of his jeans open. The younger boy wants to be fucked by him. And he has a means of blackmail: he has caught Butchy making love with another very cute student with whom he's in love. And Butchy is engaged to his sister. "I'll tell my sister everything unless . . . I've been wanting it for a long time. At least let me feel your chest, your belly." Close-up of the belly, hair, muscles . . . Well, this little blackmailer's not so bad after all. He's even cute. He has good thighs, he probably runs.

"Let's latch the door." . . . "But what if my roommate comes back . . . ?" Etc.

Fine, I was getting a good hard-on. We were still kissing. Alain had very soft skin. He seemed to like me to play with his chest. I kept my hands under his ass. He himself seemed rather interested by mine, slid one finger down between my buttocks. I wasn't so keen on being fucked by him. I would have been glad to fuck him, but I wasn't sure that was what he really wanted: what would have turned me on was if he had been very eager for it. My mouth was on his chest, my hips between his thighs, his cock against my belly, mine under his balls. He didn't resist, but gave no sign of encouragement either. If I put my arms under his legs, he let me raise them, but passively. The tip of my cock was against his asshole, but it was no use trying to get in like that, I would have to put some cream there, and in the time it would take to get the stuff I would lose my erection and have to start all over again. And then, it's always embarrassing to get out that cream when you're not sure your partner wants to get fucked. If he refuses, you look so dumb. I decided against it.

I suck his cock, which seems to please him. In fact, everything seems to please him, which turns me on to some degree. Besides, he is really very nice. The only problem is that he keeps changing position, we keep finding ourselves across the bed, legs sticking out a few inches, then we are at the bottom of the bed, or on our sides. I don't want him to come in my mouth. I should play with his cock. He plays with mine, but I don't like to come that way. I should come on top of him. I take his hand off my cock, but continue to play with his. This doesn't seem to turn him on much. I stretch out on top of him again, one hand under his ass, the other under his head. We kiss each other. With our legs, we squeeze our cocks together. In the dorm room of the American prep school, the star of the baseball team is beginning to enjoy his little blackmailer. Actually, it might be his real lover that he has in his arms now, the one with whom he was caught by his fiancée's brother. It's not very clear. Alain gasped with pleasure.

"Yes?"

"Yes!"

We both came together with a lot of noise, especially on my part, as usual. We lay against each other for a moment, half-asleep.

"Wait, I'll go get us a towel before we stick together for good."

Then I lie down beside him again.

"I have to leave now. I really don't want to."

"Personally, I'm damn glad I don't live in the Thirteenth!"

"Sadist!"

"Heh-heh."

"I don't want to leave."

"You want to sleep here?"

"No, I can't."

"You have to go home before you go to work?"

"Yes."

"Where do you work?"

"Avenue Montaigne. You know where that is?"

"Yes, of course."

"The traffic jams drive me crazy in the morning. All right, I'm leaving."

He put his clothes on quite fast. I didn't offer my phone number. If he had called me, I don't know what I would have done. Ultimately, things had gone quite well between us. But I had no intention of letting myself get dragged into a rematch that could only be a flop.

I got up to see him to the door. He kissed me:

"See you soon, I hope."

"Tomorrow, probably. We see each other almost every day, don't we?"

"Yes, but you don't see me. You're so snotty."

"Me, snotty? Like shit—"

"All right, I'm going. *Ciao.*"

"Good-bye."

"Ciao."

101

[*Seen him again many times. But when I ran into him in New York, during the summer, on Pier 42, I didn't recognize him, though I talked for quite a long while to the friend he was with, whom I also knew. Then I apologized elaborately, my excuse being his different hair style: his hair was longer now, or shorter. Since then, we also say hello, very pleasantly.*]

[*Sunday, September 14, 1980: Reading for the first time the English translation of this chapter, I suddenly realize who sent me a beautiful postcard from Martinique which was in my mail when I returned from my summer holidays last week. It said:* Thank you for that old glass of water and the rest . . . *and it was signed* Alain—*the name I gave him in the book—and then the real first name of my visitor from the Thirteenth. I had had no idea who could have sent me the postcard.*

Unless he is being sarcastic, he certainly is not vindictive: I had been feeling guilty, thinking he might read there was something of the bulldog about him.]

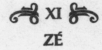

XI

ZÉ

Thursday, April 28, 1978

I am writing this on May 17: events of the last three weeks have not lent themselves to the writing of tricks. These events will probably have effects on my enterprise beyond a mere pause in the narrative and the tricks to come may well be very different, if they exist at all. As for this one, I fear I have forgotten many of the details.

I was at the *Palace* with friends. I was dancing, alone for the moment, and probably quite stoned. The floor, where the stage used to be, is slightly lower than what was once the orchestra of the theater itself. Two steps lead down to it; a little farther on, there are two more. At the top of the first two stands anyone who wants to watch the dancers. It was here that a boy was watching me, with a smile. He himself was dancing where he stood, and seemed to be as stoned as I was. He was dark, very tanned, with a moustache, and dressed in bright-colored clothes: light blue jeans which at first I couldn't see, a low-cut T-shirt striped turquoise and white, and over this an open shirt printed with huge palm fronds.

When I left the floor at the end of a number, I passed him about a yard away. (No, I must emphasize the long period of eye-contact between us while I was dancing in the middle of the stage and he was perched on his two steps: we didn't take our eyes off each other, we kept smiling fixedly, almost laughing, the communion of cheerful addicts.) Actually I could have, should have walked right up to him. But I am too French for that. I contented myself with passing close by, trusting him to make by some initiative or other, the ultimate connection already hinted at. Which he did: I don't remember exactly how, whether he held out an arm, or if he moved toward me, nor what he said to me at first. In any case, reticence was not his outstanding feature. Perhaps he asked me if I was French, if I spoke English, etc. He was Brazilian and didn't speak one word of French.

He must have been around thirty, his very black hair was wavy or curly, he wasn't as thin as he might have been, but his shoulders were broad, his dark complexion splendid, and his almond-shaped eyes handsome; his teeth were very white and his smile engaging and infectious. After a few minutes of a conversation I don't re-member at all, and no doubt rendered very difficult by the volume of the music and the sketchiness of his English, we went back down onto the floor and danced facing each other for perhaps fifteen minutes. We were, I believe, enchanted with each other, and both in very good humor.

I then told him I was with friends and that I should go and see what they were up to. I found them with some difficulty on the mezzanine, sitting opposite the bar. Philippe had met friends of

103

his, as had Jean-Cristophe and Elisabeth, so that there was a whole little group including Étienne (Trick VI), who was slightly out of it, sitting to one side and saying nothing. I took advantage of this situation to explain to Elisabeth that I had met a Brazilian who turned me on, but that I didn't know what to do next, because of Étienne. I even led her over to the edge of the balcony, to point out my new friend, quite easily identifiable, despite the crowd, by the flamboyance of his colors.

"Oh yes, not bad at all."

"Come on, we'll dance with him."

We walked down the stairs, making a detour so as not to pass too close to the others. From the top of the two steps already mentioned, it is much more difficult to recognize anyone than from the balcony, and for a moment we thought the Brazilian had stopped dancing. But no: we caught sight of him and headed toward him. Elisabeth, he and I danced together sometimes holding onto each other, sometimes without touching. After two numbers Elisabeth left us, and the two of us continued dancing, very gaily indeed, laughing throughout. At the end of a third number, he shrieked in my ear:

"All right, can we go to bed?"

"Yes, I'd really like to, but I'm with a bunch of friends, I have to go see what they're doing, and how to manage it."

So I went back up toward the mezzanine bar, where Elisabeth had already rejoined the others. Étienne had left. Philippe repeated a conversation he had just had with him: Étienne had told him he was in love with me and asked for advice as to how to *keep* me. And what, in the present situation, should he do? He was going to leave. But, Philippe had answered, I would certainly be back as soon as he had turned around, and would follow him. No, I couldn't follow him, he lived with a friend, a girl.

"Well, at least that takes care of that. Unless of course the Brazilian's left too . . ."

I asked Elisabeth what she thought of him.

"A little too much belly for my taste, and his hair is too curly, and not enough hair on his chest, but he's not bad, in your line."

I went back down one more time, and once again, because of the inveterate difficulty of finding anyone at the *Palace*, I thought that the Brazilian had left. Nonetheless I managed to find him again:

"Come on, it's all set."

We danced together one last time.

"Shall we go?"

"Yes. My friends are leaving too. We'll try to find them. Maybe they'll give us a lift. What's your name?"

"Jose-Arcadio, but everyone calls me Zé, or Zéca."

When we reached the door, we ran into Philippe, who was leaving. Yes, he'd be glad to drop us at the house. There was also little Claude, whom I hadn't seen for several months, who was probably a little drunk, or stoned too: he flung himself upon me with a lot of kisses and questions: who was the boy I was leaving with, had I known him a long time, what nationality was he?

"Oh, you've just met and you're leaving with him? Congratulations. He's very hot. I hope you tell me all about it . . . You're just the same. You always have all the luck, always the best boy in the joint! And he understands no French at all, this young man of yours?"

We had reached another row of doors, the ones that open directly onto the street and that are always difficult to get through because of all the unfortunates who crowd around the ticket-takers and doggedly wait for hours, trying to find out why they can't get in.

[*May 18. Had dinner last night with Claude, whom in fact I hadn't seen since that evening. We talked about the Brazilian:*

"*Yes, I have to tell you, I don't get it at all, not at all: I don't see what you thought was so great about him . . .*"

"*What? You made such a fuss the other night. You said he was so hot, and how lucky I was, and on and on.*"

"*No, I was mistaken. I thought you meant someone else. The one you left with was a very dark boy, lots of curls, and hair growing everywhere else—*"

"*No, he didn't have hair anywhere, except on his head.*"

105

"All right, but I remember just who he was, in any case. He was quite plump—"

"Yes. He could have been thinner, I'll admit that."

"Yes, that's the one; no, frankly, I didn't think he was so great."

Luckily I still have the photograph taken in the morning out of my balcony, and which hasn't been developed yet. For although it's certainly true that Zé was a little too fat, it seems to me that he was quite handsome, that he had a spendid head in any case, and a wonderful way of moving, of talking and smiling, very virile but not at all macho.]

There were further encounters with friends on the sidewalk, and complicated good-byes which took some time. We got into Philippe's car, Zé in front with Philippe, and I in back. During the ride, Zé stuck one of his hands between the seats to take mine, to draw me against him, my mouth against the back of his neck. Philippe dropped us in front of my door.

As soon as we came up here, I put on a record of Geneviève Waite's "Romance Is on the Rise," which my guest apparently liked a lot: he asked to see the sleeve and examined it very closely, even the serial numbers. I asked him to excuse me for a few minutes, I wanted to take a shower. I then put only my pants back on, but when I returned, he had taken off all his clothes. He said he would like to take a shower too. Meanwhile, he hugged me and kissed me on the mouth. His belly was certainly not flat, but quite solid all the same, and his whole body was a fine copper color. His arms and thighs were thick and hard, his biceps well developed, and his skin very soft and agreeable to touch. He smelled very good.

While he was in the bathroom, I lay on the bed naked, the blankets thrown off. When he came to join me, he had brushed his teeth; his mouth had the same toothpaste taste as mine. He stretched out against me, already erect. His cock was quite thick, his ass rather voluminous, smooth, but not soft. He never stopped smiling and showing his white teeth under a very black moustache

106

He pressed me in his arms with all his might. Then he sucked my cock for quite a long time while I sucked his. But his tongue shifted to my balls, then to my ass. To penetrate more deeply between my buttocks, he knelt down, lifted my legs, and stuck his face into my ass. Meanwhile, I played with myself. Then he tried to stick his cock into me. I got up to get some cream, which I put on my ass and on his cock. Then he managed to penetrate me easily, and fucked me quite a long time, sometimes with his body upright, sometimes leaning forward and kissing me, my arms behind his back, which was broad, powerful and muscular. We came at exactly the same moment, he in my ass and I, playing with myself, on my belly. And we slept very well in each other's arms.

The first time we wakened, he wanted to know what time it was—about ten—and he said he had to get up. I offered him tea, but he preferred coffee.

"Sorry, all I have is Nescafé. I'm afraid that's quite undrinkable for a Brazilian."

"It doesn't matter, it's just to wake up."

It was a beautiful day. The sun filled the apartment.

Zé asked if he could use the phone. He called the friends with whom he was travelling and with whom he was to do some shopping that morning. They were at the Hotel Bedford, Rue de l'Arcade. He talked to them in Portuguese and arranged to meet them at the *Flore*. He explained to me that he was a decorator in Rio, and that he was making a trip all over Europe to see what was new, to pick up ideas. He had already been in Milan and had arrived from Copenhagen the day before yesterday. He was leaving Monday for London, I think, before going on to Spain and Lisbon. His parents were Portuguese, he had been born in a small town near Coimbra. But for the last twenty-four years he had lived in Brazil, and he felt much more Brazilian than Portuguese, though he was a Portuguese national.

He went out onto the terrace and looked down at the traffic in the street and at the intersection. That was when I took two photographs of him, and he insisted on taking one of me, which I was to send him. He then wrote down his address in Rio with a great many details, including all his phone numbers, at home and at work, and even directions on how to get there. He had a very resonant last name, very long and tinkly. He asked me if I had done the Twombly drawing hanging over my desk.

I had to go to the Rue des Beaux-Arts to pick up some photographs I had had framed a few days earlier, and I suggested I accompany him as far as the *Flore*. On the way, he asked if the *Palace* was the best place of its kind in Paris.

"Yes, probably. There's also the *Sept*, which was the first bar the *Palace*'s owner had: it's much smaller, but also much more gay."

"No girls?"

"Yes, a few, very few—friends of the regular patrons, or girls who have had dinner upstairs. But the *Palace* has been such a success that everyone goes there now, even tourists. It's not specialized any more, there are as many girls as boys. That's why lots of fags are going back to the *Sept* now, to be more with their own."

"Is that where you usually go?"

"No, it's not really my kind of place. I like going to the *Palace* now and then, with friends and if I'm stoned. But if I'm alone and sober I get bored there. Besides it's too expensive for me. I never have a *sou*. The *Sept* is the same. The waiters chase you around to get you to buy a drink. It's really uncomfortable."

"But where do you go then?"

"I go quite often to a bar near the Boulevard Saint-Germain, over there, to the left. But it's not the same kind of place at all. I don't know if you'd like it."

"What kind is it?"

"Oh, pseudo-butch—you know, and vaguely leather, but with less and less conviction."

"Pseudo-butch? No, I don't like that at all, I can't stand guys who turn themselves inside out to look virile."

"Well, I like fake butch types better than real ones; the real ones are a pain in the ass. Besides, I like fakes. I like guys who look

108

very male, physically, but who are actually very sweet and nice, and not aggressive at all."

"Yes, then we mean the same thing, actually. What's the name of your place?"

"The *Manhattan.* Another advantage, for me, is that the people who work there don't hassle you to make sure you drink something. They don't pay any attention to you whatsoever. I call that elegant."

Zé, from all appearances, had never considered the pecuniary aspect of Paris nightlife.

As we walked past, I pointed out the *Compagnie de l'Orient et de la Chine,* where he had said he wanted to go, but apparently it wasn't this store he had heard of, but another, larger one.

"Don't they have another shop somewhere?"

"Yes, they may, but I'm not sure, I only know this one."

We crossed the Boulevard in front of *Le Drugstore* and separated in front of *Les Deux Magots.* He told me I should come and see him in Rio, and I encouraged him to call me as soon as he was back in Paris. We shook hands, laughing, as though at a good joke. He headed for the *Flore,* and I for the Rue Bonaparte.

When I passed by again, ten minutes later, my framed photographs under one arm, he was sitting alone on the *Flore* terrace, and invited me to join him there. No, I had to get home. But what had happened to his friends? He didn't know, they must have got lost, though it wasn't very hard to find the *Flore.* But he didn't mind waiting, it was quite pleasant here, out in the sun. Was I sure I wouldn't sit down? No, I had to get to work. As I walked away, I turned back, and he waved at me with a great flourish.

Yesterday, or the day before, I received a card from him, postmarked Lisbon, a reproduction of a Murillo from the Prado. He had wanted, he said, on the last day of his European trip, *to thank me for my attentions,* and to tell me he hoped to see me again.

[*Never seen again. But I received another letter from him recently. He asked for the promised photograph. I answered immediately. Un-*

109

fortunately, I had lost the film with his picture on it, and mine as well.

A few days ago I received a phone call from a friend of his, another Brazilian, who came to see me, bringing a present from Zé, a record by Aparecida, and a note of introduction, written in Portuguese, oddly enough, which sounded very beautiful. This is how it ended:

E um cara das calçadas, das madrugadas ou de qualquer momento ou lugar.

Um beijo et um queijo,
teu chapa,
Zé.

Obs.—Ele mesmo vai traduzir esta carta. Se puder.]

◈ XII ◈

FRANZ'S FRIEND

Tuesday, May 30, 1978

It was early on a sunny afternoon, on the rocks along the beach between Cannes and Golfe-Juan. To reach them from the highway, you have to climb over a little cement wall opposite a huge service station and then cross the railroad tracks.

I was with Elisabeth. As we came out from the thick strip of bushes which line the tracks, the first thing we noticed, far down below, just above the waves, which were quite lively that day, was a very tan man clad in a bikini. He was staring up at us. He might have been thirty-two or thirty-three. His brown hair was very short, but divided by an extremely straight, almost military part. His moustache was much lighter, almost blond. His regular, clear-cut features were very energetic, very virile. His shoulders were broad, his hips narrow, and his whole body was bronze and muscular. Elisabeth and I agreed he was a very hot number, and we took up a position about fifteen yards away, a little higher up the beach. We put on our bikinis. From where we were, even sitting down, we could occasionally catch sight of him in a gap between the rocks. Moreover he seemed quite interested in us, and I met his eyes quite often. But we noticed that he wasn't alone. He was accompanied by a boy whom at first we hadn't seen: also with a moustache and just as tan, his hair longer; he was younger, but too thin and much less handsome.

Elisabeth went to inspect a little creek of white sand that separates the rocks where we sat from the rest of the shore, which is steeper and punctuated by defense posts, blockhouses, all kinds of minor structures put up by the Germans during the war and full of garbage. I walked back up toward the bushes. The two friends glanced after me, especially the older one. I went into the bushes. There was a fat boy of about twenty in there, very ugly, perhaps a little feebleminded, who stared at me while playing with his cock and running his tongue suggestively over his lips. I paid him as little attention as possible and continued to watch, between the branches, the sunbather with short hair. Whereas earlier he had been stretched out on his rock, he was now sitting up, and while he had been facing the sea, he was now scanning the coast behind him. We kept our eyes fixed on each other almost all the time. Nonetheless he didn't move. I made my way into a kind of little glade, which would have been very propitious for furtive encounters, if someone hadn't recently used it as a latrine. But only the fat boy with the busy tongue followed me, and I left him there. I returned to the place where Elisabeth and I had left our things. She had come back too, and we began reading, she a text on political economy and I *The Wings of the Dove*.

Since she was sitting a little higher up than I, and turned toward them, I asked her to keep an eye on our neighbors' movements. A half hour had passed, or a little longer, when she informed me that they had stood up and were now going toward the bushes. As soon as they were out of sight, I followed them. There was already someone there, another boy besides the fat one, much more attractive but, like him, fully dressed, with even a tweed jacket slung over one shoulder. He was looking out at the sea, the rocks, the bathers, and the movements of the shore with an interest difficult to interpret. Since I found myself between him and the two friends, it was not easy to know who was looking at whom, and for what purpose. They seemed to hesitate, and pretended to be interested in the trees, the foliage. They stopped at the edge of the little glade, examined it carefully, turned back toward me or toward the newcomer, and finally climbed up toward the railroad tracks. But the better looking one came back down almost immediately, and this time he went into the tiny clearing where his friend followed him. They established themselves there in a recess from which they couldn't see the fourth person, nor be seen by him, which encouraged me to follow in their footsteps.

The first clearing overlooked access to a second one of the same general shape and size, but still smaller, hence better protected from view, and I headed for this. But they didn't move. One turned his back to me and affected to be deeply absorbed in the contemplation of some leaf, insect, or butterfly, while the other, the one who turned me on, kept his eye on me. Then he began playing with himself, under his bikini. He got an erection, which produced, under the light-blue nylon, a cylinder of considerable size curving toward one hip. I imitated him. Then I walked over behind him. He came closer to me, gradually. My cock, quite stiff now, was against his thigh. I touched his. He touched mine, and took it out of my bikini. With his other hand, he grabbed the arm of his friend, who was giving us only a few quick glances, and pulled him toward us. The friend also had a hard-on. I pulled out both their cocks from their bikinis at the same time. But the friend did nothing for me, nor, moreover, for his friend: he merely stood there, hesitant, looking off somewhere. At first I made some effort to suggest that my interest was equally divided, then I gave that up. The friend left us, went over to post himself at the entrance to the little glade, and plunged once more into an intense contemplation of the branches. The handsomer one tried to make him come back, and called to him in a slightly muffled voice: *"Franz, komm! Komm! Komm, Franz!"* while making gestures to summon him with one hand. With his other hand, he was pressing as hard as he could on my shoulder, or on the back of my neck, so that I would go down the length of his body to his cock, which was absolutely enormous, but very beautiful and perfectly proportioned. I kissed him in the hollow of his neck, without getting any reaction. I slid

112

my mouth to his chest, where the hairs turned from chestnut to blond according to the movements of a tiny breeze that shifted the foliage filtering the hot, golden afternoon light. But he continued to press down on my neck more gently but still firmly, directing my lips toward his cock. I resisted only as long as it took to brush my tongue down the blond line that divided his belly vertically. Then I took his cock in my mouth, playing with his balls with one hand and with the other working up the shaft of his cock. He continued calling to Franz: *"Franz, komm, komm!"* But Franz stubbornly remained at the edge of the clearing, turning his back to us most of the time and occasionally glancing furtively in our direction. I don't know if he had decided to mount guard in order to protect us from some outside incursion, or whether he hoped that his friend would rejoin him. The latter showed no such intention, but on the other hand he scarcely compromised himself with me. His cock was of such volume that I couldn't have sucked it for long without dislocating my jaw. So I straightened up. I wanted to kiss him again, but he was as stiff and motionless as a statue. His very clearly articulated pectorals, blond and very hard, turned me on a lot. I would have liked him to put his arms around me, and to put mine around him. But nothing of the kind occurred. Besides, the slope of the ground was not in my favor, he being taller and also standing above me.

Then he began to play with my cock very energetically. I played with his with one hand, putting my other one on his shoulder and my mouth against his chest. I was very excited, I knew I was going to come, and I didn't really want to come like that. I tried to interrupt him, but he had apparently decided to make me come that way and nothing would make him change his mind. So I spurted out over the leaves, the upper part of my body leaning back, one arm on the small of his back, the other hand on his belly. He immediately tucked his cock, which was still fully erect, back into his bikini as best he could, and went to rejoin Franz. Then they went back to their rock.

I too rejoined Elisabeth, and briefly recounted what had happened. This German was certainly very handsome and very exciting, but quite disappointing in action. Perhaps, though, his behavior was a consequence of his situation. It was clear that things weren't going well for this particular couple. We could observe, from where we were, a very lively discussion going on below us. Franz, moreover, was now putting on his clothes quite impulsively. But when he was fully dressed, instead of leaving, he went over and sat down on another huge rock, about four or five yards away from his friend, and opened a huge German newspaper behind which he disappeared.

"Yours must have the keys to the car," Elisabeth said. "In any case, the other one seems really angry. You should go and talk to him, tell him you had no intention of taking his man away from him, nor of setting up house with him in their little suburban villa in Düsseldorf."

"Sure! And all of it in German, right? Given the mood they both seem to be in, they'll reach an agreement by breaking my neck. Anyway, they don't live in Düsseldorf."

"How do you know where they live?"

"They must live in some tiny little town. They're too ill-matched. In big cities, there's always a kind of equivalence of merit between the members of a couple, tit for tat. It's only in godforsaken holes, because of the poor choices, that couples like that get put together."

"How fery inderesdink!"

"Precisely."

We went back to our reading. *The sense was constant for her that their relation was as if afloat, like some island of the south, in a great warm sea that made, for every conceivable chance, a margin, an outer sphere of general emotion; and the effect of the occurrence of anything in particular was to make the sea submerge the island, the margin flood the text.* I underlined certain passages of my book with a pencil. The sun was still high over the islands facing us. It was just beginning to sink now, already easy to trace, however, toward the steep cliffside of the Esterel.

"There's a big white villa, a little higher up the hill behind us. That's called the Villa Orion, doubtless because it's facing east toward the rising sun. Which shows to what degree the middle-class around the beginning of the century still had, in spite of everything, a classical culture which is now completely dead. . . ."

"I really love the old bore in you."

"Yes, I should have been a colonel in the cavalry. In any case, I would have been very concerned with the happiness of my subordinates."

Franz must have stayed there a good hour reading the same page of his newspaper, around which we could see only his fingers and his feet. Once or twice, I caught the other one's eye, but very briefly. He wasn't smiling. Finally, he too put on his clothes, not without an interminable struggle with the zipper of his fly, which sent Elisabeth into uncontrollable hysterics that, doubtless, prejudiced our case even further. They collected their things scattered over the rocks. In order to get back up to the highway, they had to pass right in front of us. I looked up from my book, but both of them were stubbornly staring in the other direction. They vanished between the bushes.

[*Never saw him again.*]

ꙮ XIII ꙮ
RED MORGAN

Friday, June 2, 1978

I had already noticed this little red Morgan crossing Cannes at night toward the *Palm Beach,* down the Croisette, and particularly, on several occasions, in the big parking lot just in front of the jetty and its two lighthouses. Its driver, the night before, had passed close by me twice, slowing down and examining me, but without stopping. I could scarcely see him.

That night, rather late, I noticed a young boy, twenty or twenty-two, dark, fairly tall, emphatically upper-middle-class:

Shetland sweater, corduroys, moccasins. He was standing at the corner of the Square Mistral and the Boulevard Jean-Hibert, talking with a much older man, bald and rather vulgar. They seemed to be old acquaintances—members of the local gay establishment discussing the situation. I didn't pay much attention to them. I crossed the avenue along the sea and above the beach. Several men were out cruising, one of whom, quite interesting from a distance, incited me to walk behind him in the direction of La Bocca. I had covered about a hundred yards when a huge clamor broke out: shouts, doors slamming, motors being raced. Someone ran past me as fast as he could, jumped over the parapet on the beach side of the sidewalk, fell onto the straw roof of one of the shelters along the edge of the beach, and from there jumped onto the sand, vanishing into the darkness.

Such excitement, I decided, could only signify some punitive outbreak of queer-bashing, one of many incidents that the police treat with utter indifference or even, according to some, with approval. I began by turning around and heading back toward the Square Mistral, intending to get my car, but since that way I ran into those fleeing the spot, I decided it would be better to follow behind them, and I started out again in the direction of La Bocca. This was when I was passed by the red Morgan moving very slowly. The driver stared at me a long while, then stopped and parked fifty yards ahead. He got out of his car: Shetland sweater, corduroys and all; it was that proper young man I had noticed earlier.

Still staring at me, he walked into a rather dark driveway next to a modern apartment building which led, as far as I could then tell, to a kind of private parking lot behind the building. From the sidewalk I peered as hard as I could into the darkness, intensified by the distance, but all I could see, less and less distinctly, was "Red Morgan" (as I had immediately nicknamed him) disappearing down that driveway without turning back.

I went on walking down the avenue, as far as a service station which was closed. The excitement back at the Square seemed to have calmed down. Everyone who had scattered away from it was now heading back, and I did the same. I returned to the entrance of the driveway. Looking to my left this time, I saw Red Morgan standing at the edge of the shadows, where he vanished as soon as he saw me. His tactics intrigued me. I followed him down the driveway, not so much to look at him—he was really not my type—as out of curiosity about the place itself, which perhaps functioned as a stronghold for habitués in case of attack or danger, and where, I assumed, he might not be alone.

The driveway, I have already noted, led to a rather large parking lot on the right. But further on, slanting a little to the left, it turned into a narrow alley sloping slightly downhill, whose dense, close-planted trees formed a veritable tunnel. Seeing me approach, Red Morgan turned down this alley. I followed him very slowly, seeing absolutely nothing. When my eyes began to get used to the dark, I realized that the alley, on a lower level than the parking lot, widened a little, and that Red Morgan was standing on the left side of the turnaround thus formed, facing me. I stopped on the right side. For two or three minutes, we both remained motionless, each of us waiting for the other to make the first move. I had no difficulty holding out in this little game, since Morgan, once again, was not at all my type. But in the provinces, in small towns, types tend to blur, and desire accommodates itself quite naturally and quite rapidly to the more limited opportunities it has for satisfaction. And when Morgan came toward me and immediately put his hand on my fly, he could perceive that I already had an erection. Despite his youthful appearance, he was a solidly built boy, quite broad-shouldered, narrow in the hips, with a massive cock of considerable length. He unzipped my pants before I had a chance to unzip his, took out my cock and immediately knelt down in front of me to suck it. He had taken off his sweater, and tied its sleeves around his shoulders. Leaning forward, I caressed his chest, which was very smooth, quite muscular, and very well articulated.

Suddenly we heard, in the darkness just behind us, the panting of a large dog and then, very close by, the steps of its master. The two of them arrived from the part of the driveway we couldn't see.

We hurriedly readjusted ourselves and returned to the avenue. The man, five or six steps behind us, could have had no doubt about our activities, but either because he was used to this, the place being a frequented rendezvous, or broad-minded, he seemed quite indifferent, as did his dog, a splendid red setter which had not barked once but had sniffed at us quite amicably.

Above the beach to the right, opposite the closed service station, seven or eight very young motorcyclists had gathered. In black leather jackets and with slicked-down hair, they were making their for the most part modest engines roar as best they could. I wondered if these were the ones who only a few moments ago had scattered the cruisers in the square. But apparently they were paying no attention to anyone or anything but themselves.

Closer to us, a man of around forty with gray hair had noticed our emergence from the driveway with much interest. Once the man with the dog had crossed the avenue to the beach and we were ready to return to our dark passageway, he now stood in our path. To discourage him, I remained in the drive and even started back toward the avenue. But he walked past me, as well as past the parking lot, and went in under the dark vault of the trees, where Red Morgan had already gone. Counting on the latter to discourage the newcomer and to make him realize what my disturbed expression had not been sufficient to explain—that we had just been interrupted and now wanted to be left in peace—I waited a moment on the sidewalk. Then again I was a little wary about getting stuck in what seemed a literal cul-de-sac so close to this band of young motorcyclists, whose intentions were not clear. But since they paid no attention whatever to the driveway, and since no one came back out of the covered alleyway, I finally returned to it as well. Red Morgan was standing at the opening to it, and he stepped farther back into the darkness when he saw me returning. The man with gray hair was in the middle of the turnaround, his eyes fixed on us. We remained motionless a few minutes, doing nothing, waiting for him to go away. Instead of this, he came over to me and put his hand on my fly. I immediately turned away and rejoined Morgan. We caressed each other, our shirts now opened to the waist, and took out each other's cock. The gray-haired man, standing about ten feet away, had also unzipped his pants and was playing with himself. We decided to act as if he wasn't there, to ignore him completely. We kissed, groped each other, sucked each other's cock. Morgan's was straight, heavy and voluminous. But the gray-haired man came over and began touching both of us. This time we pushed him away somewhat sharply, and Morgan said: "Why don't you get the hell out of here?" which finally discouraged him. He left. Then Red Morgan crouched in front of me again to suck my cock, which he apparently preferred doing. But no sooner had we been alone for two minutes than we heard footsteps again. I quickly put my cock back in my pants and zipped up. Morgan stood up, murmuring: "It's nothing—just the guy with the dog coming back." All the same, I stepped farther back into the darkness of the alley. The tunnel of branches gave way to another enclosure, this one even darker, over which passed the railroad tracks. Then came a new widening of the alley and the open gate of some private property, a kind of development sloping down, whose roads, between the villas, were faintly lit. Red Morgan had joined me and was standing a yard or two away. The man and his red setter, both still indifferent to our presence, passed us. We walked back under the tracks and returned to the part of the alley where we had been before.

Without beating about the bush Morgan resumed his earlier posture, kneeling in front of me, my cock in his mouth. He sucked it very skillfully, completing the work of his lips and tongue with his thumb and forefinger, playing with himself with his other hand. Each time he felt I was about to come he slowed down his movements or licked my balls, the top of my thighs and my belly. But I didn't want to come in his mouth, anyway, and I made him get up. His corduroy trousers were around his ankles and my jeans had slipped down to my knees. Our shirts were again completely open. He had put his sweater on the grass or on a branch. We kissed, cocks and torsos pressed together. But I shifted my position slightly to his side, my cock against his hip, and he, immediately understanding this sign, indeed as if he had been expecting it, turned completely around and presented his ass, toward which he directed my cock, still wet with his saliva. His buttocks were quite tight but, contrary to what I feared, I penetrated between them

119

without any difficulty for his asshole was perfectly lubricated, either by someone else's come from earlier in the evening, or because he had put some sort of cream there himself before leaving home. So the entire length of my cock went into his ass with a single thrust. He leaned forward, and with a hand thrust between my legs, pulled me against him. I was still just about to come and wouldn't move much. In order to create a diversion and to distract myself I wanted to play with his cock. He let me do this a minute or so, but preferred doing it himself, in his own rhythm. Sometimes he straightened up, and then I could caress his belly and his chest, or nibble his neck, and sometimes he bent over until his body formed a right angle, his loins and back stretched out flat, or even forming a slight concavity over which I ran my hands. Several times I came out of his ass altogether, only to then thrust in again, slowly and deliciously. I alternated these movements of penetration and withdrawal with lateral or circular movements of my pelvis which, being less exciting, permitted me to postpone the orgasm longer. But Morgan suddenly gasped very urgently: "Now, come! Come!" I touched his cock with one hand and realized that he had just come, without a sound. I immediately moved more vigorously between his buttocks, and in ten or twenty seconds I ejaculated, trying to make as little noise as possible.

Red Morgan straightened up, slowly stepped forward in order to disengage my cock, and took out of his back pocket two carefully folded paper napkins, one of which he handed me.

"Thanks."

We wiped ourselves off in silence. We pulled our pants back up, buttoned our shirts. I was ready first. He seemed to pay no attention to me now. I put one hand on his shoulder and smiled at him in the darkness:

"So long!"

"So long!"

And I headed toward the Square Mistral, where I had left my car. I had been stupid enough not to lock the doors. Since my car was parked closest to the public urinal, which serves as a center for the cruising in this neighborhood, it was the one chosen for the attentions of the fag-bashers. They had played a little trick on the car which is apparently very widespread on the Riviera: they had torn off one of the foot pedals which they then left on the driver's seat.* I was furious. I left the car where it was and asked for help from some of the men cruising the Square. One of them took me home. He was a militant leftist, very nice, very talkative, and possibly a little paranoid. According to him, the fag-bashers act with the complicity of the police. For the police, the homosexuals are the shame of the Côte d'Azur, a plague to be eliminated by any means. Getting rid of it is much more important and deserves much greater force and effort than, say, fighting against theft. Moreover, the newspaper *Nice-Matin* shares these sentiments and encourages them. When a fag is found dead, or hurt, in the morning in some park in Nice or Cannes, the headline is always something like: *Another Homosexual Scandal*. Then again my informant had noticed that when there were police raids on the pier, for instance, you never saw the queer-bashers, and when the thugs were around, no police in sight. According to him, they divided up the job between them.

* One of my friends, a militant leftist, teaches in a lycée on the Côte d'Azur. He was very popular with his pupils until two of them caught him one night coming out of a gay bar in Cannes. These two turned all the rest, boys and girls, against him, and from that moment on he was literally tormented. His whole class would follow him down the street shouting obscenities, insults were scribbled on the blackboard, endless questions were "innocently" asked about Verlaine and Rimbaud, and allusions to his preference were worked into the themes handed in.

"But couldn't you try to talk to them, since you had a good relationship with them before? Couldn't you explain what it's all about, try to make them understand that there is nothing shameful about it?"

"You're completely crazy. You don't know what it's all about. These kids are not little liberal bourgeois from Paris. These are little proles, and Mediterraneans besides—which means they're obsessed by every possible macho myth, and by homosexuality as well. It's all they can think about. It's a real obsession. Their favorite insult, from twelve or thirteen on, is *cocksucker*, or worse, *he takes it up the ass!* Once you've said that you've said everything. So go on and explain to them that after all, maybe . . . That's a Parisian intellectual for you. There's absolutely nothing in the culture of these kids which allows them to accept or even to consider such a thing.

"For me, you see, the worst is that almost half these kids belong to extremely underprivileged and exploited families, like immigrant laborers—whom I've worked with politically—even socially, you could say. The day I really broke down was when a little Arab kid of fourteen—a kid I really liked, very bright, and whose family I had tried to help, someone who really knew something about what racism is and what it does—well, one day this kid followed me down the street, all

[*Saw Red Morgan again the next night near the base of the Cannes lighthouse at the end of the pier. He was sucking the cock of a very young, very cute and slightly drunk boy whom I was fucking at the same time. We are all very giddy. Opposite us, on the dark front of La Croisette, flashed the names of the great hotels. A few yards away a launch passed, carrying quite thoroughly intoxicated sailors back from an American warship, whose high, steep outline was silhouetted against the sky of the bay. But we were interrupted by thugs who were attacking a lone fag near the parking lot and we were forced to hide between the enormous blocks of stone scattered off the pier.*]

❧ XIV ❧

JEAN-MARC LAROQUE

Wednesday, June 7, 1978

I was dancing on the tiny floor of the *Crazy Boy,* in Cannes, where I had come with Jean-Christophe. I was cruising a boy who turned me on and whom I had seen several times on previous evenings. I was dancing close to him, staring at him but without managing to

the way home, about thirty yards behind me yelling '*Faggot! Faggot!*' It was as if he had finally found someone onto whom he could project his resentment, someone he could hold in contempt with complete peace of mind. And that really wiped me out. I had to stop. Then, afterward, in the spring, things were going a little better. I have this girl friend, the gym teacher at school—a wonderful-looking girl, besides—and she helped me a lot. She knew what was happening and she offered to help me persuade them we were having an affair—we went out together, showed up together everywhere, and of course that counted for a lot—they didn't know where they were then. There was one girl in my class who actually asked the gym teacher: "But isn't M'sieur what's-his-name more interested in—" And my friend looked at her sort of dreamily and smiled and said, "You know, that's not at all the impression he gave me." And that went down very well. At least so we thought. The kids were the way they had been before—nice, curious, not at all aggressive. Then came June and the last classes. Every year, you know, they give the French teacher a present, something they chip in to buy. And one day, sure enough, I came into class and on my desk there was a gorgeous package, fancy paper, red ribbon, everything. I was really touched, you know, after all that had happened. I opened the package, and you know what was inside? A bicycle pedal. . ." [*Translator's note: pedal=pederast*] attract his attention. In fact he had an almost emphatic, though passive, way of discouraging my advances. Stubbornly refusing to meet my eyes even when this would have been the most natural thing to do, he seemed determined to make me understand that I was of no interest to him whatsoever.

Suddenly I noticed the presence of another boy who also avoided looking at me but who appeared to be constantly in my field of vision, whichever way I turned. I would not have been interested in him on my own account, but he seemed interested in me, though his eyes avoided mine. He wasn't unattractive: rather slight, very dark, with long black curly hair, a black moustache, slightly olive skin, and fine dark eyes. There was something in his face that suggested Rome 1630, something reminiscent of certain Bernini portraits. He was wearing a print shirt with short sleeves, open over his chest, and wide trousers with a transparent plastic belt. What I could see of his torso and his forearms was very hairy and very suntanned.

Still dancing face to face, we gradually moved closer to each other, until one of my legs was between his. It wasn't until our thighs touched that he consented to meet my eyes, and if he smiled then, it was just barely. Yet our hands quickly met and then moved toward our hips. We pressed together. I kissed him on the side of his neck. He turned his head, our mouths met, and we exchanged a very long and deep kiss while continuing to dance. My interest in him was greatly enlarged by his first contact. For there was something very voluptuous in this rhythmic embrace, as if our bodies had been designed for each other, our mouths destined to meet. We were dancing very giddily, glued together inextricably now, our erect cocks pressed against each other. I had both hands behind his neck, my fingers in his curls.

When we suddenly pulled apart, I had to make certain readjustments—I was wearing rather loose white pants, and no underwear. My cock, completely stiff, was pointing way down my right thigh, and I moved it up against my fly, so that it would be less obvious. This maneuver did not escape my new friend, and for the first time we exchanged a distinct smile.

We went on dancing together for about twenty minutes, for the most part separate and not touching each other, but occasionally brushing against each other again, for a moment or so, when we would kiss. Then I went over to lean against the nearest wall, and he immediately came and joined me. I put my elbows on his shoulders:

"What are you doing later?"
"I'm here with friends. They live near Grasse."
"I'm with a friend too. You want to come home with me?"
"What if you were to come with us instead?"
"I can't. I have to take him home."

The music was too loud for long conversation. He leaned toward me, and we kissed again. His arms were covered with thick dark hair, yet the upper part of his chest was smooth. I touched him between his shoulder blades and under his shirt. I then moved my hand down under his belt and over his very round, hard and extremely hairy buttocks.

Instead of continuing to discuss the problem of subsequent activities, we went back to dancing. But every night at the *Crazy Boy* the dancing stops at a certain moment for a drag show. In fact, the first part of this show had already ended, and it was during the intermission that our encounter had taken place; the second half was about to begin, and the mistress of ceremonies at the microphone was announcing it now.

We found each other at the edge of the platform which serves both as dance floor and stage.
"So what do we do now?"
"Come to Grasse with us."
"But I can't. I'm with this friend and I can't abandon him."
"But I'm with three friends."
"Do you have to end up with the three of them?"
"What do you mean?"
"They depend on you? You're their chauffeur, they can't leave without you?"

124

"Oh. . . yes. I'm the one who drives."

"You're going to stay and watch the whole show?"

"Yes."

He seemed to be distinctly turned off. As soon as the first drag queen appeared on the stage, he rejoined his friends, and I went over to Jean-Christophe, who had been dancing furiously for an hour, was ready to leave, and wanted to know if I was too.

"I don't know. No, not really. I'd like to do something with that boy, the one I've been dancing with, but he's with a whole group of friends. I don't know what he wants to do. I think he wants to watch the show."

We had already seen the whole thing on another night, and it wasn't a tempting prospect. The notion of watching it once again didn't particularly appeal to me, and absolutely horrified Jean-Christophe:

"Oh no. If we have to wait until the end for your friend to make up his mind, he isn't worth it. Besides, if you want my opinion, he's not such a hot number."

"You have to kiss him to appreciate his virtues."

On the stage, a tall blond with a German accent, who must have been a transsexual rather than a transvestite, was showing off her tits. There was also a certain adipose and fiftyish Miss James, who was suffering tonight from a sore throat and who stubbornly refused to play her usual part as mistress of ceremonies. The blond was distressed by the silence separating the different numbers and begged Miss James to say something, tell stories, anything. But Miss James, lips pursed, would do nothing but repeat *Ca-ca, Ca-ca*.

It was as pathetic as it was boring. Jean-Christophe, quite stoned, was now in an inert phase though he had been overflowing with energy before, and could think of nothing but going home to bed. Bernini no longer glanced in my direction, and besides, his words hadn't been very encouraging. So I agreed to leave. Jean-Christophe and I walked to the car, which was parked in the Rue d'Antibes, just behind the statue of Lord Brougham. Once in the car, however, I was seized by regrets:

"Would you mind very much if I went back there and asked this boy what he wants to do? Once and for all?"

"You won't even be able to speak to him in that crush. He's on the other side of the room. You won't be able to get near him."

"Yes, you're probably right. But it bugs me to leave like this. It seemed in the bag . . ."

"Listen, we're not going to subject ourselves to the whole show, Miss James and all the rest!"

"All right. I'll just go and see what's happening, OK? Give me five minutes."

"I don't feel like sitting here alone. If I have to wait, I might as well wait in there. I'll come with you."

"You sure you don't mind?"

He merely gave me a black look.

So we went back to the *Crazy Boy*. Miss James was now a fat explorer in a pith helmet, being seduced by an orangoutang. She was raising her skirt to reveal her cardboard cunt, swollen with purulent excrescences. We were in the middle of the room, and Bernini was near the stage, on the right, with his friends. At no moment did he turn around. [*Thursday, June 19: interrupted here by a phone call from him; he has invited me to join him in July at the house of one of the girls he introduced me to in the Lozère.*]

When the show turned unbearable, I asked Jean-Christophe if he wanted to leave, but he answered stoically that now he could hold out to the end. So we waited it out. Once the final scene was over, the dancing started again on the "stage." Jean-Christophe seemed to have got his second wind and flung himself into wild, complicated steps that seemed to surprise the local public. The little Bernini shot me the ghost of a smile and started dancing again too. I imitated him, but some ways off. Nonetheless, in five minutes, we were face to face again, and in ten in each other's arms, my tongue in his mouth. At the first record change, I drew him toward the edge of the floor. But even there it was impossible to hear anything clearly. So we went to sit down at the back of the room. I was determined to bring matters to a head:

"So what are we doing?"

126

"Come with us to Grasse. You can sleep there and I'll drive you back tomorrow."

"No, I told you, I can't—I have to take this friend home."

"Well, take him home, and join me in Grasse."

"Impossible, we live at Cap d'Antibes, and it's four in the morning. Why can't you let your friends take your car, and I'll bring you back to Grasse tomorrow?"

"No, tomorrow we have to go to Nice, I have a girl friend who works there, I have to go with her."

"Let her have your car. Can she drive?"

"Yes . . . no, come to Grasse."

"No, I really can't."

"If you wanted to, you would."

"It's not a question of what I want. I just can't abandon my friend, that's all."

"Well, that's it then."

"But it's a real shame . . ."

"Yeah."

"Well? See? You have to come home with me."

"All right, listen. I'll go ask my friends what they want to do."

"Terrific!"

And he went over to talk to his friends, just three girls, and not the larger group I had thought he was with earlier. He came back very soon:

"OK, it's all right with them about the car. So I'll come with you."

"Great. I really wanted you to come. Shall we leave?"

"Yes."

I went to tell Jean-Christophe, and Bernini got his friends together. They went out ahead of us. Near the door, outside, there was a slight confusion in the crowd that delayed us. Bernini, who was already out in the street, and who was animatedly talking with the three girls, came back toward me with an embarrassed look, in which I detected another problem:

"What's happening?"

"Listen: I'm not looking for a three-way."

127

"Who is? Are you completely nuts? Was that your problem?"

"Yes."

"But what made you think *that?* I never suggested anything of the kind! Poor Jean-Christophe isn't at all interested in stuff like that . . ."

"But earlier you said something like *ending up all three*—at least that's what I heard—"

"No, I didn't say anything like that. You're crazy. . . . Oh, yes, I remember what you didn't understand; I asked you—I was speaking of your friends—if you had to stay with them, if you were riding in their car, if you had to take them home, all that . . ."

"Oh, that's what it was, I didn't hear you. In fact, I was a little shocked."

"And that's why you made such a face, and never looked at me once during the whole second part of the show?"

"Yes."

"Well, I'm glad I came back and insisted. At least we've cleared up one misunderstanding."

Jean-Christophe joined me:

"What's so funny?"

"Oh, there was this tragic misunderstanding."

Bernini had gone back over to his friends on the other side of the street. One was a very tall, pale, thin girl with long blond hair, the second was shorter and stockier with a very healthy expression, and the third was doubtless the prettiest, but she had a kind of sullen look. She and the tall one were talking in Italian.

"OK, it's all aranged, they're going to take the car."

"Splendid."

The car was British, I think, maybe an MG.

The sexes separated, with smiles all around. I made introductions among the three of us:

"Jean-Christophe, this is . . . uh, I don't know your name . . ."

"Jean-Marc."

"Jean-Marc. I'm Renaud. Where are you from?"

"From Montpellier. I'm on vacation at Colette's—one of the girls you just saw. She and I both come from Nîmes."

"You come from Nîmes but you live in Montpellier?"

"Yes, I'm a student in Montpellier."

"What are you studying?"

"English."

We drove to Juan-les-Pins, then the Cape, following the lower road along the seashore. Jean-Marc spoke very little, and the conversation was mostly between Jean-Christophe and me. We wondered why so many gay bars in the provinces felt obliged to offer their clientele these shows, which tend to be so depressing, always too long and apparently exactly the same every night.

"And this one is even somewhat professional, so to speak, more than the one we saw the other night in Nice."

"Barely."

"Well, but the costumes are newer and flashier. It must have cost more."

"That's right. It looked a little more . . . convincing, provided you weren't too close. But the costumes aren't at all convincing up close. It's all a little less painful from a distance. Still tonight it seemed to me better than the other day, oddly enough."

"Yes, to me too. Even so, it's always a pain in the ass. It cuts the night in half; I still don't understand why they do it."

"They think they have to justify the price of the drinks."

"But they don't cost any more there than anywhere else."

"Those drag queens want to show off, that's all."

"Actually, the taste that provincial places have for shows like this matches the grotesque image people still have of fags, and which fags still have of themselves—it's contagious."

"And it helps get them accepted—straights come and see it the way they go to the zoo."

"I saw a strange thing—I don't know if it was just my imagination, but I don't think so. There was a couple in the place. The woman seemed on the verge of tears. Her husband was trying to console her, but he seemed overwhelmed too. They both seemed very friendly with one of those drag queens—the tall one who sings sentimental songs, the one who takes herself most seriously . . ."

"Yes, I know who you mean: she was dressed as a Pierrot for a while there."

"Yes, that's right. I might be wrong, but I got the impression that the girl was his sister, and he wanted to show her what he did, and the whole thing was turning out very badly."

"Pathetic."

"Yes . . . of course, something entirely different could have been going on . . ."

Because of his insistence on seeing the whole show, I had been afraid that Jean-Marc had liked it. But no, he too had found the whole thing very annoying. He was sitting to my right on the front seat. On the whole, he seemed a little distant.

As we left Cannes, we passed by the house of the famous Florence Gould. We wondered why, when she was on the Côte d'Azur, she chose to live *there,* so close to the highway, rather than in her villa at Juan-les-Pins, which looks like a little fort. As we left Juan-les-Pins, it was the Shah's sister who was discussed. We passed the place where one night, coming back from the *Palm Beach,* Cannes' summer casino, she escaped an attack. One of her ladies in waiting was killed.

At the house, I didn't know where the light switches were. We crossed several big rooms in the dark. I guided Jean-Marc between the pieces of furniture, holding him behind me by one wrist:

"This house is a tomb."

"Yes, it's really very dark."

"Wait, there's another room that's even more sepulchral."

We headed for the kitchen which we finally found. I was very thirsty and wanted to find something to drink.

[*Friday, June 30, three-thirty in the afternoon. I am falling farther and farther behind in this chronicle. Walter (Trick XVI) is taking a bath. I have been trying to convince him for two hours that I have to work, but first he wanted to make love again and turned me on without too much trouble, despite all my resolutions. Next I had to call his hotel to ask them to bring down his baggage, and then he asked me to try to put in a phone call for him to Kuwait. On the one hand, he didn't have the number he was calling (the United States embassy); on the other, he wanted to know how much the call would cost, so he could pay for it. But it is impossible to find out how much the call costs, because it's a direct line. Finally Walter decided that it must be eight or nine at night in Kuwait and that the person he wanted to call would have finished his day's work by now, in any case. Confronted by all these complications, he gave up on Kuwait and decided he would go directly to Ceylon.*

He's just come out of the bathroom, walked stark naked through this room, while I was writing the procedure paragraph, and has gone to lie in the sun, in a desk chair out on the balcony.]

The three of us, sitting around the table, drank some tonic. Then I told Jean-Christophe that Jean-Marc and I were going up to bed.

"So am I."

We crossed the downstairs rooms again, single file toward the stairs, and separated at the door of my room. As soon as he was inside, Jean-Marc collapsed on the bed. I turned on a light, and closed the shutters.

"Excuse me a second."

I went to piss and brush my teeth. Meanwhile, Jean-Marc undressed. [*Walter is now getting dressed. If I don't write this down immediately I'll forget that he's wearing a bright braided belt with tassels. Otherwise he's in khaki, pants and shirt sleeves rolled up. Now he's tying a tiny red necktie with a tiny pistol on it, with flames shooting out of the barrel. The tie was bought in Hawaii for ten cents. That is to say, Walter bought ten of them for a dollar.* [Interruption: he's getting dressed again after an absurd episode. He was leaving. I accompanied him to the door. He began kissing me. I told him to stop, that he was getting me all excited, that he never thought of anything but sex, that he was obsessed, [*Interruption: it's become a game. I repeat that I have to work. I am sitting at my desk:*

131

"What are you writing?"

"I'm writing that I can't work because you keep interrupting."

"No, seriously."

"Seriously."

"But you have to explain to me about French money."

"I already explained it to you yesterday. Now get out of here!"

"All right, this time I'm really going."

"You mean you're still here? I thought you had gone an hour ago!"

"Don't work too hard."

The door is still open, since he was almost out on the landing a while ago when his prolonged good-byes turned me on; he realized that he had turned me on, began undressing me and seeing my resistance, undressed himself almost completely. I was writing, or trying to write, that his little red tie with the firing revolver on it, that he had bought ten for a dollar in Hawaii, instead of being knotted around his shirt collar, was tied around his neck itself; so that as soon as he took off his shirt, the little tie remained on his tanned chest among the thick hair that extended in a dark line toward his belly, which for some reason turned me on extraordinarily. But then he took off the tie as well, and [Interruption: new telephone call from Jean-Marc. Nothing special to tell me, but he had a lot of change in his pocket, so he decided to call me from a booth in the hall of his school. The house in Grasse belonged to Corinne, the tallest of the three girls, and not to the one I had supposed, Colette, I think it was (I get their names confused). It is also Corinne, that is, her grandparents, who own the house in the Lozère where I am apparently invited.] noticing that I had an erection, he undid my fly, despite my protests, and knelt down in front of me in the doorway, to suck my cock. I took refuge at my desk, but he followed me there, citing my condition as an excuse to ignore my rebuffs. He sucked my cock while I was writing the previous page. I managed all the same to rebutton my fly somehow and to convince him to do the same, telling him that Philippe was going to stop by any minute to take photographs. Walter was supposed to go to the Air France office near the Opéra. I told him how to get there.

132

*"No doubt you'll meet lots of guys when you cross the Tuileries,
so you can go fuck for the rest of the afternoon."*

*"No, I'll wait till tonight and fuck with you. A bird in the
hand—"*

"I'm no bird, I'm an angel."] and that I had to work.]]

I opened the bed for him, and was about to join him in it. I like
getting undressed as if for the night, so that you get into bed for
good, rather than gradually pulling off each other's clothes and
getting into bed only after a sometimes tiresome progression.

"Wait a minute, this lamp is too bright. Should I put on this
little one, or turn them all off?"

"Whatever you like."

"I know what I'll do. I'll turn them all off and open one of the
shutters—there'll be light from outside."

Reflections from the moonlight on the waves surrounded the
shadow of the palms on the ceiling with silvery shimmers, regularly erased by the two beams from the lighthouse, one very slow,
the other longer and broader.

I lay down on the bed beside Jean-Marc, against him, on top of
him. Immediately the pleasure promised by our kisses at the *Crazy
Boy* overwhelmed me in all its violence: unforeseeable agreement
of bodies, harmony of every movement. Our mouths glued together, our cocks against each other, we wrapped each other in our
arms with an increasingly energetic enthusiasm. His legs, his buttocks, his arms were covered with thick fur which thinned out
over his chest. His rather short thighs were convex and hard, as
was his ass, toward which all my desires converged (when I made
a joke of this a week later, one morning in Montpellier: "Anyway,
I only love you for your ass," he answered quite seriously: "Yes, I
know . . .").

[*Interruption (July 1): visit from Didier (Trick VIII), who drops
in almost every day, these days. Yesterday he went through the ordeal
of his French orals. He brings me two prints of collages by Rodolphe*

133

Orlando, whom he ran into at the Manhattan last night and who gave them to him for me.

"Well, I'll let you work."

But as he's leaving, virtually the same scene at the door as with Walter yesterday. He licks my neck, my chest, caresses my fly. I get an erection, so does he. But finally, a manly handshake and:

"All right, man, so long, give my best to your old lady."]

[*Another interruption: phone call from Jean-Pierre (a trick not related here). I am writing with the phone in one hand while he's talking. He was in the Square Jean-XXIII last night, absolutely stoned, and was still there when day broke. He doesn't have enough money to leave and join his friends in Morocco. Maybe he will call back later, tonight, to go see* Young and Innocent *with us.*]

I am incapable of relating chronologically everything that happened the first time Jean-Marc and I made love. In any case, it lasted more than a hour. We must have made a terrible racket, for Jean-Christophe, who was in the next room—and the walls in this house are thick—remarked the next morning: "Judging from the sound track, everything went well." Which is putting it mildly. Of all the European tricks I have included here, I think I can say that this is the one that gave me the most physical pleasure. I asked Jean-Marc, at some point or other, if he liked poppers, if he wanted me to ask Jean-Christophe for some. Charles had bought more than a litre of amyl nitrite in some Parisian laboratory, a very powerful and especially devastating combination. He had given some of it to us. I had put my own little flask in the drawer of the night table, and three or four days after I had used it up the whole place still reeked.

"No, I don't really think we need it, this is so good . . ."

"That's just it. You never need it. It's when it's good that the poppers make it sublime."

But I didn't insist, though I returned to the charge much later on:

"Sure you don't want me to ask Jean-Christophe for his bottle?"

"No, I don't want you to leave for a single second."

I licked his whole body. I remember lying on my stomach between his thighs, the tip of my cock between his buttocks, his cock against my belly, my tongue on his chest. I licked his ass for a very long time, first [*Interruption: Jean-Christophe telephones about coming for dinner tonight. I tell him that I am writing about my first night with Jean-Marc, and I remind him of his morning remark—which I've just written down—about the sound track.*

"Yes, it was very impressive. Especially since during it all I was reading the first chapters of Tricks *in the next room. The creaking bedsprings really added to the effect . . ."*] lifting his thighs, then turning him over onto his belly and pushing my whole face between his buttocks, and finally turning him back to face me again, just before trying to fuck him. At his first little grimace of pain, or of fear of pain, I grabbed the tube of Hyalomiel that was in the drawer of the night table, and put some of it in his ass and on my cock. The penetration went very slowly, as he wished, but without difficulty. I have the impression of having fucked him without interruption for at least a half hour, most of this time in my favorite position, that is, the crooks of my elbows behind the backs of his knees, his shoulder blades in the palms of my hands, my mouth on his, or in the hollow of his neck, or on his chest. In my enthusiasm, at one point I burst out laughing, which intrigued and perhaps disturbed him:

"Why are you laughing?"

"Because I feel so good."

"So do I."

"It's fantastic."

"Yes. Is it always like this when you make love?"

"Oh no, I'm not always this inspired."

His whole body, like mine doubtless, was full of the stored-up heat of a day in the sun, on the beach, and merely putting my hand on his side produced a delicious sensation of sweet, dry warmth. Later in our play, this burning dryness was transformed into a moisture that was no less agreeable: sweat, saliva, and the vague honey smell of the lubricant.

Sometimes, too, I was on my knees, my buttocks on my heels, chest straight up, my cock still inside him, his thighs around my hips. My hands free, then, I caressed his torso and he mine. I was on the verge of coming a hundred times. I would tell him to stop then, not to move, and then he would become completely motionless, when the slightest movement of the least muscle of his ass would have precipitated my orgasm. After quite a long while, my cock, as though disappointed at having been on the brink of releasing its semen so many times, began to get soft. I withdrew from Jean-Marc's ass, stretched out on my back, put some cream in my own ass, and he fucked me in turn for about five minutes. His cock was rather small and very hard. He himself was constantly just about to come, so that several times he had to pull out abruptly.

The third or fourth time, I turned him over on his back, squatted between his legs, and thrust my cock into him again. We resumed all previous positions. But I was afraid we would end up exhausting ourselves and decided that I had to end it for this session. I set the soles of his feet against my chest, which left my hands free, and I began playing with his cock. With the thumb and forefinger of each hand, he pinched my nipples. By the light of the moon, I could see my cock moving back and forth in the forest of hair between his buttocks. Sometimes I made it come out all the way, its tip then seeking the opening for a second. Jean-Marc held my hand back. But after about ten minutes, I pushed his hand away, and we came together, at great length, with shuddering orgasms that shook us both to the marrow for about three minutes, even after I had already fallen back onto the bed and we were kissing, our bellies glued together by his sperm.

We remained motionless for a long while. Perhaps we even slept a little, wakened then by my cock's sliding out of his ass. He was lying across me. He got up and walked to the sink. He also asked where the toilet was, and went to it. He brought me back a towel and a glass of water. But I stood up to close the shutters. It was beginning to get light. From a palm tree came the loud and uncouth throat-clearing of turtledoves, or perhaps they were perched on the roof. I was suddenly dead tired. But not Jean-Marc, apparently:

136

"You know what we should do? Go to Grasse now, instead of going to sleep. Then we could sleep there until noon."

"But we can sleep here until noon, too."

"But your friends are going to get up, they'll wake us."

"You won't hear them. In any case, they get up very early. Around now, in fact. And besides, I don't think I really have the strength to go outside, get the car, everything. And we'd have to get gas, find a station that's open . . ." He didn't insist. He moved closer against me, caressed me and kissed me:

"I feel very good with you."

"So do I. You see what we almost missed?"

We were both getting erections again. Lying against each other produced the same effect as it had an hour before. We kissed with as much enthusiasm, our legs and arms mingled as tightly around our bodies; our bellies, our cocks pressed together. I could no longer see him. His skin had the same delicious taste of salt, sand, and the sea, and I never tired of running my mouth, or the tip of my tongue, or my whole tongue over his hips, his sides, and his chest. As soon as I stopped, he did the same to me. He nibbled my left nipple very gently, my hands were in his hair, his cock against my thigh. I made him penetrate me, and he fucked me slowly, frenzy replaced now by gentleness. But he was so close to coming that he had to hold absolutely still or even take his cock out of my ass, and we exchanged positions. Then I fucked him again, playing with his cock, and made him come almost at once, despite his protests, myself coming again and at exactly the same time.

This time we didn't even get up, and quickly fell asleep. We slept very well pressed one against the other, he with his back to me, until around ten. Waking, we made love once again, face to face, me lying on top of him, and we came, simultaneously again, between our bellies. Immediately afterward he said he had to get back to Grasse: the girls would be waiting for him. So I got up and dressed and went down to the kitchen to make some breakfast. But Angelina the cook was there, and I didn't dare ask her to make two breakfasts, nor even to make two myself right under her nose; I went back upstairs, having failed completely, and proposed to Jean-Marc that we stop in some café on our way.

"No, we can have some breakfast at Grasse, at the house."

"OK. Forgive me, but you understand, this isn't my house, I can't compromise my friends by having their cook wondering what's going on."

I had been careful on my way back upstairs to close the door that connects the rooms downstairs with the hallway at the foot of the stairs. We reached the garden without being actually seen by Angelina, thanks to this precaution which must have surprised her somewhat, as much, no doubt, as hearing me leave the house so soon after my first appearance, and without breakfast. But if she thought I had slept with someone, there was nothing to make her suspect it wasn't a woman.

We drove through Antibes, jammed with traffic, and got some gas outside town. Then we went up into the hills, toward Mougins through a well-preserved countryside covered with pine groves. Jean-Marc was talking about the exams he had just taken. He and his friends had been assigned a text by Conrad, which seemed to him perverse on the part of the examiners, since Conrad was after all, a Pole, and his English rather special. In any case, Conrad was very boring.

"Yes, I've always thought so. He has fanatic admirers, but all those ship stories bore me silly."

"That wasn't the only ship story we had. Melville was on our list this year too. We spent months on *Billy Budd*. I don't know if you know that one. It's not much fun either."

"Oh, I like *Billy Budd*. All those secret loves, that way of circling around the subject over and over again."

"If you had studied it page by page for three months, you'd get a little tired of it too."

"Yes, probably. But I also like another one of Melville's stories, something quite close to it in certain respects—*Benito Cereno.*"

"Never heard of it."

"Not many French people have. It takes place on a boat, too. All kinds of mysterious seductions . . . It's never very clear—"

"What I liked a lot on our syllabus this year was *Richard III;* that was really wonderful. It's a lot better than *Hamlet,* don't you think?"

"I don't know. I don't think I'd go that far, but it's certainly very fine."

"Oh yes. Richard's a much more complete character than Hamlet, much richer and more interesting."

"I prefer *Richard II,* but that may be because I once saw a wonderful production of it, one of the best things I've ever seen in the theater, maybe *the* best—Chéreau's production."

"Never heard of it."

"You've just finished your exams?"

"Yes, a week ago. We went to Italy for three or four days, because Corinne wanted to see her friend Laura, the one you saw yesterday. Remember?"

"Yes."

"The grand passion."

"Oh, really? I didn't realize that."

"Yes, and we were in Verona . . . You know Verona?"

"Yes."

"I loved it. I'd never been there before. It was terrific."

"I like it too."

"We were there for three days, almost without sleeping. It was mad. We went out every night, you know, to those huge bars they have in Italy."

"Gay bars?"

"Sure, but gigantic, really gigantic."

"I know one, in Milan, which I like a lot. It's called the *Rosamunda.* I didn't know there were others."

"Well, there's one near Verona. It's absolutely wild. And then there are these parties out in the country, in the open air, along the Adige. There was a big fire, everyone was drinking and singing. It was great."

"It sounds just like *1900.*"

"Yeah, it was just like that."

"And how long have you been in Grasse?"

"Since the day before yesterday."

"The house belongs to one of the girls?"

"Yes, it's Corinne's. I've known her since we were kids. We're from the same place near Nîmes."

"A village?"

"No, a very small town."

"What's it called?"

"Beaucaire, you know it?"

"Yes. Well, no, I've never *been* there. I've only seen Beaucaire from Tarascon."

"That's about all there is to see."

"I like that whole region—Nîmes, Arles, Aigues-Mortes, Sainte-Marie, Saint-Gilles-du-Gard—"

"My grandmother lives in Saint-Gilles-du-Gard."

"She does? My favorite postcard in my collection is the municipal baths in Saint-Gilles-du-Gard. If you visit your grandmother, you'll have to buy me some."

"You think there are any left?"

"Yes, of course there are. It isn't an old card, it must still be for sale."

"You like postcards?"

"Yes. Well, I'm not exactly a collector, but I do like them. Too bad they don't make very nice ones anymore."

"Why not?"

"Because in the old days, each village had its own postcards which showed just local things, and did it very well. Now all you find anywhere are the famous things, even if they're forty kilometers away. In Paris it's the same: until the sixties, more or less, each part of town had its own postcards. Every neighborhood, even the cafés and the tobacco stores, had their own postcards made. Now you find the same cards everywhere—Montmartre, the Eiffel Tower, when it isn't the Loire Châteaux . . . You said you had to go back to Montpellier today?"

"No, to Nîmes. There's a kind of flea market and I have a friend who has a stand there. But he has to go to Spain, so he asked me to watch it for him."

"What does he sell?"

"Oh, a little of everything—furniture, objects. I have to go back for that. Before that, I have to go to Nice, and I'll stop in Montpellier too. Actually, it's a lot of driving."

"Sounds like it."

When we reached Grasse, instead of entering the town, we turned off, according to his directions, toward Draguignan.

"The house isn't in town?"

"No, just outside. It isn't far."

As a matter of fact, it wasn't exactly nearby. After a few kilometers, we turned right a few times, then left, taking smaller and smaller roads. Finally we stopped at a wooden gate where Jean-Marc's green car was parked.

We could see, above us, an overgrown terrace garden with dense trees covered with blossoms, and between the branches a big, plain, white house.

"This is really very lovely."

We walked toward the house and up several stone steps. Over the door, a date was carved in the pale stone: 1719.

"A pretty house around here is really rare. Most of them are so ugly."

We went inside. One of the girls, the smaller of the two French ones, was in the first room. Jean-Marc embraced her:

"I see my car's here: didn't Corinne go to work?"

"No, she's still asleep."

"Can we make ourselves some breakfast?"

"I'm making some tea and coffee now." She turned toward me: "Which would you like?"

"Tea, if it's no trouble."

Meanwhile, Jean-Marc and I made the tour. In front of the house, the terrace ended in a low wall of masonry. To the right an old fountain bubbled up, very clear. Down below, at the corner of another paved terrace, stood a long table covered with a white cloth. There was a pool built along the length of the terrace: it was absolutely transparent.

"A pool like that is really wonderful. Not like those horrible turquoise things you see everywhere."

The water circulated through it from the fountain and flowed on to irrigate, through various sluices, the garden espaliers.

We climbed up to the side of the house. An outside staircase led up to the first floor. Jean-Marc knocked at the door, then opened it.

"Still sleeping?"

Behind the house, higher up the hillside, ran a little canal, clear

141

to the bottom, the water moving swiftly along. About a hundred yards away to the left, an old stone bridge arched over it.

"Funny, the bridge looks much older than the canal."

"That's because the canal was recently cemented, dummy!"

"I just figured that out."

He was walking in front of me, when I embraced him from behind, kissing his neck.

When we reached the door, Corinne, the tallest girl, and her Italian friend emerged, the latter wearing only the bottom of a two-piece bathing suit. Corinne immediately went over to the pool, took off all her clothes, and dived in. She took two or three strokes, smoothed her very long blond hair, and came out again with exactly the same air of unthinkingly performing a daily ritual. She wrapped herself up in a big white towel that she knotted over her breasts.

We sat around the table or lay down on the little retaining wall. The shorter of the two French girls had brought out a teapot, a coffeepot, some milk, sugar, dry toast, bread, several pots of jam, honey, and some heavy cookies (from Italy, judging by the bag they were in), that were shaped like fat, grinning men. The Italian girl, almost completely naked, was lying in the sun, her torso raised by one elbow so she could drink her coffee. Her body was a lovely peach color touched here and there with pink. She had the face of a sulky Pomona. Her broad, solid contours and her voluminous heavy breasts made a striking contrast with the tapering lines of her slender lover, a Maillol next to a Giacometti. The light and my mood were those of a whole period of gardener-artists: Renoir, Monet, Matisse, Bonnard, who strolled in straw hats between the trellises of their flower-beds.

Jean-Marc and the girls discussed their plans for the day:

"You should telephone Christian. Maybe he's not going to Spain—or not until Saturday at any rate. You might have another day to spend with Renaud."

They seemed to regard us as married.

The other French girl stood up, took off all her clothes in turn, and walked over to the pool. But she merely dipped one foot into it.

"Oh! Oh no, not me." And she put her clothes back on.

We brought the remains of the breakfast back to the house.

"You want to pack your things, Jean-Marc?"

He went up to his room, and gestured for me to follow him. He began taking off his pants and underwear to change. This was the first time that I saw him partly naked in daylight. His thighs and his ass were even more exciting than I had thought from just touching them.

"What is this, a dare?"

He touched my fly:

"Yes, and it looks like it worked . . ."

We pressed against each other. Both of us were completely erect. We kissed and he led me to his bed. He was beginning to unbutton my pants when we heard one of the girls' voices. We had left all the doors open:

"All right, you guys, no diversions. We're closing up the house. Let's get things in shape up there!"

Jean-Marc packed his bags very quickly. We exchanged addresses. The various rooms I saw were all very pretty, with old but very simple furniture, mostly Louis-Philippe in style, and windows that overlooked the countryside. Over Jean-Marc's bed hung a nineteenth-century gouache depicting a Venetian house, not quite a palace, on an isolated little canal. The splendid rich red color of the facade seemed to flow into the water— a reflection perhaps, or a cavalier indifference to detail on the part of a minor but gifted artist.

We went back downstairs.

"You want to help me here? We have to put everything away . . ."

143

I carried a few dirty plates from the last night's dinner out to the kitchen. Jean-Marc began washing them. I carried a few bags of garbage to the big can outside:

"I can't do much more. I don't know where things go, what you're taking away and what stays."

I left Jean-Marc to his sink and walked down toward the pool, where I stretched out in the sun. From the windows of the house came the laughter-filled voices of the girls, pretending to quarrel as they put things away.

After a quarter of an hour or so, Corinne came to join me:

"Jean-Marc has telephoned Nîmes: his friend isn't going to Spain until Saturday, so he can stay until tomorrow."

"Ah, that's great."

"Can he sleep at your place?"

"Yes, of course."

"What are your plans for today?"

"Oh, I'll probably go to the beach, down from where I'm staying. Maybe I'll sleep a little. Want to stop by this afternoon?"

"Wait. Don't make invitations so lightly. We're harpies, and where we pass, the grass doesn't grow again. No, seriously, that's nice of you, but I have to work this afternoon."

I went up to find Jean-Marc in the kitchen. He was going to go with the girls to Nice.

"And afterwards you'll come by my place?"

"When?"

"Whenever you want. I'm not going anywhere. I may get some sleep. If I'm not in the house, I'll be on the beach just below."

"Good. Around four this afternoon?"

"That's perfect. Whenever you want. And you'll have dinner with us?"

"You want me to?"

"Of course I want you to. I'm asking because I have to let them know."

"OK, I'd be delighted."

"See you later, then."

"You're going already?"

"I have to pull myself together a little . . ."

"Later, then."

I went back upstairs to say good-bye to the three girls.

"You're leaving? Why not stay a while?"

"No, no, I'll just get in the way here, with all this packing. I'll go down to the beach awhile. But if you want to come by this afternoon, that'll be fine."

"Your friends will be shocked to see us descending on the place, no?"

"Oh, they've seen worse things happen!"

"So long, then!"

I walked down to the gate, through the garden, from one level of steps to the next. A faint breeze stirred the leaves, green on one side, silver on the other.

[*He came for dinner with my friends that evening, and virtually didn't open his mouth. We spent the night together again, every bit as agreeably as before.*

A week later, I went to see him in Montpellier. We walked together to Le Peyrou. He asked me to stay to dinner. I slept at his place, a studio in the university district, amazingly comfortable.

Later, he telephoned me often, and invited me, as I've already noted, to spend some of the summer with his friends in the Lozère or in Grasse. I did not go.

Precisely at the moment when I was getting ready to recopy here the pages concerning Jean-Marc, he came to spend three days with me. The evening of his arrival, I was watching L'Herbier's Inhumaine on television and I was so absorbed in it that I couldn't tear myself away. It was endless, and, according to Jean-Marc, ridiculous. This

145

trivial incident, and several others for which I was almost always responsible, cast a certain shadow over his stay, especially since he turned out to be a very moody boy. The enthusiasm of the previous spring was gone. Nonetheless, we parted good friends.]

❧ XV ❧
DOMINIQUE AND ALAIN

Sunday, June 25, 1978

Between Dominique and me there had been, in fact, a certain past consisting of looks, hesitations, and missed opportunities. I had first seen him at the *Apollinaire,* I think, almost a year ago. He was sitting on the terrace, and when I passed by on the boulevard, his eyes had followed me insistently. He had a beard, brown hair, and pale green eyes set very deep in their sockets. His forehead, level with his brows, was noticeably rounded, emphasizing his very virile, somewhat primitive look, confirmed by his large size, the solidity of his build, the breadth of his shoulders. He wasn't, on the whole, my type, but I was flattered by his attention because I thought he was handsome. Nonetheless, to make contact with someone who is sitting on a café terrace, even the *Apollinaire*— especially the *Apollinaire,* perhaps, where everyone is scrutinizing each of your movements—is not so easy. I walked past in the other direction: a new exchange of prolonged glances. Then, five minutes later, I passed again in my original direction. But now the boy with the beard was having an elaborate conversation with someone else at his table, and so I gave up trying to speak to him.

A few weeks later, I had seen him at the *Sept.* I had met someone else that evening, and we had decided to leave together. This boy first had to tell his friends he was going or something of the kind, and I was waiting for him at the foot of the staircase. There just opposite me was the bearded boy, staring at me hard. I had smiled at him, he had barely responded, but he continued to keep his eyes fixed on me. I remember that the other boy, the one with whom I left that night, was very aggressive and half-crazy. As we were crossing the Tuileries and he was explaining how much he detested fags who were queens and sissies and never even said hello to you three days after you had slept with them, I greatly regretted not leaving him there and going back to the *Sept* to get to know my bearded boy better. As it turned out, this Jacques, with whom I had spent the night at the house of one of my friends, was a total masochist, and everything he said was no doubt designed exclusively to turn me against him. Contrary to my expectations, our relations were very successful in sexual terms, though in a perverse mode somewhat unfamiliar to me. And exactly as I had expected, a week later he no longer said hello.

The third encounter with the bearded boy occurred two or three months ago, again at the *Sept*. I was with Tony, who agreed that he was attractive. Once again we exchanged long stares. But he never once smiled, seeming absolutely determined to remain where he was and not take one step in my direction. At this point, Daniel Boudinet had gone over to speak to him, they had started up an intense conversation, and Tony and I had left.

The following episode goes back to Sunday, June 18, shortly after my return from the Côte d'Azur. It was on the afternoon of a relatively nice day for this spring of 1978, which in Paris was exceptionally rainy and cold. Tony and I were sitting on the terrace of the *Apollinaire* in the sun. I had gotten up to go inside and take a piss. Crossing the café, I saw a boy with a moustache sitting in the rear of the room and staring at me. He looked vaguely familiar. But it was only when I came back upstairs from the toilet and examined him once again that I recognized him: it was the bearded boy of the missed opportunities. I smiled at him. He smiled back. I touched my cheeks with my hand to explain that it was the disappearance of his beard that had kept me from recognizing him right away. He signalled that he understood. He was sitting across from a shorter boy with light hair and a moustache and a round face, who also stared at me and to whom he might have been describing the story of our abortive contacts.

147

I returned to the table outside, where Tony sat. I told him about the ex-bearded boy, reminded him of his last appearance at the *Sept,* and explained that he was here, now, with a friend.

"Ask them to dinner if you want to," he said.

We separated. Before leaving the café, I went inside. The two friends didn't see me. I decided that there was no hurry, and left for my usual rounds, taking the Rue de Buci and the Rue de l'Ancienne-Comédie to the Odéon, and returning down the Boulevard Saint-Germain. But when I returned to the *Apollinaire,* determined to proffer my invitation, its intended beneficiaries had vanished.

I saw them again that same evening, though; they were still together at the *Manhattan.* From which I concluded that they were doubtless lovers, and that they probably lived together, especially since the shorter one, it seemed to me, was jealous of the other, who was the object of a great deal of attention. I spoke to him myself two or three times, but it was difficult, given the crowd and the noise. Contrary to what I had concluded from his sporadic appearances, he lived in Paris. But this was about all I managed to learn about him. A friend of mine, Gilbert, lavished his attentions upon him, and he himself seemed to be quite actively interested in someone I have known by sight for a long time, a thin, balding fellow with a moustache, who frequently appears with the same boy; and who, moreover, is a great friend of that Jean-Rémy, whom I have already mentioned and who nearly made me quarrel with Etienne (Trick VI). There were all kinds of pseudo-departures, which I interpreted as the sign of paraconjugal difficulties. The ex-bearded boy and his friend left together, the former returned and talked to me and Gilbert, and especially to Jean-Rémy's friend, then the second boy came back as well, and once again they left together. This happened two or three times. The situation seemed too complicated, especially since I was with Tony myself, and I stopped paying any attention.

On the afternoon of the following Sunday, June 25, the same situation exactly: I was having a drink with Tony on the terrace of the *Apollinaire* and the ex-bearded boy was inside with his friend. But when Tony left me, not without having urged me, as before, to invite them to join us later, instead of first taking my little stroll, I went into the café. There, at a table next to theirs, was one of my friends, an American to whom I began speaking in English. He told me about his summer plans, which took a good five minutes. During this conversation, the ex-bearded boy, who sat with his back to me, frequently turned toward me and smiled, which made it easy for me to approach him and his companion:

"You have your little rituals, I see."

"Oh yes, every Sunday afternoon these days, two good hours at the *Apollinaire*."

"And always inside?"

"It's cooler. The problem is deciding where to eat afterward."

"Yes, that's always a problem on Sundays. As a matter of fact, if you'd like, you could both come to dinner at my place. It won't be much of a feast, a little improvised, but you'd be very welcome."

The ex-bearded boy looked at his friend:

"I don't know. What do you think?"

"I don't care. You decide."

"Well, you two don't seem very enthusiastic about my proposition—"

"No, it's not that. It's just that we don't want to impose on you just like that."

"You're not imposing at all. It won't be anything complicated. I'm not even the one who'll be doing the cooking. And my cook will be very glad to see you." They still seemed to hesitate.

"Listen, it's very simple, I'll leave you my phone number. That way you can take your time and decide. In any case, I have to go home now."

"No, that's not what it's about . . . All right, what shall we do? Shall we go?"

"Sure."

"All right, so we'll come with you?"

"OK."

149

We left the café together, followed by the eyes of the entire terrace. We crossed the boulevard and walked west on the left sidewalk.

"What's your name?"

"Dominique."

"And yours?"

"Alain."

"My name is Renaud."

"That's a really unusual name . . . I've never met a Renaud before."

"I live near here, Rue du Bac. But I should warn you, there are a lot of stairs to climb."

"How many?"

"Six flights."

"Oh, that's all right. There are five at my place."

"You live together?"

"No, but we live near each other. I live off the Avenue de la République and he lives near the Place de la Bastille. We're always in one place or the other."

Indeed they seemed so close that most of the way they talked only to each other, which irritated me a little. And, although physically they were both quite butch, especially Dominique, they had rather queenly turns of expression, and even designated each other, eventually, in the feminine. There was a lot of discussion about a certain François. Each time Dominique saw François, something happened to him:

"If we dance together, you can be sure he'll kick me in the shins. The first time I slept with him, next day, I got a big pimple on my forehead. Last Sunday, we took a taxi home: he gets out first, and bang! closes the door right on my nose. Sorry, he says, I forgot. Forgot! And in the morning the alarm goes off, he tries to turn it off and bang! another sock in the face! A regular barrel of fun, François!"

"He must be something, this guy, if you keep going back, in spite of all these catastrophes."

"Don't ask. She can't keep her hands off him."

"No, that's not true. All I know is, every time I see him, I don't know why, I feel something inside."

"You'll see him tonight."

"Yes, sure. He'll be at the *Manhattan* later on, all right. But I'm not sleeping with him tonight. I have to get up early tomorrow. I have to look for work."

"You on welfare?"

"Yes. Well, no. I work in a bar, but it's only for a month. I'm through this week. And besides, it's not my real line of work."

"And what is your *real* line of work?"

"I'm a nurse."

"How do you find work, when you're a nurse?"

"What?"

"I mean, how do you go about looking--in the want ads?"

"Yes, of course."

"What do you do, Alain?"

"I work in a food store."

"Near where you live?"

"Yes, right next door."

"All right, kids, here's where the climb begins."

It was about twenty to eight. No one was at home.

"Oh, this is nice. You have a terrace."

"Yes, it's nice this time of year. But with the weather we've been having this year, we haven't used it much. Make yourselves comfortable. Excuse me a second, I have to telephone my cook to ask him to buy some bread."

But the line was busy.

"I don't have much to offer you, I'm afraid: Perrier, Coca-Cola—yes, there's some champagne, if you'd like some. Yes, let's have that."

While I was washing up the first three glasses I could find in the kitchen, they went on with their conversation. I uncorked the bottle and tried to phone Tony again. The line was still busy.

"What a bore. I have to go back down and get some bread, before they close up."

I was gone for five minutes and took advantage of the occasion to buy a cake. They seemed to pay as little attention to my return as to my departure. Dominique was talking:

"The whole thing's a bore. It pisses me off. I don't know what to do. You know, I don't like asking my grandmother because she'll try to make an appointment for me with her doctor. I know him. He knows all about me, I'm sure, but I hate having to explain all that to him—dotting every *i* and crossing every *t*. Not because he minds especially, but because *I* do. I'm going to ask my grandmother if she knows some other doctor."

"You're going to come out to your grandmother?"

"Sure! That's no problem. I always tell her *everything*. Besides, she always asks for details. She's *fascinated* by stories like that. She always wants to know all about the guys I sleep with."

"That's really rare. Mothers are one thing, but grandmothers . . ."

"But it's the same with my *mother*, you know. We *cruise* together! Last summer at Saint-Tropez, she'd put on whites, pants and a jersey, you know, a sailor outfit with the collar and the cap, and she'd go out with me—down to the harbor, everywhere. Everyone thought she was a *dike*. She got cruised right and left. My mother's very young-looking. She's forty and you'd say she was maybe twenty-five at the most. She used to tell me which guys to go home with."

"It's nice to have that kind of relationship with your parents."

"And with my uncle and my aunt, it's the same way too. Every time they have me over for a meal, they ask if I want to bring a friend, everything. The other day, there was this guy, we were at their place. You should have *seen* him. He sat in my lap, right in front of them. My uncle was a little surprised, of course. But they laughed it off."

"Mine aren't like that at all. They don't know a thing. Well, probably they do, but we never talk about it. Never. God, what a scene *that* would be!"

"Where are they? Are they Parisians?"

"No, they live in the Mayenne."

"The Mayenne . . . near what town, Mayenne itself?"

"Yes, near there. Laval."

"Oh, sure."

"Do your folks know?"

152

"Yes. There were a lot of terrible scenes. Now, we never mention it. But whenever I go there it's all very strained, there are long silences . . . You're really lucky, you know that?"

"Of course, my father isn't like the rest of them. It's hard for him to swallow."

"Do your parents live in Paris?"

"No, Marseille."

"You come from Marseille?"

"Yes."

"Funny: you don't have an accent at all."

"No. No one has an accent in my family . . . My father, though, when he has a chance to make some nasty little comment, don't worry, he makes it, all right. Whenever there's some queen on television. It never fails. My father trots out the whole song and dance."

"Sure. Well, television is terrible when you have to watch it with your folks. Every time I go see mine, it's the same thing. You can bet your ass the television will mess it up. Now they've got me terrorized, whenever they turn it on, you can be sure there's some nasty story about fags, sooner or later. It makes for a *charming* atmosphere, let me tell you."

"Of course, it's not *all* my father's fault. I've done some pretty stupid things, too, that's for sure. One day, there were about ten guys over at my place. We'd all had something to drink, the music was real loud. The telephone rings. I pick it up and I hear a man's voice. I thought it was this guy I knew. He asks me: 'Who's on the line?' I couldn't hear a thing, of course, with the music, and I say: 'This is Dominique. What can I do for you, gorgeous?' 'It's your father,' he answers. You can bet that sobered me up right away. The next day, I got *some* lecture from my mother! He's going to kill me one of these days. I'm sure he's going to kill me. Last year, when I brought Jean-Marc to visit, you should have *seen* the faces they pulled! Of course, this year I told him I was coming with François. No problem. He said: 'All right, fine, but I warn you. You sleep in separate rooms, because of your brother.' That was a good one, because where we go, to the shore near Lavandou, our house there, it's tiny, you know, just three

153

rooms. So I said to him: 'Where are you going to put *him*, in Jacques's room?' My mother broke up over that. But Christ, *he* didn't think it was so funny."

"François is the boy you were talking about just now—the walking catastrophe?"

"Right."

"You're spending your summer vacation together? This is a grand passion!"

"No, it's not, but I like him a lot. He turns me on. When I look at him, it does something to me. My *legs* get all funny. I'd do anything he asked."

"Mmm . . . Was he at the *Manhattan* with you last Sunday?"

"Probably. He's always there. Last Sunday—wait a minute, sure. That was the night he closed the taxi door in my face."

"A skinny boy with a thin moustache and a high forehead?"

"Right. I'm sure you know him, he's always around."

"Isn't he usually with a boy named Jean-Rémy?"

"Yes, that's right. Jean-Rémy. That's the one. I don't know what he'd *do* without his Jean-Rémy."

"Then I know which one your François is. By sight. He looks very nice."

"You can say that again. It's like this: as soon as I see him my heart starts pounding. You know this Jean-Rémy?"

"No, I don't know him. But I've had some funny contacts with him. Before, we used to say hello, because we kept seeing each other all the time. Besides, I knew his brother. But one thing, Jean-Rémy and I, we have exactly the same tastes. It's very simple: each time I see him looking somewhere, I look too, and I can be sure it's a guy who'll turn me on. Well, I thought it was funny because there wasn't any rivalry; on the contrary, it was a kind of bond, a kind of complicity. Besides, I thought he seemed so nice and everything. And then, one day something very nasty happened. I'd met a boy I liked a lot, and Jean-Rémy was cruising him. And then I went out of town for three days. When I came back, I found my boy completely transformed, icy . . . I tried to find out what had happened. I insisted on knowing, and finally this boy tells me: 'I've heard terrible things about you.' Of course it was Jean-Rémy. I didn't think that showed much class, that kind

154

of behavior. He'd told the kid I hung out all the time, that I never stopped cruising."

"That's Jean-Rémy, all right. And if he sees *you* hanging out, it's because *he's* there cruising too. Right?"

"Right. He wasn't exactly in a position to criticize. And besides—I don't know—if you're cruising someone, it seems to me the least you can do is not put down your rivals, even if what you have to say is true."

"Yes, that's pure Jean-Rémy, through and through."

"Why does he always do that? Is he always this nasty?"

"I don't know. I'm not one of his friends. But every time he finds some way to badmouth some queen, you can bet he'll do it."

"François spends a lot of time with another boy, doesn't he—quite tall, maybe not French?"

"What? Watch your language!"

"I don't know. I don't mean they're a couple or anything. I just saw them together a lot, that's all."

"Oh, I know. Yeah. Tall and sort of heavy, with curly hair. Is that the one?"

"That's right."

"Oh, that's his ex. They used to live together, but it's been over a long time . . . You're right, they're together all the time."

I'd called Tony several times during this conversation. He was supposed to be at Roy's. The first few times the line was busy, then there was no answer. It was now after nine o'clock.

"All right, listen. We'll have something to eat anyway. I'll see what I can do. It won't be a feast, because I never do the cooking. I have no talent for it. But we can't go on waiting for hours. It'll be a strange dinner. There's enough food here for several meals for *two* people, but nothing for four. It doesn't matter though. I'll put it all together, and everyone'll take what he wants." And I went out to the kitchen to get the food ready. From time to time I came back into the main room to set the low table. "We'll sit on the floor, if you don't mind. It'll be a kind of picnic."

But Dominique and Alain were in the middle of a conversation and paid no attention to me. There were two lamb chops that I put under the broiler, some ham, some sliced roast beef, salami, sau-

155

sage. I arranged the whole thing on a platter and combined a can of peas and a can of carrots, which I heated up:

"All right, take whatever you like. It's not a very well-planned meal."

Just as we began to eat, the telephone rang. It was Tony. He had picked up an Iranian boy on the street, could he bring him home for dinner? I wasn't very hospitable—he could have called earlier, there was nothing for his Iranian to eat, I was with two friends, we had waited for him over an hour, etc. But he was coming up anyway.

Ten minutes later there he was, along with his Iranian, a short dark boy, not really handsome but quite sexy, with wonderful eyes—the kind my American friends call *bedroom eyes*. He was studying architecture in the States, cultivated, elegant, very upper-middle-class. And spoke not one word of French. Dominique and Alain couldn't speak any English. In any case, they had resumed their private discussion.

When we had finished the cake, Tony turned on the television because he wanted to see some Lon Chaney film. Since it was a silent film, he supposed that all our linguistic problems would be solved. But the film hadn't started, and for the moment there was some kind of very heavy talk show which seemed to delight Dominique and Alain: just watching it sent them into irrepressible hysterics. I was sort of interested. Tony stared at Dominique and Alain with a puzzled smile:

"What's the matter with those two, are they completely smashed or what?"

"Yes, listen, try to behave. You're impossible! I can't take you anywhere, you're a real whore," Alain said to Dominique, who immediately burst into hysterical laughter all over again.

They were sitting side by side on the low bed, virtually bent double, collapsing into each other's laps in turns. The Iranian seemed surprised, vaguely disapproving, as if he wondered where he had landed. Some friends were expecting him, he had to call to tell them he would be late, but when he managed to reach them by phone, they absolutely insisted he come right away, so he decided to leave. He said he would call Tony the next day.

There was news on the television now. Dominique asked if there weren't anything else to drink. We had finished all the wine in the house, three or four bottles.

"No more alcohol, unfortunately. Oh yes, there is some Cinzano, but you don't want to drink that now, after dinner."

"Sure I do. All I want is something alcoholic. Anything. Cinzano will be fine."

"You don't think you've had enough?"

"No. Alcohol has no effect on me."

"All right."

I brought him the Cinzano bottle. Meanwhile Tony rolled a joint, which we passed around. The film was beginning. I've forgotten the title. Lon Chaney played two parts, two brothers, one bad and the other virtuous, in the lower depths of London. The good brother, "the bishop," was a cripple: his body was completely deformed and he had no legs. The film was very slow, rather depressing, and not at all the kind of thing I felt like watching.

I was sitting in an armchair not far from the little bed across which Dominique and Alain were sprawled. To tell the truth, I had decided there was no longer any question of sex between us, given the stories about François and their plan to go to the *Manhattan* later on. But while Tony was in the kitchen or in the bathroom, Dominique knelt down beside my chair, stuck one hand into my shirt, caressed my chest, then drew me toward him to kiss me. Then he pulled me toward the little bed. He had an erection and so did I. I was lying on top of him. Beside us, Alain was caressing my thighs. When Tony came back, he sat down on the floor, beside the sofa. The next moment, Alain and he were kissing. So for a moment we were paired off, then Tony began undressing us all, beginning with the shoes. Since we had to stand up to get rid of our trousers, I took advantage of the situation to lead Dominique into the bedroom as soon as we were completely naked.

157

Undressed, he seemed even bigger and stronger: his torso, arms, thighs, and cock had the same massiveness, the same heaviness, the same solidity. In fact, we were not very well suited to each other. Alain was much shorter than I, hairy, with a good-sized cock, but he had something of a potbelly.

Alain and Tony soon came to join us on the big bed in the bedroom. We were all playing with each other, but the original combination was nonetheless maintained on the whole, despite certain temporary permutations. Tony and Alain seemed in better sexual agreement than Dominique and I. Quite rapidly they were fucking each other, while we were still only kissing or sucking each other's cock. Tony had emptied the contents of a whole tube of lubricant among the four of us. But I still couldn't manage to get my cock into Dominique's ass, and as usual, difficulties of this kind made me lose my erection. Dominique lost his, too. Tony then handed us a bottle of amyl nitrite which he and Alain had already sniffed. Dominique grabbed it very enthusiastically, and kept it under his nose for a long time before handing it to me. He became absolutely frenetic:

"Beat me! Beat me!"

I was surprised by this request, and embarrassed by the presence of the others. But Tony was fucking Alain, and neither of them was paying any attention to us.

"Go on, beat me!"

So I slapped him a few times, not very hard, on the biceps and on the shoulders. But that wasn't enough for him:

"On my face, go on, hit me!"

I was lying on top of him, my cock against his. Again, we were both getting hard. With my left hand I grabbed the hair on the back of his head, and with my right I slapped him, first with my palm, then with the back of my hand. Then I raised his thighs, which I kept up with my arms. My cock was against his balls, which were very large and heavy. I nibbled his chest, still clutching his hair in my left fist, closed on the nape of his neck.

"Yeah, you bastard, hit me. Hard!"

Tony and Alain, beside us, were both coming, with a lot of sound effects. When they fell back, side by side, breathless, Dominique asked them for the bottle of amyl. His voice sounded strange, disembodied, as if he were talking in his sleep, but child-like, too. He began inhaling the bottle intensely every three min-utes, meanwhile urging me ever more insistently to beat him. I couldn't do much more than knead his sides and back or bite his pectorals, holding his head back by the hair. He kept encouraging me to more violence, but I was getting a little tired of this game. Each time he inhaled the amyl, he seemed to have an epileptic fit, arching his whole body, hollowing his hips, touching the bed with only his heels and his shoulders. His cock wasn't altogether hard now; neither was mine.

Tony and Alain had left the bedroom to get something to drink, to change the record, and to clean up. Suddenly Dominique went completely stiff and motionless.

"What's the matter? Is something wrong?"

"No, it's nothing. Wait. Don't move."

"You feel sick?"

"Yeah, I feel like shit!"

Alain came back into the bedroom.

"I think he's sick."

"Something's wrong?"

"No wonder—mixing everything, the champagne, the red wine, the rosé, the Cinzano. Then a joint and the poppers on top of all that. What do you think!"

"Bring a bowl, quick!"

"I don't know what's wrong with me. I don't know what's happened. I've had this before. This isn't the first time. I'm sick of it, sick of it. I'm going to kill myself, and this time, don't worry, I won't fuck it up. I'm a nurse. I know what to do, what to take. I'm sick of this life. Sick of it. And what does anyone care anyway? The guys cruise me because I look good—or I don't know why. But if you have problems, if you're unhappy, the hell with you. A lot *they* care. They couldn't give a fuck. They shoot their wad and good-bye. Thanks, *ciao,* take it easy—"

"No, that's not true. They're like everyone else. Some are bastards and some are very nice. Some people *do* give a fuck whether you're unhappy or not."

We were sitting on the edge of the bed now, I on his right and Alain on his left, one arm around his shoulders.

"Look. We just met you today, and *we* give a fuck about your feelings. We'd like to be able to help you. And your buddy Alain, he gives a fuck too. I think it's just that you feel bad right now because you've had too much to drink, and it doesn't mix with the grass. Lie down, try to sleep. Maybe you'll feel better in a little while."

"No. I don't want to lie down. I want to go home. I want to be alone. I don't want to hassle you. What the fuck do you care about someone like me? What do you want with me? No one wants anything to do with me! All I want is to be done with it. I want to kill myself. Besides, it's nothing new. I've tried more than once. A long time ago I tried. Look. You can see for yourself. Look at that."

He showed me his wrists, where I could in fact see three parallel horizontal scars.

"That time I came close. But next time I'll do it right."

"No. Listen. You see everything that way now because you're sick. Tomorrow you'll feel different about it."

"No, I know what I'm saying. Besides, you shouldn't believe that people who keep telling you they're going to kill themselves will never do it. That's not true. One day or another they'll do it. They *always* do it. There was this guy, he lived on my floor. He was just like me. Exactly like me. We understood each other. We understood each other right away. He said he was going to kill himself. No one believed him, but *I* believed him. Well, one day we smelled gas, the guy I lived with and I. You can be sure, we knew right away. We went to his place, he had his head in his oven. He was lying there in his kitchen . . . Well, I'm just the same. The same thing will happen to me. Why should I go on living? You tell me. Why should I go on living? What's the use? A guy like me! Why should I?"

"Wait a while. Lie down. Rest a little. Try to sleep. Come on now . . ."

We stretched out side by side, his head on my shoulder. He continued his monologue about his complete uselessness: guys like him had no reason to live. Nonetheless he was getting harder and harder, and so was I. He pulled me against him. When I realized

160

that both of us were very aroused again, I stopped his talk with a kiss. And we went back to making love, more or less. A new attempt to fuck him was a failure. Tony and Alain rejoined us and stretched out on the bed beside us and began making love together as well. I was lying on top of Dominique who was moving around a good deal in a convulsive and jerky way. Alain then stretched out on my back and stuck his cock into me, while kissing Dominique underneath me. He came in my ass, quite quickly. Dominique again demanded the bottle of amyl nitrite. We hesitated to hand it to him, but he insisted on it. After having inhaled it deeply, he again begged me to beat him. I obeyed this request, but without enough determination for his taste. He kept encouraging me to be more violent:

"Hit me! Go on! Hit me hard!"

I realized that I would never manage to satisfy him, and I was pretty tired of all these exercises. Taking advantage of a lull, I decided to come in the simplest way possible, lying on top of him. I bit his neck, twisted one of his arms against the sheet, putting all my weight on him, and expelled my sperm against his belly with a good deal of pleasure.

But I would have had a clearer conscience if he had come too, and I concerned myself with that almost immediately. I took his cock in my mouth and sucked it methodically, accompanying myself with my right hand. He wanted more poppers, which again produced the same effect, a kind of apparently epileptic fit which made it impossible to go on blowing him, for he twisted and jerked his body like a man possessed. I lay down beside him again. He asked me to beat him some more. I did what I could. But either because he got the same pleasure from it, or because he was trying to get me really angry, he began to return my blows and to give me others with much more skill and force than I had demonstrated. It was a dreadful mess. Tony and Alain were trying to squeeze against the wall to escape the rain of blows coming from all directions, while Dominique, who was a good six inches taller than all three of us and much more solidly built, was throwing himself around with a frenzy which he revived with poppers every two minutes. After I got a good thrust of the elbow under my

161

chin, which made me bite my tongue, and a terrific punch on the hip, I had had quite enough of this little session. I fell back onto the pillow, and Dominique with me.

Then virtually the same scene began again, the words and gestures following each other now in a flexible, continuous way, joined together frictionlessly, like the necessary elements of a well-oiled machine. First he asked me for something to drink, alcohol, any alcohol, some Cinzano—

"No, absolutely out of the question. You're going to make yourself really sick."

"But I *am* completely sick. A little more or less won't matter! You can see what a wreck I am. All I can do is hassle guys who don't give a fuck about me. I'm no good, I'm no use. I spoil everything."

"I don't want to disappoint you, doll, but you hardly look like a wreck."

"I'm sick of it, sick of it, *sick!*"

"You have to sleep awhile. Stretch out now. It'll be better tomorrow."

"No, I want to go home."

"But you can't go home when you're like this. You can hardly stand up."

"Yes, I want to go home. I want to be alone. I don't want anyone to see me . . ."

"No. Sorry. We're not going to leave you alone."

"I want to go home."

Alain intervened:

"All right. If you want to go home, I'll go home with you."

"Can you sleep at his place?"

"Yes."

"You're sure the two of you wouldn't rather stay here?"

"No, I want to go home. I don't even need him. Look. I can walk perfectly well. Wait, leave me alone. I have to move. Let me walk a little."

He stood up and went into the next room. But he stayed there only a moment, and went out onto the balcony. I immediately followed him there.

"Leave me alone. Go back inside. Leave me in peace."

"What are you doing?"

"I'm going to jump. I'm going to be done with it once and for all. That way at least I won't bother anyone anymore."

"You're *not* bothering anyone! Now stop! If you jump, yes, then you'll be bothering quite a lot of people."

"I'm going to jump. It's easy. What's this? A little railing. All I have to do is step over it and then that's that. All the shit is over and done with."

"All right, stop. Come on now. Let's go back inside. You're going to go to bed here. Or if you absolutely insist, you can go home with Alain. Come on now."

"No. I want to jump."

He was clutching the railing and I was pulling him back by the waist. We were both naked. Although he was much stronger than I, I managed to make him let go, and we went back into the bedroom, where he lay down on the bed again. We remained there in silence for a moment. I caressed him and talked to him in a low voice as if he were a child. I went to get him some water.

"Feel better?"

"Yes, a little. I have to go home."

"You want me to call a taxi?"

"No, it's all right. We'll find one."

"Wait a minute. I can see from the balcony if there's one at the stand . . . Yes, there are a lot."

Alain and he got dressed again quite quickly.

"Are you all right? Can you stand up?"

"Yes, of course. I'm fine. Fine."

"Anyway, Alain's with you. He can help you."

"Yes. Lean on me."

"Don't fall down the stairs."

"No, we'll be all right."

"Telephone me when you get there. Wait! I'll write down the number for you. Here, I'll give it to *you*. It'll be safer. Call us right away!"

"Yes, sure."

"Good. All right. I think he's feeling a little better."

"Yes, he's better. I'll take him home and put him to bed."

163

They began going down the stairs. Dominique, who seemed to be asleep already, was leaning on Alain, who, a step below him, barely came up to his chest.

[*Alain telephoned a half hour later. He had left Dominique, quite calm now, at his house, where there was someone with him.*

The next day Dominique called. "I was absolutely smashed, wasn't I? Did I make an asshole of myself?"

I saw Dominique two or three times more, the following week; he was always very calm, nice, and good-humored. Then he vanished. I meet Alain very often, always with the same boy. He is only half-friendly, and affects, like his companion, an emphatically conjugal manner.]

❦ XVI ❦
WALTER IRVING

Thursday, June 29, 1978

[*New York, at F.H.'s, Sunday, July 23, 1978.*] I had arranged to have dinner with Philippe and I was supposed to meet him at the *Petit Saint-Benoît* at the end of the Rue Saint-Benoît. As usual, I was early, so I strolled down the boulevard as far as the Rue de Buci. When I walked back, I noticed at the corner of the *Flore* a boy who immediately turned me on: short, very dark, short hair, a moustache, tanned. He was wearing rather loose khakis with a narrow belt, a short-sleeved beige shirt open at the neck, and incongruously, a tiny reddish tie. He had a lot of long black hair on his forearms and at the pit of his throat. Looped over his shoulder was a good-sized canvas bag, also beige. Obviously he was a foreigner, but it wasn't easy to identify where he was from.

He met my eyes, which were doubtless rather insistent, and smiled. But I couldn't tell if this was a pleasant or perhaps amused way of acknowledging the attention I was paying him, or a sign of interest in return. I walked as far as the central door of the *Flore*, glancing over the terrace, and then returned to the corner. We were two or three yards apart, he standing near the door at that corner. I glanced in all directions, including his, and toward the Rue Saint-Benoît. He looked at me as well, but this time without smiling. He went a little ways down the street, I followed him, he turned around and sat down at one of the tables of the *Flore* that are set out there, where no one else was sitting. I passed him and continued walking, very slowly, toward the Rue Jacob. He got up and started walking in the same direction. I crossed the street and came back a few steps to glance into the side windows of *La Hune*. That was when I caught sight of Philippe, who was walking up from the bottom of the street, and I signalled him to stay away for the moment. Philippe saw the foreign boy who was then—his big bag hoisted over his shoulder—in front of the door of the Hotel Montana, and he passed in front of me without coming any closer, but with a little pout which indicated that he did not share my interest.

Meanwhile, the foreign boy and I were still walking down the Rue Saint-Benoît, each on his own side of the street, he on the left, I on the right. I stopped at the corner of the Rue de l'Abbaye. Then he crossed the street and passed right by me. I smiled at him, he made no response, but he stopped a couple of yards away, sitting down on the fender of a car and putting his bag on the ground.

I went over to him and said in English: "You looking for something?"

"Oh, you speak English! I was afraid no one spoke English."

"Oh yes, a lot of people speak English. You look a little lost."

"No, just looking around. I've just arrived in Paris."

"Where are you from?"

"Guess!"

"I don't know. Iranian?"

"No."

"Lebanese?"

"No."

"Oh, I don't know. You could be a lot of things."

"I'm half-Ceylonese and half-Portuguese."

"That I'd never have guessed! And where have you just come from?"

"London."

"You live there?"

"No, I live in Australia."

"Half-Ceylonese, half-Portuguese, coming from London and living in Australia—now that's exotic."

"I only live in Australia half the year. The rest of the time I live in New Zealand."

"Wellington?"

"Auckland."

"And in Australia?"

"Sidney. You ask a lot of questions."

"I know I do. Forgive me. It fascinates me. And you just got to Paris?"

"Yes, three hours ago. I went to my hotel and came back out right away."

"Where's your hotel?"

"Wait." He took out of his pocket the card of a hotel whose name I've forgotten, somewhere near the Place de l'Europe, in the Rue de Léningrad, I think.

"How did you ever find a hotel over there?"

"Oh, a girl I know gave me the address. But it's too far away."

"Yes, it's hardly central."

"I should have found a hotel around here. If I were going to stay in Paris, I'd change."

"How long are you going to stay?"

"Oh, I don't know, two days, three. I haven't decided—I'm thinking of going to Florence."

"To Florence? Why Florence?"

"I don't know. It's a good place to go, isn't it?"

"Yes, a very good place to go. But why Florence especially? I mean, rather than Venice or Rome?"

"I don't know. That's just the way it is. I have a friend who told me Florence was good . . . Maybe I'll go to Switzerland, or else to Kuwait."

"To Kuwait?"

"Sure. Why not?"

"Why not, as you say . . ."

I was sitting beside him now, on the same fender at the corner of the Rue de l'Abbaye. Philippe, who was coming back down the Rue Saint-Benoît, slowly approached us.

"I can't introduce you. I don't know this young man's name."

"Walter. What's yours?"

"Renaud."

"Rano?"

"Yes, more or less. Philippe, Walter. Philippe and I were going to have dinner together, down the street on the left."

"Yes, but I just went by the *Petit Saint-Benoît* and it didn't seem very lively tonight. I thought we might go and have a bite somewhere outside . . ."

"How about the *Cour Saint-Germain?*"

"I just came from there: I reserved a table. I thought it would be more fun."

"Yes. That's fine. Would you mind if I made a last-minute invitation?"

"No, of course not."

"Well then, Walter, will you have dinner with us? We're going to a restaurant just down the boulevard from here. We'll eat outside."

"Yes, I'd like that."

"Walter just got here from London."

"Today?"

"Today."

"But how did he discover the Hotel Montana?"

"He's not staying at the Montana."

"Oh, I thought I saw him coming out of there with his big bag."

"No. No, he's in a hotel in the Ninth Arrondissement."

"Really. Why?"

"Someone gave me the address. It's ridiculous—it's so far away."

"A little remote from the scene, as they say. You've just come from London? But you're not English, all the same, with a color like yours?"

"No, he's Ceylono-Portuguese."

"That's an original combination. You're the first Ceylono-Portuguese I've ever met."

"Is it your father who's Portuguese?"

"Yes."

"Of course, it's not all that amazing. The Portuguese are great travellers."

"Yes. And besides, the Portuguese were the first Europeans to set foot in Ceylon, right?"

"It's even more complicated than that—my father's mother was Irish, and he had a Dutch grandmother."

"Fortunately the Dutch part hasn't left many traces."

"Why fortunately?"

"I can't say I find the Dutch very sexy, as a rule."

"Oh, *I* do. In London I met a Dutchman who happened to be just that. Really wonderful, actually."

"There are exceptions, of course. I just meant that as a nation, it's not a physical type that turns me on. That's all. A little too buttery . . ."

We were walking slowly toward the restaurant. It was a warm summer evening. On the square and the boulevard a huge crowd milled around, habitués, tourists, and strollers forming circles around the various booths and performers, jugglers on a platform, fire-eaters, chamber musicians, guitarists, someone playing the zither, someone selling phosphorescent necklaces that shone green in the moist night air. Walter was very interested in all of it.

Walking alongside the church, we passed the famous Jean-Rémy, who didn't even see me, so busy was he staring at Walter, even turning to look back at him. This attention confirmed my own interest, of course, despite the reservations expressed earlier by Philippe.

[*November 29, 1978: the original manuscript of this chapter ends here. At the time of writing, last July, I decided that it was preferable to devote my energies to the American tricks as I experienced them, before I forgot the details. So that now, several months later, my recollections of the encounter with Walter are somewhat vague.*]

Philippe had reserved a table for two at the restaurant. We were now three, and the table reserved was no longer suitable. We waited a little while, leaning against the cars parked at the curb. Walter had with him a little list of Parisian restaurants drawn up for him by friends. He showed it to us: it continued into a list of bars, which Philippe and I took it upon ourselves to annotate. *La Mendigote*—yes, it was still going, but I found it a little depressing; you always felt you were a dirty old man there, since everyone else was eighteen. *Le Nuage*—I hadn't set foot in there for years. *Le Rocambole* sort of fun, sometimes, but only interesting as a commentary on the other places, if you knew them; it wouldn't be where I would go if I had only one or two nights to spend in Paris. *Le Sept* might amuse Walter, and so might the *Palace*. It must have been rather late, almost eleven, because I remember having pointed out some boys who were walking up or down the Boulevard Saint-Germain, heading for *Le Manhattan*—they seemed the *Manhattan* type. Or was it only nine, and was I saying that these boys would probably turn up later at the *Manhattan*? It doesn't matter. Walter was curious and wanted to know which of these places we thought would interest him the most. *The Palace* was impossible on weekends, it was just too crowded, busloads of tourists, and besides, it was really not very gay these days. Which left *Le Sept* and the *Manhattan*. Very different, from every point of view: "I don't know which you'd like best, I don't know your tastes well enough yet; in any case, you'd certainly be popular in either one. From the way you're dressed, I'd say you were very *Sept*, but physically—dark skin, moustache, short hair and so on, and a new face into the bargain—you'd have the *Manhattan* at your feet. . . ."

169

Thanks to Philippe's habitual skill, we didn't have to wait too long. We were quite quickly settled, Philippe and I side by side, and Walter facing us. At the next table sat a fat dark man wearing a suit and tie and with a guide to Paris beside his plate—the book in English. He looked like an Indian, seemed to understand English and be very interested in our conversation. Philippe and I were a little irritated by his intrusiveness, and I was afraid he would be shocked by what we were saying. After the bars of Paris, we went through those of London and Walter's stay with his Dutchman, which he described in detail, and the English, whom we all agreed were not very stimulating from a sexual point of view. We had decided that the Indian's interest was explained by curiosity about Walter's race—he might easily have taken Walter for one of his compatriots. But as the allusions in our remarks grew more explicit and his smile more marked, it became evident that his sympathy was not exclusively of a patriotic nature. Despite his suit and tie, and the shifty expression of a shady Congress Party member, and despite the rather aggressively heterosexual aspect of the diners on the restaurant terrace, the Indian, quite simply, was cruising. And when we thought we had finally outraged him by a discussion about the *Catacombs,* flavored with allusions to Holland Park and the public urinals of Piccadilly Circus, just as Walter asked us to explain the French monetary system, he actually interrupted our conversation and launched into a discourse on the equivalences between francs and pounds sterling. We did not, I must say, receive this intervention very warmly. Fortunately, he was eating his dessert.

During the entire dinner there was a regular parade of friends moving down the boulevard who came over to say hello to Philippe and me, or of strangers cruising us, or whom we could have been cruising. There was one empty chair at our table, and Philippe would have been glad to fill it with someone invited out of the crowd.

Moreover, at the corner of the boulevard and the Rue de Buci, an acrobat—a blond boy in black tights—was doing his number. Walter had his back to him but was very interested in his tricks.

He wanted to take photographs of him, especially when the acrobat got up on the roof of a tiny newspaper kiosk, closed at this hour. But each time the camera was ready, the acrobat jumped down from his roof, because he could spot the police approaching. The picture was never taken. On the other hand, some drawer in Auckland must contain many shots of Philippe and of me, eyes closed and mouths wide open on our advancing forks.

However, Walter regaled the two of us with the long, comical narrative of his trip around the world in three weeks. When he had left New Zealand, Walter apparently wasn't sure what he might expect to find where, nor what his itinerary would be. Nonetheless, everything delighted him. He couldn't stop praising San Francisco and New York. But what he preferred, by far, was Hawaii, where he intended to return. He spoke enthusiastically about the beauty of the landscapes, the beaches, and the boys, noting their simplicity and sweetness.

I had supposed, from his curiosity about the Parisian bars, that Walter meant to explore them tonight, and that basically he regarded Philippe and me as useful informants. I changed my mind when he began squeezing my knee and looking straight into my eyes while declaring that as far as French boys were concerned, his opinion wasn't settled yet, but that his first impression was very favorable.

"Well, well, I'm sure we're all ready to do our best!"

"Are you?"

"You bet I am!"

After this exchange the course of action seemed clear. Nonetheless, we still managed to get down an enormous cake—a raspberry charlotte, I think.

Philippe left us when we got up from the table. Probably he had some sort of idea between his legs. Walter and I walked as far as the Place Saint-Germain in the undiminished crowd, talking about one thing and another. We stopped near the doorway of the *Deux Magots*.

"I've got three alternatives. We can go to the *Manhattan* for a while, to see what it's like, or have a drink in one of the cafés around here, or go to my place, if you want to."

"We can go to my hotel, too."

"No, I can't because I have a friend staying at the house. He's having dinner with friends but I told him I'd be coming home early. He might phone, so I have to get back pretty soon."

No, I remember a fifth possibility was mentioned, with a certain insistence: that of an automobile ride through the city. Walter was still considering leaving the next day for Switzerland or Italy and he wouldn't have seen anything of Paris, so I offered at least to show him the illuminated monuments, at a great clip. I had my mother's car at the time, but the keys were at my place.

"Oh yes, that would be great. In any case, let's go to your place. We can decide there."

So we came back here. The apartment was empty, but Tony might return any minute. It can't have been later than eleven, for I remember thinking that the lights were turned off the monuments at midnight, and if we wanted to make the tour as planned—Invalides, Eiffel Tower, Arc de Triomphe, Place de la Concorde, Louvre, Notre Dame and maybe the Panthéon too—we would have to leave now. But apparently Walter had other ideas. He was very enterprising, this boy who, while kissing me, managed to open my fly.

"Wait a minute. This friend I mentioned, the one who'll be coming back—it would be better if he didn't find us naked. You want to see the sights, don't you?"

"Sure I do, but I want to see something else, too. I don't know. All right, let's go."

"All right."

"Kiss me first."

"But if we start kissing, we'll never get out of here."

"Kiss me anyway."

"All right."

"You turn me on."

"Wait."

"I have to take a shower. That'll cool me off. I need one in any case."

"Unfortunately, the showers here aren't much. They don't work very well. Is a bath all right?"

"Of course."

"Wait, I'll turn it on for you."

He immediately undressed. His whole body was extremely tan, quite muscular, and hairy, especially the legs and ass. He had an erection.

The telephone rang. It was Tony. His dinner was just over. He wanted to know what my plans were. I told him that we had a visitor, a Ceylono-Portuguese, who was getting ready to take a bath.

"A bath? Then he's already been . . . tried, as it were?"

"Not at all. He's a traveller. He's just come in from London, and he wanted to take a bath, that's all."

"Hmmm."

"No hmmm."

Walter and I flirted a moment on the daybed, he completely naked and I fully dressed. His cock was quite thick. Then he went into the bathroom. Tony, who had dined a hundred yards down the street, came back in a very good mood, a little drunk and a little stoned. I introduced him to Walter, who wore only a little towel around his waist. Joints quickly appeared, and five minutes later all three of us were in the big bed.

I don't remember the night itself in detail, except that it was very lively and very satisfying to all parties concerned, I believe. This three-way was a success, one of the best I can remember. I think that Tony and I mostly fucked Walter, at least twice apiece before we fell asleep, once in the middle of the night, and then again when we woke up. He may have fucked us too, for a while, but without coming. It's no longer very clear. We were all three quite done in—poppers had been circulated—a great enthusiasm reigned, every imaginable combination was attempted.

173

In the morning Tony invited Walter to stay with us for the rest of his Parisian visit. I suggested that he nonetheless do some sightseeing during the day, because I had to work. He smiled. We then made love once again toward noon, just the two of us. We had lunch together here, in the sunshine out on the terrace. As for what followed, I have already related it in snatches in a preceding chapter (Trick XIV).

[*That evening, I took him on the ride around the city we had planned the night before. He seemed delighted, but just as much by the illuminated Quai d'Orsay as by Gabriel's palaces, and much more by the Hôtel de Ville than by the Invalides. He spent the night here. The next day he left for Ceylon. I never saw him again. But he has written several letters. If ever Tony or I should be passing through Auckland . . .*]

❧ XVII ❧
RALPH

Wednesday, July 26, 1978

I was at the *55th Street Playhouse* in New York. This is a porno movie house, exclusively gay with regard to its films and its clientele, and to what happens off-screen in the auditorium and particularly in the toilets. There weren't very many people there. I was standing in the right aisle, leaning against the wall, when I saw a tall blond boy with a moustache moving down the left aisle. Slowly but deliberately, he went over and sat down in the second seat from the left of the fourth or fifth row.

I went over to the left side of the house, walked down so that I was standing opposite him, and leaned against the wall. He immediately began staring at me in the semi-darkness. Sometimes I kept my eyes on the screen, sometimes on him, sometimes on the rest of the house, but he did not once look away from me. His light hair was quite long, parted down the middle, and fell over each side of his forehead. His moustache was very protuberant. He was wearing a shirt unbuttoned all the way down his chest, the sleeves rolled up to his elbows, and jeans.

After two or three minutes of reciprocal observation, I sat down next to him. He immediately put his left hand on my right thigh. I caressed his forearm, which was very broad and powerful under thick blond hair, each clearly defined muscle responding to the movements of his fingers. Then I touched his broad, muscular, and rather hairy chest. He shifted his hand to my crotch. My cock was hard. So was his. Turning further, he moved his right hand across my body and unbuttoned all my shirt buttons down to the belt. My cock was against my thigh; I shifted it up against my belly. He took it out and began playing with it. I was already so excited that I had to stop him, and I smiled at him. He smiled back. I discovered he was very handsome, with his thick hair that almost covered his eyes and his heavy, open face, the features lacking delicacy but very regular and well cut, especially his chin and cheeks. Above all, I found him very nice: he seemed to be happy and having a good time. There was nothing shamefaced, embarrassed, or furtive about him. And contrary to many Americans, he did not consider the kind of sexual relations to be had in a public place—a bar, a baths or a specialized movie-house—as something physically localized, destined for an immediate and specific goal, but rather, as an exchange as complete as the environment would permit. I don't like the way so many boys in the United States just blow you, for example, devoting themselves entirely and exclusively to the relation of their mouth and your cock. This boy was different; he seemed to enjoy and to want a total physical relationship, so to speak, and moreover to be very little concerned by our neighbors or by the theatre staff. A foreigner just passing through, I didn't know how far one could go in this context. In the toilets upstairs, I had observed all kinds of cheerful copulation, but in the house itself I had been able to see only some reciprocal masturbation and a very few discreet fellations. But my neighbor was totally indifferent to these tacit rules, whose rigor I may well have imagined. When he discovered that by playing with me as he was doing he would make me come too quickly, he put an arm around my shoulder, drew me close to him; we kissed for a very long while in sight of anyone who took the trouble to look at us.

[*San Francisco, in the sunshine of Lafayette Park, August 11, 1978.*] As for me I put my right arm behind his back, and with my left hand I opened his shirt and then his fly and took out his cock, which was quite thick, and which I played with for a moment. Then he got up, knelt between the two rows, and began to suck me, very nicely. Unfortunately I was so aroused that I kept having to worry about coming in his mouth. I concentrated on moderating his ardor, to the point of pushing his head away from my crotch with both hands. When he got up and came back to his seat, I in turn sucked his cock, holding it in my right hand and his balls in my left. Far from holding me back, he encouraged me. He had as extreme an erection as was possible, and his cock gave evidence of that kind of particular tension which indicates the proximity of orgasm. But I didn't want him to come.

When I got into my seat again, he smiled broadly, as did I. We were obviously delighted with each other, and his pleasure intensified mine, as mine did his. We kept kissing each other, our mouths endlessly exploring, our hands pressing us together. Several times he leaned over to suck my cock some more, but I always interrupted him, determined not to come. He seemed not to mind this, and continued smiling and laughing, looking me in the eyes:

"Wow! Feels good, huh? Isn't it great?"

"Yes. You're so nice . . ."

The film program consisted of several shorts; the one just being projected was more ambitious then the usual fare, and, oddly, sentimental. For once, the sexual acts represented were set in a more or less coherent narrative. It was the story of an affair between a professional photographer, a tall, dark, very handsome fellow with a moustache, and a blond student, who is at first extremely innocent. They meet one winter day in Central Park, where the pho-

176

tographer is posing two or three female models, then literally fall into each other's arms at an intersection. The dark one doesn't know if the blond is gay or not, but courts him assiduously, so that the slightest gesture of advance, given the suspense, assumes an enormous importance, as when their hands touch for the first time in a restaurant.

Of course we weren't following the plot very closely, and it seemed to have accelerated considerably during one of my disappearances under the row of seat backs, with my neighbor's cock in my mouth. Not only had the blond and the dark boy become, when I resurfaced, intimates to the point of sharing an apartment, but their infidelities were already multiplying on both sides.

Both of us were now largely undressed, our shirts completely opened and barely hanging on our shoulders, our pants pulled down to mid-thigh. [*Same day, at six in the afternoon at Mary-Ann's. I am sitting opposite the big window overlooking Golden Gate. Under a sky still perfectly blue, the fog is solemnly making its entrance across the bay.*] Our positions became increasingly acrobatic. Sometimes I tried to extend my body over his, one way or another; then he slid down to the extreme edge of his seat and I tried to straddle his legs, a movement which my trousers around my ankles rendered extremely difficult. Sometimes it was he who tried to lie on top of me, and given his size this was even less likely. We kissed each other passionately. Then he knelt beside me again in order to blow me, and again I held him back. He then sat back in his seat and leaned toward me:

"What's the matter, don't you want to come?"

"Wouldn't you rather go somewhere else?"

"Where?"

"My place, for instance?"

"Where is it?"

"Lexington Avenue."

"Lexington and what?"

"And Eighty-ninth, I'm afraid."

177

"No, I can't, it's too far. I don't have time, I have to meet someone for dinner."

"Oh, hell."

We kissed each other some more. I caressed his chest with my left hand, then ran my tongue over it, moving down his belly to his cock which I sucked, holding it at the base between my thumb and forefinger. I was kneeling between the rows, my right hand on his belly. He was arched in his seat, legs folded back underneath, shoulders against the top, head back, one hand on the nape of my neck, the other on his right thigh. He came very copiously, and I swallowed his sperm.

I sat up and met his eyes, smiling. He looked back into mine, smiling too, eyes half-closed. Then he in turn knelt, in a position equivalent to mine a moment before, and took my cock in his mouth. I had one hand in his hair, the other gripping the hair on his chest. Strangely enough, now that I was determined to abandon myself to my excitation, it was less powerful, and whereas before I had made tremendous efforts in order to postpone my orgasm, now I was trying to hurry it because I did not want to make him wait, now that he had ejaculated. Certain movements of his tongue tickled the tip of my cock somewhat uncomfortably. Nonetheless I released my sperm into his mouth quite soon, and experienced enough pleasure to let him know about it.

We were sitting side by side, smiling, sweating, and completely disheveled. On the screen, the blond, now quite certain of his preferences, was following a black boy into a cellar and undergoing all kinds of humiliations at his hands. We sat there motionless for five or six minutes, only our thighs touching, then with some difficulty we readjusted our clothes. We kissed each other once more. Then he said he had to leave.

"OK. Good-bye."

"You don't want to leave with me?"

"Sure, if you like."

It must have been between six and seven. In front of the movie house on Fifty-fifth Street, the daylight was still bright; we were dazzled by it. We headed east, watching each other without seeming to do so. He was not as handsome as I had thought, in the darkness, actually more of a redhead than blond. But he certainly wasn't plain, far from it, and he had a very appealing expression.

"What time is your dinner date?"

"Oh, not before eight, but I still have to do some last-minute shopping."

"Oh, it's your dinner—I didn't understand that."

"Yes. No big deal. Just two friends. But it's not my place, so it's a little complicated."

"You're not from New York?"

"Well, no, I used to live here, downtown, and then I went to live in the country—at the shore, near Providence, in Rhode Island. I just came back. Too many people this time of year. Now I'm looking for an apartment. Where are you from?"

"I'm French."

"Oh. I thought you had some kind of accent. But you live in New York?"

"No, I'm here on vacation, staying with friends. I've only been here three or four days."

"My name is Ralph. What's yours?"

"Renaud."

"Wono?"

"Yes, something like that."

"No, seriously. What's your name?"

"Renaud. You know, like the cars. It's pronounced like the French car. The company that makes *Le Car.*"

"Renault?"

"Yes, that's right."

"And that's how you write it?"

"Yes, almost. Not quite. With a *d.* But it's a terrible name to have here. No one understands it, and Americans are so polite, they all want to know your name. You have to explain, spell it out. There's no end to it. Sometimes I pretend my name is Bruno, it's simpler."

We were crossing Fifth Avenue.

"I'm going to take the Lexington subway at Fifth-ninth Street. You going in that direction?"

"Over to Third Avenue. Are you staying in New York all summer?"

"No, I'm travelling with a friend. We have one of those circular tickets, you know, you can go wherever you want, to seven cities at least. It's for foreigners, or for non-residents anyway; you buy it in Europe and it really doesn't cost much. Less than a round trip ticket to San Francisco."

"Where are you going?"

"Well, first to Detroit—"

"To *Detroit?*"

"Yes, to see friends. And then to San Francisco, Los Angeles, Houston, Memphis, Washington . . ."

"Have you been to California before?"

"Yes. I'm crazy about San Francisco. Los Angeles too. But San Francisco especially. Are you going to be here in the city?"

"Yeah. I have to find an apartment and a job. But I hope to get to Europe in the fall—France, as a matter of fact."

"France? You've been there before?"

"A long time ago. Seven or eight years. I was very young. I have friends who've just come back, but they weren't very enthusiastic—first of all, they said it's incredibly expensive."

"Yes, it's true. Especially in the last two or three years. It's gotten completely crazy."

"Much higher than here?"

"Yes, probably; well, it depends, not the hotels and restaurants, but even that, now. It's all very expensive. Two or three years ago, there were a lot of little restaurants where you could get a very decent meal for three or four dollars, but now that's absolutely impossible. And the food you buy in stores, and clothes—all that kind of stuff is ruinously high. And it will be worse in the fall; every year they take advantage of the summer vacations to raise all the prices."

"My friends told me that a drink in a bar cost them seven dollars; could that be true?"

"Oh yes, it's possible. Probably at *Le Sept.*"

"That's absolutely crazy."

"Yes, I know it is. Americans who are used to paying seventy-five cents or a dollar are outraged, and they're right. There's a new bar, called the *Palace,* that costs you ten dollars just to get in. . ."

"You're kidding."

"No, I swear."

"But aren't there any cheap places?"

"The *Manhattan* is much less expensive, three or four dollars."

"Three or four dollars for a beer! That's just ridiculous!"

"Yes, I know. But in Paris that's not considered so bad. Especially since at the *Manhattan* they're pretty decent; if you don't want to buy anything you don't have to. But in New York guys are used to having four or five beers a night. They can't believe it. In any case, sexually speaking, Paris isn't much fun if you come from New York. The poor bastards who think they're going to find another Christopher Street are in for a bitter disappointment. It's ridiculous, because for most people, now, a vacation is something sexual, certainly for young people, and from that point of view, Paris is very repressive. There are dancing bars but no fuck bars any more, except one that's quite sinister. The *Manhattan* closes at two in the morning, and in any case there must be fifty bars in New York as good or better. At night there are police all over the place, and thugs. Of course London is much worse, and you can forget about Rome. But it's embarrassing sometimes, American friends think they're going to have such a good time in Paris—they come once and then never again."

"Are there movie houses?"

"No. Well, there are, but they're completely sordid, and the films are ridiculous, too. The ones we just saw are nothing special, but compared to the films shown in France they're extraordinary. You understand, the ban—the taboo—is so powerful that to work in fag porno films you have to be a wreck with nothing left to lose. It's not the gorgeous guys, like here. It's anyone they can find."

"Have you been to the bars here?"

"No, not many this time. I've only been here since Saturday. I went twice to *Chaps*, because it's practically next door to where I'm staying, but that's all. You know the place?"

"Yeah, I went there once. But I don't like the bars much. I get bored unless I know someone."

We had reached Lexington Avenue and turned uptown toward Fifty-ninth Street and the subway station.

"If you have a piece of paper, I'll give you my address in Paris—if you want."

"I don't have anything to write on. Let's go into a store and ask."

We went into a little candy store, where someone let us use a pencil and a sheet of paper. I wrote down my name and address:

"Call me up. It would be nice to see you again."

"OK, I will."

We had reached the subway entrance, opposite Bloomingdale's.

"You're going up Lexington too?"

"To Seventy-fourth Street."

"OK. Then I can walk with you, if you don't mind."

"No, I'd like it. Come on."

"I'll take the subway at Seventy-seventh Street."

But when we reached Seventy-seventh Street, I decided that I might just as well do the whole thing on foot. Meanwhile we had mostly talked about the Upper East Side, for which Ralph had no use:

"I'm used to living downtown. I don't like the atmosphere up here, the people, everything—I don't feel comfortable."

"Yes, I understand what you mean. But sometimes, when you leave the Village, it's nice to get back up here, away from all that activity. And then, it's so pretty up here, so clean and everything . . ."

"I don't like the way it looks, it's too . . . too polite. I don't know. Like the people. They look like models, mannequins, puppets. And to get anything up here takes all day. And it's so expensive. And it's no better, either. Downtown, I know the stores, I know where you have to go for fish or cheese or this or that. Here I feel like a foreigner."

"I once lived with some friends near Greene Street, but the last three times I've stayed up here, around Eighty-ninth Street with this friend. He's very nice, and the subway goes straight downtown. There's an express stop close by and you're downtown right away if you want to be. I like being close to the park, too."

"You come to New York often?"

"Yes, quite often. Usually twice a year."

"Always on vacation? Or for work? You work here?"

"No, not for work; well, I work some, but not much."

"What do you do?"

"I write."

"You're a writer?"

"Yes."

"What do you write?"

"Novels."

"What kind of novels?"

"Oh, the kind that comes out in an edition of three thousand copies."

"Me too—when I first came to New York, I wanted to be a writer. But nothing came of it."

"Where are you from, originally?"

"I'm from Texas."

"Oh! You are? And what are you doing now?"

"Oh, a little of everything, I putter around, I paint, I do plumbing, I apartment-sit. And I do horoscopes."

"You do?"

"Does that interest you?"

"Yes, of course. But I don't know anything about it."

"What's your sign?"

"Leo."

"What's your rising sign?"

"I don't know."

"I'm going to do a book on the signs of the zodiac and diets."

"What a good idea. Combining the two American passions . . ."

"OK, I turn off here, I have to get moving."

"OK. Have a good dinner."

"I will. *Merci*. You take care!"

"I will. *Ciao*. Come and see me in Paris."

"OK. Good-bye!"

He turned to the right at Seventy-fourth Street, and I walked home.

[*Never heard from him.*]

❧ XVIII ❧

THE COWBOY

Thursday, July 27, 1978

It must have been about five, maybe five-thirty. I was coming back from Pier 42, on the Hudson, where I had spent the afternoon in the sun rereading Rousseau's *Confessions*. I went into the "book-store" on the corner of Christopher and Hudson Streets, only because a boy who vaguely attracted me, and who was walking ahead of me, had gone in there first. He glanced through some magazines, as did I, and then went out again.

I was about to do the same rather than proceed, for a dollar, through the subway-like turnstile to the other section of the establishment, where a dark narrow corridor, which circles back on itself, gives access to a row of tiny projection booths.

But as I put *Luscious Dessert* or *Chicken Lickin' Good* back where I found them I felt someone looking at me. I turned my head. Standing on the other side of the turnstile was a rather pale-skinned boy with a thin, black moustache, wearing a red plaid shirt and a cowboy hat with its broad brim turned up. He was standing quite still, but as soon as I noticed him, he stopped looking in my direction and moved away, disappearing from my field of vision.

I had only glimpsed him for a few seconds. He had seemed very handsome to me, so handsome that it scarcely seemed likely he could be interested in me. He was undoubtedly checking out the front room with the books, magazines, and the door, to see if anyone new would appear on the other side of the turnstile. And he was probably standing there because there was no one interesting in the back room. So I did not immediately resolve to go and join him. But I also did not leave the magazine rack as quickly as I had intended. I contented myself with opening another book at random, and turning my head toward the turnstile at the end of each paragraph. Three or four minutes later, the cowboy was back and this time—there was no doubt about it—he was staring at me.

Of all the tricks I describe in this book, this one was uncontestably the handsomest; and except for Jeremy, the only really handsome one, maybe, according to all possible and objective criteria, and regardless of what one's *type* might or might not be. He was fairly tall and rather muscular, but quite naturally, so to speak; and without excesses; very virile, but not rhetorically so. His cowboy outfit, which could easily have been completely ridiculous, on him was very alluring and, although I couldn't explain just why, somehow touching. He perfectly incarnated the myth, and yet he didn't have the traditional physique of the role: his hair, one lock of which hung down below his hat over his white forehead, his eyelashes, his eyes, his moustache were too black; he seemed more Latin, or better still, gypsy. What was most remarkable about him was his face, to my mind a perfect one: energetic, finely cut, luminous, made paler still by the dark lustre of his eyes.

This time he gave me a chance to see him better. But, as before, he moved away from the turnstile and vanished among the booths. At the moment he shifted position, his eyes were on me. This seemed a clear invitation. I had a hard time believing my good luck. But now I was determined to test it, so I handed my dollar to the man behind the counter. He released the turnstile, and I was inside.

The corridor off which the booths open forms a square, so that if you follow it you end up back where you started. I didn't follow the cowboy. I took the opposite direction from his, supposing I would meet him halfway through. But he had turned around, and I made the complete circuit without catching sight of him. There were ten or fifteen boys there, several of whom I had seen a moment before along the river, two or three of them very appealing. It seemed to me wiser to concern myself with them rather than with this cowboy of mine, who definitely intimidated me. He was too handsome. But I also knew that I would greatly regret not having pursued this adventure to its end.

When I next saw him, he was stepping into a booth. He left the door wide open and leaned against the wall opposite it, his thumbs in his jeans pockets. He was looking at me. But I still couldn't take the plunge. Stupidly, I turned away again and walked off. When I turned back, he was at his door. He checked that I had seen him, that I knew just where he was, and resumed his position inside the booth, against the wall. I made a complete circuit of the corridor, but quite rapidly this time, and stopped opposite him. We stared at each other; I again turned my head away once or twice, then I made the decisive step and joined him.

My apprehension was that he was the type who receives the homage he inspires without the slightest impulse to return it. And I was worried about being too sexually intimidated to get an erection: what if he put his hand on my crotch and was anything but impressed by the modest dimensions of my cock in repose? But these anxieties were not confirmed in the slightest degree. He touched me at the very moment I touched him, he was just as exciting as he was handsome, a rare combination, and I hadn't been with him for fifteen seconds when I already had a most enthusiastic erection.

His jeans were old and worn. On the inner side of his right thigh near the top was a hole with frayed edges. He wasn't wearing undershorts. When I first put my hand on his crotch, the tip of his cock was quite far from this hole—about two inches. But while his cock was stiffening, it came closer to it, and soon the entire glans was visible. This apparition turned me on: I pulled the sliding door shut behind me, but not all the way, so that a little light continued to reach us: I had rarely wanted to see one of my lovers so much. I knelt in front of him and ran my tongue over his cock, through the intriguing hole. With my right hand I began undoing his belt and his fly. He helped me. I stood up again. He opened my pants and took out my cock. I unbuttoned his shirt, whose sleeves were rolled up over his well-developed biceps. His chest was covered with brown hair very precisely confined by the outline of his pectorals, although a thin line of hair ran down the middle of his belly and joined his cock—a perfectly straight line except for the hollows and bulges of his stomach muscles. Nothing was very emphatic, but everything perfectly hard, perfectly well defined. His cock, which I held, was bigger than mine, long, thick, very neatly circumcised, and I am tempted to describe it as remarkably elegant. His balls were voluminous. His long, powerful but slender thighs joined his pelvis very high up, so that their curve was already apparent at the level of his cock: each time he shifted his position, I could see the long, clearly distinct muscles shifting as well.

He was a little taller than I. We looked at each other, smiling. Then he made that obligatory gesture—knocking back his hat a little with his fist, another lock of wavy black hair fell over his forehead. I had my hands on his hips. He pressed me against him. I had undone my own shirt, and I pulled it apart so that our bodies could be in direct contact with each other. We kissed. His legs were slightly parted, mine between them. Our fully erect cocks pressed against each other, forming an *X;* we made them oscillate very gently, from left to right, momentarily pressed and released, pressed and released.

I shoved my hands between the plywood wall and the cowboy's ass. Like the rest of his body, his buttocks were very hard and quite prominent, with a concavity on each side. They were quite hairy, but not exceptionally so, except at the asshole.

Again I knelt down in order to suck his cock, caressing his belly and his chest. His hands in my hair, his shoulders against the wall, he thrust his pelvis forward.

At the rear of the booth, to my left, was a low bench intended for the spectators of the film we had neglected to switch on. I sat down on this, drawing the cowboy toward me, his hat still tipped back over the back of his neck. His jeans were now around his knees. With my right hand I caressed his ass, and with my left hand I squeezed his cock at its base, or else played with his balls. We remained in this position for four or five minutes. Each time I felt he was about to come, I slowed down the back and forth movement of my mouth, or else I ran my lips over his balls, or my tongue behind them.

As soon as I stood up, the cowboy made me change places with him, which was anything but easy in a booth much less than a yard wide. He sat down and took my cock in his mouth. But once again, I didn't want to come. Tony and I had a whole round of visits planned for the night: *The Anvil, St. Mark's Baths,* etc., and I wanted to conserve my energy. What would have delighted me, of course, was to bring the cowboy home with me. But still intimidated by him, and by my desire for him, I didn't dare suggest such a thing.

When I was on the point of coming, I leaned forward. I raised his head, kissed him, and forced him to stand up. He leaned against the wall again, facing the door. But he was quite determined to come. He played with himself, then I did it for him with my right hand, my left forearm on his shoulder, and kissing him the while. He thrust his hips forward, bending his legs slightly. At the moment of coming, he turned his head and sighed, lifted my hand away from his cock and put it on his right nipple, my fingers on the tiny metal ring, which ran through its tip and which I forgot to mention. He finished pulling himself off, and his sperm spattered against the door in several surprisingly separate spurts. I gathered up the last drops in my mouth.

Immediately afterward he, very sweetly, wanted to make me come as well. But I began to put my clothes back on, smiling. He didn't insist and asked no questions. He had a handkerchief in his jeans with which he wiped off his cock, and rapidly readjusted his

188

clothes. I let him go out first. With a laugh, he gently poked my shoulder with his fist:

"Take care!"

I left the booth almost immediately after him, quickly enough to see him go into the toilet which was just opposite the turnstile. I stood there in the light coming from the shop itself. I wanted to see him one more time, to confirm that he was as handsome as he had seemed. He was, and more so. When he came out of the toilet, he nodded and then, near the door, he turned back with a smile and waved his hand.

I stayed in the bookstore another five minutes in order not to seem to be following him and making a nuisance of myself. When I in turn left, I walked up Christopher Street toward Sixth Avenue. As I gradually regained my confidence, I castigated myself for my timidity: I should have offered him my address, my telephone number, should have invited him over for dinner. He was one of the handsomest boys I had ever seen in my life. He seemed very nice as well. And now I had lost him.

At Seventh Avenue, I turned around. I had to find him again, it was so stupid not to. Luckily, with that hat, it was easy enough to spot him, even at a distance. He must be wandering around in the neighborhood. I went into several bars—*Boots and Saddle, Ty's,* and walked back as far as Hudson Street. On my way, I met a French friend, Patrick, and asked him if he hadn't seen a boy in a cowboy hat.

"Yes, earlier in the afternoon."

"A really beautiful boy?"

"Yes, not bad, yes."

"No, this one wasn't *not bad.* This one was one of the wonders of the world!"

"I'm not sure he was that . . ."

"You would have been sure if you had seen him. All right, I guess he's gone home, damn it all!"

And I went home.

[*Never saw him again.*]

Here the original manuscript of Tricks *breaks off for good. For the chapters which follow I had only a few notes, whose extent varied, according to the circumstances, from three lines to a page. These narratives have therefore been entirely rewritten in Paris, in December 1978, several months after the episodes they recount. Their ultimate interest, then, does not consist in the freshness or the acuity of the relation, but in the revelation, maybe, of what fades and what is engraved, twenty weeks later, in the recollection of such encounters.*

XIX

JIM

Sunday, July 30, 1978

Here begins, or intensifies, my pronounced uncertainty about names. Was it, as I think, at *The Stud*, or at *The String?* In any case, it was in that bar I rather like and which is at the corner of Greenwich and Perry Streets. These two street names had caught my attention since Perry, the British explorer who discovered Melville Island in 1819, was the governor of Greenwich when he died, I believe. Or was that Peary? And perhaps Peary Street? Yes, more likely. Besides, it's not Perry, but Parry, Sir William Parry, who died at Greenwich. Peary, the American explorer, was the first to reach the North Pole, in 1909. It doesn't matter.

The *Stud*, then, if it's *The Stud* that I mean, as I think it is, encompasses two good-sized rooms. The first is a bar, the second, where they project films, is also a fuck room. The interesting feature of these premises is that the films projected are not exclusively pornographic, rather what's shown here, every night, are classics of the cinema, more or less minor and generally very old. I could not identify this evening the film that was showing; I had missed the title. It must have dated from the late forties, judging by the cars and the women's dresses. It was a detective story set in Los Angeles or some other Western city; certainly it was not in New York or even in San Francisco. The hero, or rather the protagonist—for he seemed a quite mediocre person—had a new car, whose surprising luxury awakened the suspicions of his mistress, or of his wife. One scene took place in a supermarket parking lot.

Facing the screen, the crowd of boys was so thick you could scarcely move, the noise deafening, the heat terrible. Behind two or three rows of attentive spectators there was nothing but groping, sucking, simple or complex fucking, all in the powerful stink of poppers. You couldn't actually stay there very long, for fear of smothering.

The second room of *The Stud* also has a bar, like the first, though it plays only a minor role here. I saw or glimpsed a boy leaning against it who seemed entirely my type: not very tall, quite muscular, light hair and thick moustache *à la* Kitchener. I think he caught sight of me at the same time I noticed him, and apparently I kept his attention, as he did mine. At first glance, he represented exactly what I was looking for that evening, and which I had not found in the melee from which both of us had momentarily withdrawn; so exactly, in fact, that I immediately decided I had no chance with him, according to a system of deduction which is a specialty of mine. Nonetheless, he was looking at me. At the bar, where he stood, we couldn't have entered into contact as directly as I wanted. We would have had to talk first, and I had no desire for that. So I remained where I was, waiting for him to make the first move. Apparently he had adopted the same resolution, but my determination won out over his. He didn't come toward me but went yet somewhere else, where I immediately joined him, an admissible compromise. Although to reach each other, we had to shoulder and elbow our way through all kinds of people—and it took a good five minutes to cover a yard—we pretended, against all likelihood, that if we were pasted up against one another, we owed it merely to chance.

By then we were considerably disarrayed, our shirts open to the waist. His torso was covered with thick blond hair. No question about it, he turned me on, especially his smile, which seemed to take into account and faintly deride our tacit maneuvers. We kissed each other, we pressed close together, and unzipped each other's trousers. I sucked his cock, he sucked mine. Since he was crouching in front of me, I knelt too; we kissed on the floor, and could easily have been trampled or smothered. It was very difficult to get back up. Hands from unidentified sources brushed over our chests, our asses, mouths appeared in the vicinity of our cocks. We pushed these away as best we could, not without eliciting protests from visible and very stoned suitors. In five minutes we were

covered with sweat, our jeans somewhere around our ankles. I
whispered into his ear:

"Let's get out of here for a while."

He agreed. But we managed to get away only from the mêlée,
not from the room. We reached a calmer zone and pulled ourselves together, adjusting our clothes.

I would have liked to go to his place, but he did not invite me.
He would have liked to go to mine, which was impossible. I no
longer remember how quickly these various points were made, nor
if this occurred in the place we had first withdrawn to or in the
corner to which we later retreated, a recess formed by a door that
opened onto the street. This door was blocked, but nonetheless a
little fresh air managed to get in.

Once it was established that we were not, unfortunately, going
to be together in a bed, despite our mutual desire for each other,
we decided, I think, to take very possible advantage of the available
opportunities. We kissed each other, licked each other, hugged
and rubbed against each other. We sucked each other's cocks, took
each other's balls between our teeth. We were soaked with sweat
and at the height of enthusiasm.

He came in my mouth, I swallowed his sperm. I came in his, he
swallowed mine. We kissed again, mingling with our tongues the
drops that remained.

This time, we really needed air. I suggested that we go out onto
the street. He followed me. We sat down, on Greenwich Street,
on the ramshackle railing of some basement. Around us, on the
sidewalk, the stubborn weeds grew up as high as our knees.

No, I was not American, I was French, I was on vacation, I
would be leaving New York the day after tomorrow for a tour of
the States, especially the West Coast, but I had had a violent
argument two hours ago with my travelling companion, and I now
intended to let him follow our itinerary by himself.

"You're going to stay in New York?"

"Yes, I think so. But I'm not sure. The problem is I don't
have much money—only two hundred dollars. Here in town we're

staying with friends, but they're really friends of the fellow I'm travelling with, I can't stay with them if he leaves. I have one of those 'circular' tickets that lets you go to seven cities in the United States. I'm going to try to turn it in, but I'm not sure I can—you can only buy them in Europe. Or in any case, outside this country. If I do, I'll have enough money to spend three or four weeks in New York, of course, since I already have my return ticket."

"But how do you know you won't make up with your friend? Before Tuesday a lot can happen. Then maybe you'll leave with him after all."

"I'd be very surprised."

"As bad as that?"

"Yes. It was quite an epic battle, just now."

"Is he your lover, or just a friend?"

"No, he's not 'just a friend.' "

"He caught you with someone? You look notoriously cruisy to me."

"No, I'm good as gold! And besides, I'm only interested in certain spiritual nuances . . . No, it wasn't exactly that. Actually, it was all very typical."

"You live together in Paris?"

"Yes. At least when we aren't breaking up. Recently we've been apart more than together. I'll have to try to reach some friends here who can put me up eventually—if I go to some hotel, I won't be able to hold out very long, given the prices they charge. Unfortunately, a lot of people are out of town . . . And you, are you leaving on vacation?"

"No, not me. This year I'm not taking a vacation. I just moved into a new apartment. I have to get it all together, finish furnishing it, everything. I don't have the time or the money to go anywhere."

"You're not taking any vacation at all?"

"No."

"That's really a shame."

"Oh, you know . . . Even last year, I only took a week or ten days. That was all."

"Yes, I know. Americans take much shorter vacations than the French. Back home, it's a kind of national obsession. Everyone takes a vacation, three weeks, a month—at least, about fifty per cent of the population . . . And where's your new apartment?"

"In New Jersey, like the old one, but it's much better."

"Is that where you're from, New Jersey?"

"Yes."

"That's funny, I have a kind of erotic fixation on New Jersey."

"You do? Why? You must be the only one!"

"In Europe I'm turned on by Italians: physically, they're just my type. But psychologically or socially, they're a pain in the ass. It's not their fault, it's society's fault, or the Church's. All that. But on the whole, the Italian trip is tough to take. You know—the kind of guy who says to you next day that it was the first time he ever slept with a boy. Or I do this but not that. Or I have to go home now, my mother is waiting up for me, etc. Of course it's all changing very quickly now. And in the north especially, things are often quite different these days. But on the whole, they have a tendency to be rather stuffy. On the other hand, psychologically, I'm really crazy about Americans, their way of not making a big deal, of taking things as they come. So I fantasize about New Jersey because it's full of Italian-Americans, isn't it? Physically they're my type, and culturally, psychologically, as well, because they behave like Americans."

"Oh, that's true, all right. New Jersey is full of Italians. My landlords—the owners of my new apartment, they're Italians. Their name is Santangelo."

"Just right, a perfect Italian name. By the way, what's your name."

"Jim."

"Mine's Renaud."

"It's stupid, tonight I came with a friend. Just a friend. You know, someone I've known a long time. We do the same kind of work. But I have to drive him home. Otherwise I could have taken you home with me. Unless you have to get back tonight."

"No, not at all. As a matter of fact, I'd really prefer *not* to go back. I'd really like to go with you."

"So would I—I'd like to spend the night with you."

"But I don't understand: if it's only a friend, why can't I come with you? I could take the train back tomorrow."

"The car only has two seats."

"Oh, that doesn't matter. I can squeeze in somewhere."

"No, it's impossible tonight. But if you stay in New York, you can telephone me. Or when you come back, if you do go on your trip. You have something to write with?"

"No."

"Can you remember a phone number?"

"Maybe."

"Wait, there's an easier way. You said you like the name Santangelo. I don't have my own phone yet, I live on the top floor of their house. You can telephone them, they'll call me, or if I'm not there they'll take a message. It's in Passaic."

"But I don't have a New Jersey phone book—"

"It doesn't matter, you just ask Information. All you have to remember is 'Santangelo, Passaic.' "

"Santangelo, Passaic, Santangelo, Passaic. Santangelo, Passaic . . ."

His friend joined us. For "just a friend," he seemed quite worried, even annoyed by Jim's "disappearance." I was introduced to him, but he paid very little attention to me. After that, he came back every five minutes.

Parked in front of us was a black sports car, impeccably clean, gleaming in the darkness.

"Pretty car. What kind is it?"

"A Corvette."

"Really, only a Corvette? I didn't know they were so sleek. I thought it was a Maserati or something like that. It doesn't look very American, the lines, I mean."

"Yes, it's well designed. This one's the best I've ever seen."

At the wheel was a young guy, sort of plump, with a heavy moustache who was staring hard at us both. According to Jim, he was a hustler.

"But he doesn't really think we're going to pay for him?"

"No. I think he's cruising you."

"Or you."

"No, you. It's you."

"He's not my type, in any case."

"What's your type?"

"Well, if worse comes to worst, you, conceivably . . . almost."

From time to time, the glossy black Corvette drove around the block and came back to the same place, between the garbage cans. One of its absences was longer than the rest. On its return, a passenger got out, a rather elegant man of about forty who went into the bar.

"There. He scored."

"Really, so quickly?"

"The bare minimum, I think. Probably a quick blow job in the car."

We must have stayed on our railing for about an hour. Now and then it swayed under our weight, and we lost our balance. A cat ran past, mewing. Jim talked about his life, about New Jersey, about his nights in New York. He came in two or three times a week. It didn't take him much more than an hour to make the trip. The *Stud (String?)* was his favorite bar. He had a regular friend, but that was over—besides, you know, it's a rare thing in New York for couples to stay together long. And how long had I been with my lover? That was a long time. He didn't know anyone who had lived so long with one guy.

The friend reappeared, stayed two minutes, left again. The black Corvette went around the block, and its driver began staring at us again. According to Jim, he was ready to split his night's profits with me.

"Thanks, but no thanks. In any case, you're the one he's cruising."

"That would surprise me a lot, considering the way I look after all our calisthenics inside."

"No, not at all. You look fine. You look like a young Kitchener."

That didn't seem to mean much to him. I should have said Teddy Roosevelt. But he took it as a compliment. And in fact, I really liked his looks. He was more of a redhead than a blond—or more precisely, Titian. I liked the golden reflections of the hairs on his forearms. Sometimes, while he was still sitting on the railing, I stood between his legs, which he pressed around my hips. We kissed each other.

"I never know what you can or can't do out here."

"You can do whatever you want. No one gives a damn."

"Even kissing each other for five minutes in the middle of the street?"

"On this street, at this hour, people would be surprised if we *weren't* kissing. There'd be something suspicious about it."

"Well then, if it's to reassure the public! But it's too frustrating. I'd like to be in bed with you."

"So would I. But we can do that tomorrow. Or the day after, if you don't leave with your lover."

"I'm not leaving with my lover."

"Oh, that's what you say now. Lovers' quarrels. We all know what that means!"

"You'll see. All right, I'm going home now."

I must have said these words five or six times before convincing myself to go. As a farewell, I kissed Jim again, caressed his chest. The friend appeared on his tour of inspection. The boy in the Corvette kept staring at us.

"All right, this time it's for real. I'll call you: Santangelo, Passaic. Santangelo, Passaic."

"Right. Don't forget."

Walking back to the center of the Village, I stopped at the trucks parked nearby. Several energetic couplings were taking place there, in which I did not participate. No one really interested me; moreover, no one was really interested in me. I had already come, and besides, I was a little afraid of the trucks. But I lingered for a moment. On Christopher Street, when I passed an all-night ice cream stand, I saw Jim and his friends, who had their cones and were getting back into their car. We waved at each other from a distance. A little farther on, I went into *Boots and Saddle*.

[*I saw Jim again when I returned to New York at the beginning of September. I telephoned him, and he came to F.H.'s. Tony and I spent the night with him. Since then I've received a very friendly letter from him—his plan is to come to Paris if he has enough money. I wrote him he could stay with me.*]

XX

BOB

Sunday, July 30, 1978

At the *Boots and Saddle,* around two or three in the morning (Monday), there weren't many people left. I walked down the length of the room and immediately noticed, at the back, to the left, a boy I had seen earlier that night, on my way to *The Stud.* It had been at the corner of two streets whose names escape me, one of which runs into West Street a little above *The Ramrod.* I had been looking, at the time, for a place to piss, and had passed two boys talking very loudly, very gaily, so to speak. One of them had immediately turned me on, and noticing my stare, he had smiled very sweetly at me. He looked like a Lebanese, or a Greek, or perhaps a Sicilian. He was a little taller than I, but much more solidly built. His black hair was quite long, curly, and his brown eyes very dark, his rather rough face decorated with a thick moustache. I can isolate very specifically what it was in him that had released my vehement desire. He was not wearing a shirt, but only a sleeveless white T-shirt which revealed a lot of his shoulders and the upper part of his chest. He was very muscular, and his prominent pectorals showed distinctly under the T-shirt, which may have been chosen precisely to emphasize this effect. For between his nipples, which were more or less hidden, and his biceps, a part of his chest remained exposed, bulging under a forest of black, bushy hair. It was this region I would have liked to touch, to caress, to kiss, to lick. But though the boy in the white T-shirt had turned around, he nonetheless continued on his way. I found a place to piss, and then went on to *The Stud.*

Now, with his elbows thrust back, legs crossed, he was leaning against a kind of thick plank you can set your glass on which runs along the wall down one side of the room. He seemed to be alone, but two boys about a yard to his right were talking to him now and then. A third, a tall, dark, moustached man in a plaid shirt and leather vest, with studded, pointed boots, was sitting opposite him on a beam that divided the room and gave it the vaguely Western look that the name of the place implied. This man was obviously trying to start a conversation with him. I also leaned against the shelf, a couple of yards farther on.

The pseudo-cowboy was evidently in an expansive mood, and it was not easy to tell if he was talking to himself or to White T-shirt, at least until he stood up, went over to the latter and under-lined each of his remarks with a gesture of his arm which seemed to lead his forefinger quite regularly to precisely the zone dear to my fantasy. White T-shirt made no answer really, and on the whole merely went on smiling, but a single word from him was enough to stimulate the other man, launching him into a long, apparently incoherent speech meant to be both comical and seductive.

If I leaned against the shelf (but did it really exist, or is this a figment of my memory, providing a convenient detail?), if I leaned against the shelf, then, instead of immediately leaving the bar, as I had meant to do, it was because I wanted to get a better look at White T-shirt. I hadn't the faintest hope he might be interested in me. Moreover, it was very late, I was tired, I had already come an hour before, under physically trying conditions, standing up in the crowd at *The Stud* in a terrible heat. My mind wasn't on cruising.

Or barely. For after all, I had come in there, even if it had only been my intention to look around. And when White T-shirt in-vited me, with a glance and a smile, to witness the cowboy's drunkenness, my mood changed quite rapidly. But you never know with Americans. That smile and that complicity make no promises. Shit, he really turns me on. But I'm so tired that even if it works and we connect, I probably won't be able to get it up. Another smile. I return it. And again. It really looks like he's cruising me this time. But maybe he's just trying to get rid of the other one, who isn't so bad, anyway. And who's beginning to understand what's happening. Retreats. Goes away. Sulks. White T-shirt flashes me a big smile. A big smile back to him, but I don't move. All of this is too good to be true; there must be a misunderstanding somewhere. And besides, I'm so tired. He looks like the kind that requires a lot of energy. Another exchange of smiles. This is getting silly.

And now there's someone else. One of his two neighbors on the left comes over to White T-shirt, but walks past him and toward me:

"I can see that unless I do something about it, you two'll never get together. His name's Bob."

"Bob?"

"Yes, Bob. He's cute, isn't he?"

"Sure is. And what's your name?"

"John. You?"

"Renaud."

"What?"

"Renaud. Or Bruno."

"You're a foreigner?"

"Yes."

"What?"

"French."

"French? A real Frenchman?"

I laugh:

"Yes. Why? Are there fake ones?"

"Hey, Bob! Come over here. I've found you a Frenchman!"

"Really? You're French?"

"Yes. And his name's Wono."

"Wono? That's hard for me to say, but easy for a Frenchman, of course. Gees!"

"What?"

"A real Frenchman!"

"But there are lots of them—every time I go out on the street, I run into half-a-dozen!"

"Me, I've never known a Frenchman. Have you?"

"No, never."

"I once knew a German, though."

Then a gesture imitating a violin player. . .

"All right, you don't need me any more."

John walks away, and Bob and I are next to each other.

201

"Your cowboy's going to be furious."

"He's not my cowboy, and he's a pain in the ass."

"All the same, he's not bad-looking."

"I know, I know. But he's totally sloshed. I don't like drunks. Besides, you're not bad-looking yourself."

"Why, thank you, sir. But I don't think you remember me."

"Remember you? Why, have we met before?"

"Of course we have. We had a long affair. . ."

"You're kidding!"

"No."

"When? Where?"

"Just now, earlier this evening, in a dark street. I was looking for a place to piss."

"And then?"

"Then you smiled at me."

"I smile at everyone I like."

"And you forget them a minute later?"

"What difference does it make? After all, I found you again."

"I'm not complaining."

We kissed. He put his hand under my shirt, which was very rumpled and wide open. I put my hand under his T-shirt, on the right side of his chest, which was round, thick and very hard. He touched my crotch. I had something of an erection, but not as much of one as the situation required. He turned me on a lot, but mostly, it seemed, in my head. He whispered in my ear:

"Can we go to your place?"

"No, I don't have a place. I'm staying with friends, and I just had a fight with them."

"Shit! We can't go to my place either. I don't live in Manhattan."

"You don't? But where were you planning to sleep tonight?"

"At my lover's. I have a lover; I sleep at his place when I want to stay in Manhattan. The rest of the time I live with my parents in Queens."

"Shit! That's too bad. So stop turning me on if we can't sleep together . . ."

"Wait a minute, wait a minute. Let's not lose hope. I'll think of something."

He leaned to his right, arm outstretched in the direction of John, who seemed to be his great recourse, and drew him toward us:

"We can't go to his place."

"Go into a booth at the bookstore!"

"No, I want a bed to spend the night in!"

"Then go to *The Anvil*. There's a hotel upstairs."

"*The Anvil?* Are you kidding? For once in my life I find someone I like, I'm going to keep him!"

"What about that hotel at the end of the street, over the *Cock-Ring?*"

"The *Christopher?* Oh no, it's really too filthy there. I don't want to catch a lot of bugs. Which reminds me—I do know a hotel. The one where that German lived, as a matter of fact. It wasn't much, if I remember. Do you have money on you?"

"A little, but I'd rather not spend too much. All I have is a couple hundred dollars to live on for a month."

"I have twenty—we'll split. It'll work, if we pay ten dollars apiece. OK?"

"OK."

"Come on. We'll try it."

We thanked our go-between. The cowboy now seemed to be in the gloomy phase of his drunkenness, and said nothing. Out in the street, we turned right and walked east, then south, without saying much. Bob wasn't sure of what the hotel might cost, and didn't know how much the German had paid for his room, which wasn't a bad one.

I was amazed at not being more excited.

He nudged me with his elbow.

"Here we are. Let's go in. You do the talking. With your accent, it'll work better."

I was taken by surprise; I didn't know we had arrived. We were two steps off Washington Square. I had never gone into a hotel with a boy, in the middle of the night, without luggage. I was quite intimidated, but we were already in the lobby, there was no turning back now.

An unshaven man of about sixty-five with red eyes came over to the counter. He was neither friendly nor curious, but seemed merely tired and indifferent. He asked us for twenty-four dollars. Bob took out a twenty-dollar bill.

"Give me ten, and I'll take the change."

"But there's no reason you should pay more than me."

"Don't worry about it."

"Thanks."

The man handed us a key:

"One-hundred seven. On the first floor. You have to leave by one tomorrow."

He gestured to the right. But Bob had already set out to the left.

"No, no, not that way, over there, at the other end."

The stairs were steep, the corridor narrow and dark, twisting around right angles with sudden shifts in direction. Behind some doors, you could hear transistor radios, more or less muffled conversations, snores, an argument.

The room was quite small, dimly lit by an imitation alabaster chandelier. The bed lamp didn't work. The double bed looked broken down, its plush spread rumpled.

Bob glanced around the room, satisfied. He went into the bathroom, talking while he pissed:

"Everything: air conditioning, shower, television. No wonder it costs twenty-four bucks. They could even ask for more."

When he came back, I went to piss too. On my return, he was already on the bed, completely naked. He had turned out the overhead light and turned on the television, but the only program he could get was some kind of talk show involving two men in turtleneck sweaters, rhythmically interrupted by a horizontal white stripe moving regularly down the screen. Bob had turned off the sound, and I suppose that the screen interested him only as a source of light. The white, trembling light flickered over the pale green walls to the hum of the tired, sticky ventilator under the window.

I took off my clothes and stretched out beside him. We put our arms around each other and kissed. Because of the heat, our bodies were already moist. His belly, thighs and ass were as hairy as his chest. I was lying on top of him, and licked him from top to bottom. I had the tip of one of his nipples in my mouth now. But he had other ideas. He lifted his legs on either side of mine. My tongue moved from his belly to his cock to his balls, to his asshole. But instead of being enthusiastic, as I would normally have been, I was vaguely disgusted without knowing why. He was very clean, his body very firm, it had nothing to do with that, only with my mood, the exasperation of the day, my fatigue, and the heat. Apparently he wanted me to fuck him. I put my cock into him, which was pleasant but nothing more. My cock was not completely stiff. He was playing with himself, and encouraged me by murmuring:

"Come on, fuck me, yeah, fuck!"

He made the mistake of calling me *Frenchy,* which made me laugh, and added nothing to my performance, which was already no better than mediocre: I immediately had the impression of having to defend the national colors, especially in this hotel, in the very room, perhaps, where he had made love with a German, to his great satisfaction, it appeared. This was too heavy a responsibility for my loins, given the state I was in after that endless night. If I moved too much, I would come out of his ass. If I moved too little, I would go completely limp. How absurd. This boy represented everything which was supposed to turn me on, all he wanted was to be fucked, and I could barely manage to oblige him.

His hand was working faster and faster on his cock. He was going to come. He came. It took me five minutes to catch up with him, telling myself stories whose characters pleased me much less than he.

I went into the bathroom again. When I came back, I asked him if I could turn off the television now. He was already asleep. I got back into bed. His back was turned to me. During what remained of the night, which is to say, of the morning, he didn't move, didn't make one gesture. I didn't even hear him breathe. Yet I couldn't manage to fall asleep. The hours passed, and in my head various scenes of this busy day, contradictory plans for the days to come, memories merged . . . I was thinking about Tony. Was it all over between us, then? I couldn't believe that. I tried not to get too upset. Now and then, I convinced myself that I wanted to piss, and that certainly I would fall asleep, once this task was performed. As I went by the window, I foolishly lifted a corner of the curtain: it was broad daylight. The window looked out onto a tiny courtyard, just below me and filled with empty beer cans, bottles, old papers and huge curls of black dust, everything coated with a heavy layer of soot. It was raining. So this was my new life? But what a fine page of *Tricks* it would make, this inert body, this insomnia, my sadness, this sordid hotel, this hideous courtyard, and through it all, Tony's face! Where was he?

I must have slept from about ten to noon. Bob wakened me when he finally stirred. He had pressed himself against me, still with his back to me. I fucked him again, but not much more brilliantly than the first time. I was even more exhausted, and had no more of an erection than before. Nonetheless we just about managed to come together.

He said we would have to hurry. He got up and headed for the bathroom, automatically turning on the television as he passed. I also went to clean up a little after he was through. When I came back into the room, he was sitting on the edge of the bed, riveted to the set. It was an old serial, I think, something more or less comical about the life of blue-collar workers. I don't remember much about the plot, but the two main themes of the episode were *camaraderie* and paternal love. The whole point was to permit a father to spend, in accordance with some tradition or other, a certain day fishing with his son, or something of the kind. The son was far away, in an elegant prep school that was ruining the father, who didn't even have enough money to join him, or to take a day off work. Or no, maybe the son *was* there, but didn't care about the fishing. In any case, the factory workers, who were the father's friends, were getting up a party to raise some money for him, a party to which, of course, he wasn't invited. But he got wind of it and so ensued a whole series of misunderstandings and gaffes which entranced Bob without making him forget, nonetheless, that the time was five to one.

Outside it was raining. Bob was hungry. He led me into a cafeteria on Eighth Street. No, I didn't want anything to eat, just a cup of tea. He wanted tea too, but with a hamburger:

"You're sure you don't want one too? I'm paying."

"No, thanks. You're nice, but I don't think I can face a hamburger just like that, first thing in the morning. I'm not very hungry."

We were sitting opposite each other, at a green formica-topped table. He was going back to Queens. And where did I live?

"Lexington and Eighty-ninth."

"Then we can take the subway together. I know that part of town—I used to work in a hospital up there."

"And now?"

"Now I still work in a hospital, but another one. Near Fifty-ninth street."

I explained to him what I had explained to Jim the night before, that I had argued with my travelling companion and that I was probably going to stay in New York. But in his opinion, as in Jim's, a reconciliation would probably take place before the next day.

"I'd be very surprised if it did. Especially after last night. Is there a number where I can reach you?"

"Yes, of course. But be careful; if my lover answers, don't say anything—or I'm the one who'll have a scene then."

"No, of course. I'm not going to say 'I'd like to speak to Bob. I'm his trick from last Sunday night.'"

"Even if you didn't say anything you could start something. He'd ask me: 'Who's that?' Especially with your accent. He knows I don't know any French people. No, tell you what we'll do: Thursday night I'll be in the *Boots and Saddle*. If you're still in New York, we'll meet there."

"Fine."

It was still raining. Finally I decided, instead of taking the Sixth Avenue subway with Bob, to see if my friend Eugene was at home. He lived nearby, in Washington Square Village. We separated. I walked fifty yards and changed my mind again. But I took the subway at another station, Union Square.

[*I left New York the next day, so I didn't see Bob the following*

Thursday. I ran into him by accident at Ty's, in September. I was then with Tony and he, probably, with his lover. He smiled and said hello, but didn't seem eager to start a conversation.]

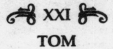

XXI

TOM

Thursday, August 10, 1978

During one week in San Francisco, I had seen him several times, late at night, in the *Black and Blue* south of Market Street, and each time in the rather cramped, always crowded passageway that serves as a fuck room. The first time, my attention had been drawn to him during a scene which had amused me. He was trying to fuck a boy of about twenty, who was very enthusiastic about the endeavor. But his cock was so unbelievably big that he was getting nowhere, as he might have expected, for no doubt he had already encountered this particular problem before. Few assholes certainly were in condition to accommodate him. Yet he seemed amazed and furious. He redoubled his efforts, swearing the while.

Standing beside him and his putative partner, I had tried to help them, as several other volunteers were also doing: spreading the buttocks of the one, directing the other's member. On this occasion I had touched him, and not only his cock, whose proportions had astonished me, but his balls, his ass, his belly, his chest. In the darkness, I couldn't see him very clearly, but I decided he had a good head, an open expression that contradicted his current anger, a great deal of energy, and a very muscular body, though more the muscles of a laborer than of an athlete. Tony, to whom I had mentioned him afterwards, and who had seen him as well, maintained that he was at least forty. It was my impression that he was about thirty. But in any case we were agreed about his most notable feature, and between ourselves we referred to him as "The Horse."

From his stubborn insistence on penetrating the ass of the poor kid, and from his rage at not succeeding, I had supposed he was interested in only the one sexual role. But the next night, or the next after that, in precisely the same place, I had seen him being fucked by a rather handsome boy—part Japanese, probably, or perhaps Chinese—and at the same time sucking someone else's cock. I was standing next to this someone else, and kissing him. Someone in the mêlée had taken out my cock and was playing with it. The Horse may have had the fantasy of mobilizing as many cocks as he could, because he began playing with me, after having rather cavalierly—so to speak—shoved away the hand already thus occupied. Then he drew me as close as he could to the boy whose cock he was sucking, and took my cock into his mouth as well. The other fellow may have found this sharing inadmissible, or else he was attracted by another of the countless combinations in the little passageway, for he moved away. The Horse then devoted his entire mouth to my cock, while playing with a newcomer and continuing to be fucked by the Eurasian, who leaned forward and drew my face toward his own. We kissed each other. I had one hand on the cock of one of my neighbors and the other on the Horse's chest. He, however, wanted to perform a variation on this arrangement: he straightened up, kissing me as he did so, turned around, and offered me his ass, into which I introduced my cock without the slightest difficulty, and he began sucking the cock of the Eurasian, whom I kissed again. Poppers were circulating from some unknown source.

For about twenty minutes, perhaps more, we gave ourselves up to permutations which invariably afforded the Horse at least one cock in his ass and another in his mouth. Tony, appearing from some nearby entertainment, joined us. For a while, he took my position behind the Horse and fucked him. No one actually thought of coming: everyone had already done so, and no one did again. This moment, moreover, never clearly came to an end. It dissolved imperceptibly: each of the participants, gradually and almost unconsciously, found himself involved in other exchanges, and if the scene continued, it was with a different cast of characters.

On the night of August 10, Tony and I were again at the *Black and Blue,* as was the Horse. He and I recognized each other, smiled, kissed, but between one in the morning, when Tony and I arrived, and two, which was closing time, there were few contacts between us. Nonetheless, he seemed quite amiable.

Closing time at the *Black and Blue* is followed by a rather prolonged period of indecision. A good half of those who have been inside remain outside on the sidewalk in front of the doors, in a radius of about fifty yards. Friends talk to each other, plans for the rest of the night are discussed, final passes are made.

Tony and I were sitting on the fender of a car a little distance away. We were in a very good mood, a little drunk, a little stoned, curious about the local customs, and reluctant to go home unaccompanied. Yet among the boys present, those who interested one of us failed to turn on the other, or vice versa, and if both of us were interested, then *they* were interested in only one of us, or neither.

A ways off, I glimpsed the Horse talking with a boy he seemed to be cruising, but their conversation led to nothing, apparently, and they separated. At this moment, Tony had altered his opinion about the Horse's age, and agreed with me that he was quite handsome. We decided I would speak to him, since he seemed to regard me as an acquaintance, and discover what his intentions might be. I therefore went over to him. He was all smiles, and asked if I was going somewhere else, to one of the clubs that stayed open all night. I didn't know yet, what about him? He didn't know either. It depended on what came up. Well, maybe I could help him out: would he like to come to my place? Yes, he would, or else we could go to his place, which would be more convenient for him in case I had a car, because he didn't. Yes, I had a car, and I would like to go home with him, but I was with a friend. That was fine with him; in fact, the more the merrier. We could leave right now, the three of us, he would go wherever we liked, dancing, or to the baths, or to our place, or to his. I brought this news to Tony, and returned with him to the Horse, whose name was Tom.

We decided to go to his place. We got into the car, I behind the wheel. He lived in Noe Valley, a stone's throw away from Castro Street, but much farther south than the *Castro Cinema* and the liveliest part of the street. No, actually it wasn't so far, but I was considerably stoned, I remember now, and I had a very imprecise sense of distances: I was driving with such extreme caution that the streets seemed endless. Sitting to my right, Tom was giving me directions with one hand, the other resting on my thigh. Tony, sitting behind us, leaning forward, had draped his forearms around Tom's shoulders.

No sooner had we come into the apartment than our problems began, though I'm not sure in exactly what order. Tony vanished into the bathroom. Tom came over to me and put his hand on my crotch. No reaction at all. His own cock was only half erect; even so, it nearly reached the middle of his thigh. It seemed to me that the ratio of size between my cock and his was at that moment about one to ten. I was a little intimidated. Then he offered me a beer. I said I preferred a glass of water, but he opened a can. I didn't like the taste on his breath.

We were in a rather large room, with a "dining room set," in it: an enormous table, six chairs, a sideboard, a serving table. Everything was in pale beige wood, in that Spanish Renaissance ("Mission") style so popular in California. In comparison, our own early Third Republic-Henri II seems light and graceful. In any case, this solemn presence was no help to me in getting an erection. It even seemed to have the opposite effect, if such a thing exists, as I believe it does. My cock was visibly shrinking, and stubbornly remained in hiding.

To gain time, I decided to suck Tom. I crouched down, my knees apart, and immediately ripped the seam of the old white trousers I was wearing. I had to stand up again to get them off. Tom then suggested that we go into his bedroom. But it was lit brighter than daylight by a very powerful ceiling fixture which spared no detail. Luckily Tony, returning, asked Tom if he could turn it off, and didn't even wait for his answer to do so.

Now we were all together on the big bed. Tony had a fine erection, Tom half a one, and I none at all. Tom was very attentive to me; kind, patient, and persistent, but he had that localized, pinpointed approach to sex which I deplore. He sucked my cock, wanted me to fuck him, constantly changed position, so that not for a moment could I simply be in his arms, kissing him peacefully before getting on to something else. He kept making a strange noise, a deep sigh of satisfaction or admiration, which I hardly seemed to deserve.

Tony fucked him quite rapidly while I was playing with his cock or sucking it. Then Tom wanted me to fuck him as well. Thighs raised, he offered me his ass, while my cock was about the size of my thumb. Finally he acknowledged the obvious and abandoned this project. The next one was for him to fuck me. I dared not refuse altogether, since I had nothing better to propose. Besides, he himself had only half an erection, and I imagined this would come to nothing. That is in fact what occurred. But there was nonetheless an uncomfortably long quarter of an hour filled with efforts which for me were both tiresome and painful. He kept trying to get his huge but not entirely hard cock into me, while Tony, somehow full of energy, was fucking him once again. Furthermore, Tom seemed to derive more pleasure from the latter than from the former. When Tony came in his ass, he gave up trying to come in mine and stretched out across the bed. In two or three minutes, and without ever managing to get a real erection, I then came on his belly, to his mild surprise. Then Tony and I tried for a very long while to get him to the point of ejaculation as well, but to no avail, and it was he who called a halt to our efforts.

His mood, despite this failure, remained excellent. Everything seemed to delight him. I don't remember how his monologue began, for that is what it was, our infrequent interventions merely serving, in the main, to keep him going. He told us that he liked us, that we were a handsome couple, and he wanted to know how long we had known each other:

"Nine years? That's incredible. That just doesn't happen here, couples who stay together that long. Well, yes, maybe, but it's rare, very rare, if it does happen. I know one guy, he works in the house, the other day I saw him in a restaurant, he was with a really hot boy, a really *hot* number. [*If I could give some idea of the way he pronounced this adjective, with the very clearly aspirated* h *and the very extended* o, *doubtless I could manage to give some idea of what Tom was like, his sweetness, his humor, and the kind of perpetual enthusiasm which seemed to be his distinctive feature.*] The next day I met this guy and I said to him, 'God, that kid you were with yesterday, wow, he was really hot.' He smiled and squinted his eyes and he said, 'Really, you think he was really all that hot?' I started to say, 'Believe me, I—' And he said, 'We've been together thirteen years.' I couldn't believe it. Thirteen years! In San Francisco! With a guy like that! There really has to be something between them, huh, something special, something strong, something unique, like between the two of you, it shows—I can tell."

Maybe it was from that, and from the life of homosexuals in San Francisco, that he went on to Proposition Six which was stirring California that summer. Or was it Proposition Thirteen? Whichever, I no longer have a clear idea of it now; in truth, it was quite dim in my mind even that August, so I confused it with the other one, of which I was a staunch supporter and which prohibited smoking in public places. Anyway, Proposition——, whatever its number was, specifically concerned homosexuals and was presented, especially by its detractors, as the local fallout from Anita Bryant's actions in Florida and on a national scale. Its goal, according to those who supported the plan, was to protect children and adolescents against homosexuals in schools. The measures envisaged were creating a great stir in the gay community. Everywhere leaflets were being distributed, petitions circulated, collections taken up to mount a counter-campaign. According to Tom, whose convictions on this point were very firm and almost violent, it was quite simply a matter of imminent Fascism:

"The Jewish community understood it right away, they know the problem, they know what they're talking about, and they're almost all with us. You understand how it works: some kid who has bad grades, all he needs to do is claim that his teacher made a pass at him, and bang, the teacher gets fired. The slightest suspicion, the slightest accusation is enough. Actually, what's involved is simply a way of keeping gays from teaching. Of course in San Francisco it's all a big joke. Three-quarters of the teachers are fags. Besides, here in the city, the proposition won't go through. Between us and the Jews—and then, too, there's a certain liberal tradition around here—it'll be blocked. But in Los Angeles they're so conservative, they're so scared, it's incredible. It'll go through. And in the rest of the state it's almost a sure thing."

Tony and I, in a kind of half-sleep, listened to him with pleasure. He spoke well, in a very lively way, with a lot of idiomatic expressions, some of which, it's true, escaped me entirely. From California politics he went on to the national scene. He seemed to regard it as no more than a spectacle, and to evaluate the principal figures solely as actors or directors, according to their presence on television, and the dramatic effects they could produce. Carter, for instance, might have been a "good guy," but he had no sense of humor, no entertainment value:

"While Nixon! Oh, those were the good old days. You can't imagine how much fun we all had! We were glued to our TV sets all day, all night. It was a national trip. No serial could compete. Every day we wondered what he was going to come up with next, what new rabbit he would pull out of his hat. The public was on edge, and he played it like a virtuoso. You could really say he was an artist with the public. The people who miss him—and there *are* some—know perfectly well he was a crook. But for the most part they don't care. And besides, in those days, even the others, the secondary figures, were good. Great supporting casts, even for the most obscure parts, down to Nixon's dog. McGovern and the Eagleton business, you remember that, that was a good one too:

I'm a hundred per cent behind Senator Eagleton! And Agnew? Agnew was incredible. They don't make them like that anymore, they wouldn't dare!"

The political and para-political serials led him to the real ones, and Tony roused himself a little to evoke, with mounting enthusiasm, dozens of soap operas of their childhood, and increasingly obscure television actors and the return of Cesar Romero, *who had been Tyrone Power's wife,* and who for ten years had publicized I don't know what, and singers that were already forgotten in 1965, and even the commercials of the fifties, which they both remembered with a certain emotion. I listened, excluded yet fascinated, amazed all over again by America's power to elaborate a complete and modern mythological fabric, etc. etc. They were punching each other on the belly, on the ass:

"And you remember Lana Carsons [*I'm inventing the name, I've forgotten them all, a good hundred must have paraded past*], who was always so unhappy because she wanted to have straight hair? And what was the one whose boyfriends always dropped her? The one who was always getting ditched? And Jimmy Montero, who kept getting inside refrigerators!

They laughed until they lost their breath, or else they became quite moved, and I realized with a certain irritation that in France, we had nothing so richly nostalgic in the same realm, and that the evocation of *Persil lave plus blanc,* of the *Famille Duraton,* or of *Thierry la Fronde* would never manage to create such an immediate solidarity between two strangers.

We left around four in the morning, perhaps five. Tom walked out onto his landing to see us off. His cock looked even more stupefying at a distance. There had been no question of seeing each other again, except by accident. He was still as merry as ever, and seemed delighted by his evening.

[*Never saw him again.*]

215

≈ XXII ≈

PLAID SHIRT

Saturday, August 12, 1978

To the west, San Francisco does not quite reach the ocean. The long straight avenues stop on the heights, and the shore remains almost wild and very steep: rocks, scrub, and maritime fir. You could easily be in Brittany. You'd never suspect a city up above, just behind the cliffs.

The California palace of the Legion of Honor, a reconstruction of the Parisian one, stands surrounded by a golf course. Beyond the last holes, down below, begins a very marked, steep, sometimes difficult slope to a tiny beach of gray sand. This is Land's End. Here the Pacific is rarely calm. The fog comes in early, around the middle of the afternoon on summer days. You can hear the foghorns of the ships coming into the bay toward Golden Gate, a little to the north, but often you can't see them at all. These austere and splendid shores are a cruising ground for boys, one of those mythical places, among the most beautiful in the world. Like the gardens of the Villa Borghese, the Tuileries, the Molo in Venice, the dunes of the North Sea at Le Touquet, the rocks of Biarritz, the hills of Griffith Park in Los Angeles, and the more modest slopes of Central Park in New York, Land's End lends some of its majesty to the search and to desire.

It was four in the afternoon. I had been reading on the beach. But the sun had now dissolved into the clouds, the waves were rough, and a cold wind had risen. I was climbing back up to the car. In the scrub, I passed a man of about forty in the rigorous uniform of a Castro Man, as the boys sometimes say out there in reference to Castro Street, their sanctuary: big hiking boots, old tight jeans, and a flannel plaid shirt, with more red than black in it; short hair, moustache, etc. He wasn't especially handsome, but a certain code, which is not precisely mine, would have called him that. His rugged face, his broad shoulders, his muscles, and his way of walking, suggested the countless ads for unfiltered cigarettes which appear in every magazine in America as well as on the signs along the highways. As a matter of fact, it was really Land's End that was turning me on, the most distant place I had ever reached, facing the most exotic ocean. I had dreamed of leaving some semen here—mine or someone else's—as an obligatory rite.

It all happened very quickly. He was coming down; I was climbing up. We turned around to look at each other. He came back in my direction. I went on walking, but very slowly. Without hesitating, he pushed aside the branches and came into a little glade where I joined him. We immediately approached each other. He unbuttoned my shirt, and I unbuttoned his. His chest was broad and prominent. Doubtless he spent a lot of time in his gym, like a good Castro Man. He opened my fly and took out my cock. I did the same for him. He knelt in front of me and sucked my cock. We were interrupted by a sound of approaching voices. It was three boys, who were coming down the path. Apparently there was nothing to fear from them. Besides, they hadn't seen us. But Plaid Shirt had stood up. Which was fine—I was just at the point of coming, and I didn't want to. I began playing with him. His cock was pretty big. He thrust his pelvis forward, and bent his legs slightly. I was at his right side, playing with his cock with my right hand, and running my left over his torso. When he came, he bit his lower lip. His sperm spattered between the bushes onto the ground of the little glade. He dried himself off with leaves.

He wanted to make me come too, but I had already begun to button up. He did the same. We smiled at each other for the first time, and exchanged a light punch on the shoulder. We had not uttered a single word.

When I reached the top of the cliffs, I turned around and saw him all the way at the bottom, alone on the little gray beach. He was staring at the sea.

[*Never saw him again.*]

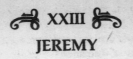

XXIII

JEREMY

Sunday, August 13, 1978

Tony already knew him, but apparently not very well. And I had seen him once in Paris, back in May at a sort of literary party where I immediately noticed him. It was just after my reconciliation with Tony, and I had assumed that this very seductive boy at whom he had smiled must be one of his lovers. We had not been introduced, and I had heard him speak only from a distance of about ten feet through other conversations: I had judged his voice, or at least his elocution, to be a little too precious, but this was probably out of jealousy and the wish to attribute some defect to him. Because to tell the truth I found him absolutely splendid. First of all, his hair was extraordinary. Black, rather long, very well cut, and incredibly thick, it formed a moving, undulating mass, which set off the beauty of his face still more: his black eyebrows, eyes, and moustache, his straight, almost classically chiseled nose, his regular lips and the strong chin which, like his hands and wrists, kept him from being merely pretty. He also had a way of looking at people, men or women, when he talked to them, which must have stirred more than one among them. Watching him for two minutes was enough to be convinced that he was, whether consciously or not, a formidable charmer.

His name was Jeremy. He came from Virginia, whence those drawling, lingering intonations which had initially irritated me a little, and which later would become, in my memory, one of his most attractive features. He was twenty-five, but had already received his doctorate in modern literature. He was one of the youngest professors in the department of comparative literature at Berkeley. He was anything but a French specialist; he spoke

French quite badly, but he was very up to date about French cultural life. He had begun a correspondence with Tony concerning several of Tony's articles, early ones on Pessoa and Roussel published in a review of Romance languages at Indiana University. Tony said he wasn't sure whether or not Jeremy was gay. At that party in Paris, he was accompanied by a very young and very pretty girl.

He had been living in San Francisco for a year or two. Tony had telephoned him when we arrived in town, and he was supposed to come for a drink that Sunday at our place, that is, at Mary-Ann's, and to have dinner with us. He had said he would probably be coming with a French friend, Pierre, with whom he lived. From that we concluded that this Pierre was probably his lover. But we would have much preferred that he not come along for both of us had designs on Jeremy.

When he arrived, around six in the afternoon, I was taking a bath. I joined Tony and him only after about a quarter of an hour. He was even handsomer than I remembered. Whereas that first time he had been wearing an extremely well cut checked suit and a tie, he was now in sports clothes, brown corduroys and a white button-down shirt, sleeves rolled up. His forearms were muscular and very hairy. In May I had admired his pale complexion, which made such a surprising contrast with his hair and eyes, but he pleased me even more as he was now, deeply tanned.

He was sitting at Mary-Ann's desk. Tony was showing him an issue of *Creatis* devoted to Daniel Boudinet's photographs, with a text by Roland Barthes:

"Renaud, Jeremy. But you've already met, I think."

He looked at me, flashed one of his famous smiles, which are absolutely irresistible, and said:

"No, I don't think so."

"But Renaud distinctly remembers having seen *you*. He never stops asking questions about you."

It seemed to me that Tony was overdoing it. But the quarter of an hour they had already spent together had done a lot for their intimacy, it appeared. They explained that Pierre wouldn't be coming, and Tony hardly concealed his satisfaction. Jeremy and Pierre had done nothing but fight for a week, even to the point of blows. The day before they had decided to break up:

"I feel much better now that it's been decided. We'd rented an apartment together, and all that is going to cause a lot of complications. But I'd rather not think about it now."

"Have you known each other a long time?"

"Five years."

I think I can remember most of our conversation that evening, or at least the various subjects discussed, if not the details, but I'm no longer sure what was said at Mary-Ann's and what at the restaurant. It seems to me that we did most of the talking at dinner. Yet we didn't go out before eight, certainly, and we must have talked about something all that time, but I don't know what. Probably about Mary-Ann, the friend who had lent us her apartment during her vacation. It seemed to us that these two rooms whose arrangement, furnishings, and decoration we considered slightly affected, required analysis. But that couldn't have taken two hours. Actually, Jeremy must have come well after six o'clock. Very likely, since Tony and I had been at Land's End all afternoon. Oh yes, we spent a lot of time choosing a restaurant. We phoned, or tried to phone several restaurants to reserve a table, but to no avail in each case, either because they were full, or because they were closed on Sunday, or even because we couldn't find their number. Finally Jeremy suggested a place more modest than the others, whose name I've forgotten, but which I had already seen on Folsom Street. It was very simple, he said, but very popular and very lively. We couldn't make reservations, or even get a real meal with courses, but the food there, which consisted mainly of different kinds of hamburgers, was good. He went there quite often, and he thought we would enjoy it.

Would we take one car or both? On his insistence, we all got into his, a big Buick that seemed quite sumptuous and in excellent condition, but which his parents had given him, he explained, over four years ago:

"It's been through hell, this car, and it'll probably break down on me soon. But not tonight."

The restaurant was quite large, very full and very lively, as promised. It had the look of a big pub: long bars, complex scaffoldings of bottles, figured mirrors, dark wood panels inset with the front pages of old newspapers. A host of framed photographs depicted views of San Francisco early in the century: the earthquakes, the fire, ships in the bay, local personalities, actors and actresses, scenes from films. There was a lot of noise and smoke. No table was free. Meanwhile, we were led to a corner where we could sit down near the bar and order a cocktail. Tony and Jeremy drank margaritas or daiquiris, I can't remember. I had asked for a martini, but Tony reminded me just in time that what was served under this name in America has nothing to do with the European martini, and that I didn't like the American variety. So I ordered whatever they were having.

We weren't very comfortably seated. They were next to each other; I was a little over to one side. I had trouble following their conversation in English, partly because of the racket in the room and partly because I suddenly felt extremely tired. I was sleepy from my afternoon's exertions on the cliff-lined beaches of Land's End and the fresh sea air, and my eyes were smarting from all the cigarette smoke. Yet Jeremy made a considerable effort to bring me into the conversation, with such smiles, glances, and even, it seemed to me, pressure of his knee, that I was beginning to wonder if he was cruising me. I decided he wasn't, but I must confess that I was silently calling him a tease and even a southern belle: another of those lovely sons of the Old South who must seduce everyone at all costs.

Our table was ready. A waiter came to take our order. Another of the specialties of the house was the chili con carne. Jeremy recommended it particularly:

"It's the best in town. Nothing to do with the chili you get everywhere." Tony and he decided to order that.

221

"No, I don't really go for Mexican cooking. It's a pure prejudice on my part, I've never eaten Mexican food in my life. But it always has connotations of Montezuma's revenge for me—I can't help myself."

"But for Mexican cooking to have that effect, it has to be made in Mexico, with Mexican products."

"Yes, of course. Still . . ."

I ordered some kind of chicken salad with a pretentious name which turned out to be something enormous and not very appetizing. The dishes took a very long time getting to the table.

During dinner there were two main subjects of conversation, and I'm not sure which came first. Maybe we talked first about Roland Barthes. Before we left, Jeremy had leafed through the issue of *Creatis* that Tony had pointed out to him, but had said nothing about it at the time. At the table, he told us that he wasn't very taken with Boudinet's photographs.

"It's hard for me to judge. All I can say is that it's very far from my sensibility, from what I like in photography. Maybe it's just because it's so . . . European. It screams Europe at you. No American photographer would ever do something like that."

"And is that so bad?"

"Nooooo . . . No, of course not. I mean, I don't know. It's so . . . romantic, isn't it? In any case, he must be pleased to have a text by Barthes, isn't he?"

"Yes, probably."

"Does Barthes do a lot of things like that?"

"Yes, there are a lot of little pieces that turn up here and there. He's very fond of this work. So am I, by the way. There are also more recent pictures, very different ones, in color—night scenes, and I think they're splendid."

"All right, but how do you feel about Barthes's text?"

"I like it a lot."

"I actually think it's embarrassing, at first glance. In my opinion, it's really not possible to still talk about photography like that."

This was the moment I chose to emerge from my silence:

"I can't agree with you there at all. I wonder if you're not mixing up doing something *still* with doing it *again*. Barthes is perfectly aware that the modern way of talking about photography is to talk about technique and framing and composition. To talk about the medium. He knows perfectly well that that's the established way of talking about photography."

"No, it's *not* the established way of talking, not enough. Listen to people talk, open any magazine. The established way of talking about photography is to talk about the subject: X is a good photographer because he's photographed something amazing, something unique, because he was in the right place at the right time, etc. That's all you ever hear, anywhere. A good photographer is a good reporter."

"Yes, yes, I know, you're right, but you have to be more specific; you have to distinguish different ways of talking, different layers of discourse. The dominant discourse among people who are interested in photography today, the established modern discourse, is the kind that talks a lot about the photographer's art—his way of working, his technique, whatever is specific to the medium. This discourse sets the subject completely aside. And that's fine, it's been fine as a reaction against the dominant discourse you're talking about. But it's this new discourse that's become the established one now. This is the established modern discourse. And Barthes isn't unaware of it, on the contrary, he knows it very well. He sees that it threatens to become dominant in turn, to forbid another possible way of talking about photography. And his position is that yes, it's all true, if you talk about photography you have to talk about the medium itself, of course, about what is specifically photographic, but we're beginning to discover that this is becoming in turn a cliché, a stereotype, in certain circles in any case. And the one shouldn't crush the other. We should also be able to talk again, today, about what the photograph represents, or about what it evokes, even subjectively. Representation, in photography as in literature, is never completely cancelled out. It was fine to contest it when it was dominant—hegemonic, so to speak—but if it is threatened now, then it has to be defended."

"Yes, but if you criticize the dominant discourse, you fall back into the clique of idiots who have always rejected it."

"No, you don't. That's exactly my point. Your objection is

the kind people use when they say you can't mention the labor camps in the USSR because if you do you're saying what all the reactionaries in the world have been saying for fifty years."

Tony smiled:

"Oh please, both of you. I don't see what poor Boudinet has to do with the Gulags."

Unfortunately, either from drunkenness or nervousness, I was off and running:

"You can't lump together people who apparently say the same thing. You have to take account of degrees. It's the metaphor of the spiral—you can't avoid it if you're talking about Barthes. Besides, that's how Barthes works in everything. After the sixties, which were massively theoretical in France—and to a large degree thanks to him, don't forget—he wrote *The Pleasure of the Text*. He reminded us that in spite of theory, there was something else in writing which was precious, which had to be preserved at all costs, and which was pleasure. I can tell you that when he wrote his piece, there was a huge sigh of relief all over Paris. No one had dared say so. And that's why, because of this method of his, that's why it's from Barthes that we can learn what freedom is, thanks to his *despite* and his *nevertheless*. He always comes to the defense of the most threatened discourse. And the threatened discourse with regard to photography today is the way we talk about the subject."

Now they were both smiling. Were they making fun of me and my flights? I was wondering what had come over me, what need to break lances for Barthes and Boudinet, as if they needed my help. In any case, if, thanks to them, I was losing this trick, they would hear from me about it!

But this question was gently abandoned. I don't know how Jeremy happened to get started talking about Pierre, but it was clear that he wanted to do so. And meanwhile there must have been some question of other things. The people at the next table, for instance, were four boys a little preposterous in their rigid adherence to the Castro Street code, who provoked Jeremy to comment that this restaurant seemed to be turning gay (which was more or less inevitable, anyway, given its geographical location). Also there was some discussion of Jeremy's stay in Paris last May:

"You stayed with friends?"

"No, in a hotel."

"Which one?"

"The Meurice. I love it, because of the view."

"Then you had one of the rooms overlooking the Tuileries? They're marvelous, aren't they?"

"Yes, it makes an extraordinary impression when you wake up in the morning: the rows of trees, the statues, the branches, the fountains . . ."

"I saw it in some movie, what was it, it was just the other day . . ."

"It was *Julia*. They were at the Meurice. Jane Fonda had a rendezvous in the Tuileries with someone from the German resistance."

"Oh yes, that's right. What's funny, if you can call it funny, is that a few years later the Meurice was the headquarters of . . . of what, was it the Gestapo or the military government of Paris? Which was it, Renaud?"

"I don't know exactly. No, not the Gestapo, I don't think so—it must have been the Kommandatur."

"It was? I didn't know that."

"But, this time you only went to Paris?"

"No, everywhere, I was with a girl who teaches with me at Berkeley; we were in Italy, then in Greece. That's where I got my tan."

"Was it your first time in Europe?"

"No, I went with my family several times when I was a kid, and then once by myself, at twenty. That was when I met Pierre."

"In Paris?"

"No, in Amsterdam. I landed in Amsterdam; I was flying KLM. And I met Pierre the second day I was there. He was living in Amsterdam in those days. I was planning to travel all over Europe, but my trip ended right there. And I didn't have the least regret. I stayed with him in Amsterdam for two months. Then we went to Copenhagen for a while. And then I had to go back to the States, because my classes were about to start. Pierre left his job and came with me."

"What did he do in America? Where were you studying?"

"In Ann Arbor."

"In Ann Arbor? I know someone there I like a lot—I mean, I don't know him personally, but I like his book a lot, about logophilia—"

"Pierssens? Yes, sure, I used to work with him. He influenced me a lot."

"What happened to Pierre then?"

"Pierre took courses in Ann Arbor."

"Really? That's funny. Of course we went you one better: Renaud taught at the university where I was finishing up my B.A."

"How'd you pull that off?"

"I'd written them to ask if they needed a French professor. They answered right away, all very friendly, but no, thanks, they would put me on file. I went there with Tony, and as soon as the school year began, some woman got pregnant or something. They needed a French professor right away. And they took me on immediately, without even asking what I was doing there."

"And Tony was one of your students?"

"No, it wasn't that good. I had mostly beginners."

"You were teaching French—the language?"

"Yes, mostly. At the end I did a course on Flaubert."

"Was that your choice?"

"No, it just happened to work out that way—it was on the syllabus."

"All the girls were in love with him. They gave him presents, they walked past the house every five minutes, and they kept wondering why none of them got anywhere. It was a good thing we left when I graduated. People were beginning to get suspicious. But you, didn't your family think it was odd? This Frenchman who signed up at Ann Arbor?"

"No, not at all. They paid for his studies."

"What?"

"Of course. They knew all about what was going on between

us. When we came back from Europe, we stayed with them first, I introduced them to Pierre."

"And how did that go?"

"At first they were a little surprised, of course, and not very enthusiastic. They hadn't suspected anything, up till then. But then they understood, and they said all right, if that's what makes you happy, that's the way it has to be. My parents are fine people. And they adore Pierre. It's always Pierre this, Pierre that. He's like another son to them. It's reached the point now where I don't dare tell them we've quarrelled and are going to break up. It's going to be a real disaster for them. They gave the car to the two of us. And the apartment too, as a matter of fact."

"Still, that kind of attitude's rather rare, isn't it?"

"I don't know. Probably. But it's perfectly natural, if your parents love you, that they'd understand, don't you think?"

"Yes, at least I tend to think so. But you know, it doesn't always work out that way. At least so I hear. More and more, maybe, it does. I hope so. Some parents even go too far. I know one boy whose mother insists on bringing them breakfast in bed each time he invites a friend to spend the weekend. All too often, I suspect, when parents have that kind of attitude, it's not so much because they're liberal, or enlightened, or independent, or because they've thought things through. It's only because they're a little disconcerted, or just odd, or else resigned to accepting everything. They would just as well put up with a perfect idiot. That mother I mentioned, in any case—it's obvious she's delighted her son's a fag. We met a boy, not long ago, who said that his parents were very understanding, more than understanding, even; he used to cruise with his mother, his grandmother wanted to meet his lovers, etc. It all sounded fine, but unfortunately he was completely bonkers. I'm not saying it was on their account; there must have been something else, but I had the impression that the whole family was . . . well, I don't know. It's not enough to be liberal. It has to be for good reasons. Knowing what you're doing, rather than doing what you do out of weakness."

"Well, as far as my parents are concerned, it's entirely different."

"No, of course, I wasn't speaking of your situation."

"They'd rather I weren't gay, of course, but it so happens that I am—there's nothing to be done about it. They weren't going to quarrel with me over that, and that's the end of it. But how do your parents react? Do they know?"

"No, they don't know anything. They'd have a fit, I think. Besides, I don't think they even know such things exist. It would be unthinkable for them. But they're very fond of Renaud. They always ask about him."

"And yours?"

"With mine it hasn't gone over at all."

"They're outraged?"

"No, not even that. It's worse than that. They're very sad, nervous depression and all. They are past the stage of the monstrous fag who has to be rejected—they're at the stage of the poor sick fag who has to be cured, which isn't much better. Well, at least now we avoid talking about it or about anything even vaguely related. For instance, we never talk about my books. Even though you can't say that they're homosexual novels because homosexuality is really very secondary in them. Of course it comes through. It's involved, and that's that."

"They've read them?"

"No, of course not! Not only don't they read them, they don't even read reviews of them. The slightest allusion is taboo. In conversation with them, I don't have any sexual life. I do nothing. I have no friends because they're all suspect without exception—at least, all men between thirteen and eighty-five, and even women now, since they're probably lesbians. My parents refuse to visit my house because it's a place of perdition, and even if I recommend a hotel to them—in Bruges, for instance, or Fiesole—they scrupulously avoid it, because of what I might have done there. I even think they've given up on Bruges and Fiesole altogether. When I'm with them, I have the impression of not really existing at all. And then, as far as guilt feelings go, it's a real burden."

"Sad."

"Yes, very sad."

We had all three ordered Irish coffee, and I don't remember what we went on talking about, yes, it was Pessoa, among other things: Jeremy had so much admiration for him that he had begun learning Portuguese just to be able to read him in the original. According to him, Pessoa would be considered the equal of say, Joyce, if he hadn't had the misfortune of having written in such a little-known language. Tony's opinion was not far from his.

Jeremy left the table for two minutes. Tony and I conspired:
"I wonder what his game is."
"So do I. It's certainly not obvious. In any case, I'm a little put off because he knows so many people I know, and all connected with work. I know it's ridiculous, but it embarrasses me."

We left the restaurant without having exactly decided what we were going to do next, but the responsibility had tacitly fallen on Jeremy, because he was more or less a native. More subtly, our desire for him, never expressed but perfectly obvious, no doubt put us in a dependent position, making him absolute master of the situation. It was actually a little irritating.

Tony suggested going to a bar whose name I've forgotten, in Haight-Ashbury. Yes, we could do that, according to Jeremy, but he had another idea, something much more typically San Francisco: in his opinion, we should go to the hot tubs.
"What's that?"
"It's like the baths, but individual."
"Everyone has his own?"
"Yes, well, several of us can share. You rent a room for an hour, and each room has a shower, a dry sauna, a hot bath, and a bed to lie down on. It's all very healthy, very good for you. I love it. You'll see."

I was completely for it, Tony a little less so, but he quickly came round. The hot tubs weren't very far from the restaurant, but we had wandered around some, while making up our minds.

It was just off Market Street. The establishment took up, I think, only one floor, and was recessed from the street, down some steps. In a huge room two or three couples waited—all men and women, a businessman and his secretary, for instance, or young lovers. Jeremy asked—smiling, as was his custom—for a room for three. He was told—also with a smile—that we would have to wait a little while, but it wouldn't be long, rooms for three were less in demand than rooms for two. We were each given a big white towel.

When our room was free and ready, a bath boy came and led us down a long, silent hallway. The bed was to the left—enormous. To the right was a round, raised cauldron set into a plank platform, the hot water pumped in very rapidly by several feverish pipes. Then the shower, and at the back, behind a glass door, the dry sauna.

No sooner had we come in than Tony discovered he had to go to the toilet. He left our room. Jeremy and I undressed and took a shower. He got into the tub first, then I joined him, facing him, leaning on my elbows, as he was. Our feet were touching. I was still not quite sure of his intentions, at least until our legs floated together, caressing each other in the very hot water. It was with my big toe that I discovered he had an erection. Without taking our shoulders from the rim of the tub, we moved closer, the way the hands of a watch do between twelve-thirty and five to one. The water floated our arms toward each other's bodies. I touched his cock and began to play with it. He touched mine. We kissed. I was very shy but also very turned on.

Tony came back into the room. He didn't seem at all surprised by this turn of events. He undressed and joined us. We embraced each other, caressed by the water as well. Our three tongues mingled.

After about ten minutes, Jeremy said that we shouldn't stay in too long, and he climbed out. He stretched out on the planks. Tony, still in the tub, sucked his cock. I went into the little sauna. Quite soon, Jeremy came in too. I sucked his cock, he sucked mine. He was still smiling, as if all this could just as well be taken as a good joke.

230

Jeremy and I came out of the dry sauna a little after Tony came in, and we stretched out on the bed. Our bodies were warm, we kissed, and took each other in our arms. His gestures were slow, languid, lascivious. Nothing abrupt, nothing hurried.

Tony came and lay down beside us. He sucked Jeremy's cock, Jeremy sucked mine, and I sucked Tony's. But apparently Jeremy preferred simpler frolics. We began kissing each other again. I was lying on top of him. Tony was on top of me, and getting ready to fuck me. But suddenly, to my complete surprise, Jeremy came against my belly with a long sigh. Almost immediately afterward, without changing position, I came against his. "No!" Tony exclaimed, "what quitters!" Jeremy kissed him, I played with his cock, and that's how he came, two or three minutes later.

All three of us took showers. Our time had just about run out, the warning bell had already rung. I was ready first, and I went to tell the man at the desk that the others would be coming right away.

Tony was still up for going somewhere and dancing. Jeremy and I in unison protested against this. We could scarcely stand on our feet. A healthy fatigue, no doubt, but we weren't in a state to face the Haight-Ashbury discos. Besides, Jeremy had to get up early, he was going to the gym first thing in the morning. Then he and Tony discovered a desire they shared for a certain cocktail whose name I can't remember, like so many others. Jeremy knew a bar where they made good ones, and anyway it was on the way to our place, where he had proposed to take us later, and not far from his, either.

This bar had a Greek name, I think, which matched its general appearance, and a terrace with pale green walls, set back from a very quiet street. But it was closing time, and we were the last customers. At one in the morning, it was no longer possible to obtain the desired cocktail; we had to be satisfied with three small bottles of Perrier. We were very thirsty, and Perrier was just the right thing. We must have talked about the absolute and lightninglike conquest that Perrier had made of the States: it was a conversation I remember taking part in, at one level or another, about ten times that summer. How much money one could have made if only one had thought of it sooner! There must be other French products that would work wonders on the American market! But was it the water that was imported or the gas? In any case, not both. And exactly what was Poland water, the main rival? According to some rumors, there were very complicated links between the two companies, the son of Perrier's director for America was the director of Poland Water, or something like that, etc.

When we left the bar, Jeremy had still another proposition to make:

"Have you been to Coit Tower yet?"

"No, never right up to it. We've only seen it from a distance."

"You want to go? It's right close by."

"But I thought you had to get up so early tomorrow."

"I do, but it's just five minutes away. You'll see. It's beautiful at night."

Coit Tower is that emphatically phallic structure which overlooks the Golden Gate on the bay side, to the northeast of the peninsula. The stories about it are contradictory, and I've never heard two San Franciscans offer quite the same version. One thing that's certain is that this tower was the gift of a local woman between the wars, and that its name is that of the donor. According to some, Miss Coit was a rich old maid eager to immortalize her patronymic. According to others, though there's nothing incompatible in the story, she was a passionate admirer of the fire department, and wanted to raise this monument to its glory. Or else Mrs. Coit was the widow of the fire chief, and it was to perpetuate her husband's memory that she commissioned this tower in its fireplug form. This last was Jeremy's thesis.

Coit Tower stands at the top of a rather steep hill. It is surrounded by a semicircular terrace and a low wall. We arrived at this terrace to find a huge black Cadillac parked with its doors wide open, emitting the smell of hash and the sound of extremely violent disco music. The light inside the car was on. A black man and woman of about thirty, each dressed in extremely loud clothes, like a burlesque pimp and his protegée, were silently passing a joint back and forth. There was another car parked but its lights were off, and we couldn't see its inhabitants.

The three of us walked on the little wall, Indian file.

"What's that island to the right?"

"Treasure Island. That's where the World's Fair was, in '39."

"And there. That dark shadow. That's Alcatraz?"

"Yes."

"And that dark shape over there, where there are no lights at all, to the right of Sausalito?"

"That's Angel's Island."

"No houses?"

"No. Oh, maybe the guard's. It's a kind of park, where people go for picnics on Sunday. You can't spend the night there. Here, I'll show you the murals."

He led us to the foot of the tower. To the west, south and east, huge bay windows with chromium frames, in the purest Art Deco style, revealed an empty, illuminated room, decorated with bright colored frescos showing men at work, vaguely in the manner of Siqueiros.

"Nice, aren't they?"

"Yes, very nice."

"I like them a lot."

I couldn't tell how serious he was:

"Not really my thing."

We stayed on the terrace a moment, in the chilly wind which had risen, our arms around each other's shoulders, our eyes on the city or the bay.

The music coming from the car was a little disturbing.

"Why don't you go over and ask them to turn it down some?"

"Thanks. I have no desire to end up with a knife in my back: *Murder at Coit Tower.*"

"It would probably sell."

Taking us back toward Pacific Heights and Lafayette Park, Jeremy showed us his house, on Russian Hill. He was full of plans for the next day:

"You know what we ought to do? We ought to leave town and go to the beach at Devil's Slide—would you like to do that?"

"Sure!"

"I'll come for you around nine, after my gym, OK?"

"Ooooh . . . Would ten be all right?"

"Yes, fine."

"Wait, I have to take our car back to *Budget* tomorrow. I'm supposed to turn it in during the afternoon, but the morning would do, of course. Could you pick up Tony at the house, and me at the garage, on Geary Street?"

"Sure. Give me the address."

"At ten-fifteen, ten-twenty?"

"OK. Good night, kids."

"Till tomorrow."

We all kissed each other. Jeremy was still laughing. At a distance, through the window of his car, he made another broad wave with his arm.

[*The next day, then, all three of us went to Edun Beach, and spent a fine time together. The following day, Tony and I left for Los Angeles, where Jeremy joined us at the end of the week. But his short stay was a little disappointing. He was embarrassed, he said, to make love with Tony and me at the same time. We had another friend with us who of course flung himself almost immediately into his arms.*

Afterward, we exchanged two or three letters and photographs taken that summer. He lives alone now, and one of the rooms in his apartment is, he writes, waiting for me, whenever I want to use it. I often think about him.]

[*September 1980: Seen him again, last summer. Made love with him again. We are great friends.*]

234

XXIV

A PERFECT FUCK

Sunday, August 20, 1978

And seek forever more
The soul's impossible bliss
                    —Gide

We had been given cocaine, we had had an excellent dinner without eating too much, and we were in a very good mood. This was the first time I had gone to *8709*, a baths in Los Angeles which Tony had already visited, and about which he had had a lot of good things to say. He seemed to have trouble remembering, though, the particularly complex arrangement of the premises.

We had barely undressed and hardly begun to explore, when, quite by accident, we happened to find ourselves in the *maze*, as it is called. I have always enjoyed large establishments with their innumerable and complicated corridors, their infinite honeycombs, where new detours, new perspectives, new doors keep presenting themselves, so that you never know, at least on your first visit, whether or not you've already been in this or that place. Constantly disoriented and lost, you never quite feel that you've discovered all the possibilities. But that such emporia, labyrinthine in essence, should further contain in their midst a real labyrinth, expressly conceived as such—that, in the state I was in, was enchantment itself. There, between the dark mirrored walls, in almost total obscurity, the most symbolic figures of myth and literature merged wildly and grotesquely in my excited imagination, their bizarre and absurd combinations a source of intoxication and delight.

Tony was next to me. We were holding each other's arm, advancing slowly, groping against the glass walls. I don't know which of the two of us happened to first put his hand, by accident, on this body. Someone was standing in the shadows—a boy completely naked, without even the ritual bath towel around his waist. A boy about my height, very well built, muscular, with some hair on his well-formed chest, and more on his forearms, his ass and his thighs. He was motionless, leaning against the wall. He had a hard-on. His hair was short, he had a moustache, but we couldn't tell anything about his face except that he was young, and his skin smooth, taut, and cool. Tony kissed him. I knelt in front of him and took his cock in my mouth.

As I've already said, we had just arrived; I had never been in this place, and this boy was the first we had encountered. Now, judging by the contact of our bodies, he was everything I liked. How could I help supposing, delightfully stoned as I was, that every corner of the maze, and the whole *8709*, was full of hundreds of boys like him, as sexy and as welcoming, the fulfillment of the kind of California dream one has in Paris bedrooms in winter, a dream of a place where each and every body is splendid and accessible? This would have incited me to continue, to advance, to touch at random so many chests, so many faces, so many cocks, to multiply so many precarious embraces. But no: the others would still be there, and since the first one was perfect, he represented them all.

Especially when he abandoned his role as a statue. While I was still sucking his cock, he held some poppers under my nose, and then handed them to Tony, and inhaled them himself. Tony knelt down beside me. We kissed each other, passing the Invisible Man's cock between us. But then he knelt down too, put his arms around our shoulders, and the three of us kissed each other. Then we lay down on the carpet between the mirrors, where nothing could be seen except our watery dim shadows. We were probably at one of the dead ends of the maze, because no one tried to step over our interlacing bodies. Unless all this happened very fast, for I no longer had the slightest notion of time. But I don't think so. We kissed each other, licked each other's nipples, sucked each other's cocks, thrust our tongues into each other's assholes. Nothing was abrupt or jerky: we shifted from one figure to another by gradual stages, and in any case we were each constantly engaged in several pleasures at once, which neither began nor ended at the

236

same time. The only regular interruptions were for the circulation of the poppers—the good yellow American poppers, in ampules you break within their envelope of cotton gauze, and which don't smell bad at all. They did not make us frenzied but diligent, almost laborious, each attentive to everyone else's sensations as well as to his own. The cocaine, too, was not the kind that sometimes keeps you from getting an erection. On the contrary, I felt absolutely light. All the heaviness in my body was in my cock.

The Invisible Man tipped Tony over onto his back, raised his thighs and for a long time licked his ass, while behind him, I licked his. Then, kneeling, he fucked Tony. He was kissing him. And I fucked the ass of the fucker.

What I should like to be able to do—I was already thinking of it at the time, and it was my only regret then, knowing that I could never succeed—is to describe precisely the sensations I was experiencing when my cock penetrated that ass. At each second they were different, and yet they all had the same, almost intolerable acuity of pleasure. First of all, there was the delicious irritation at the narrowness of the passage, and the faint, suggested, evaded pain. Then the squeezing pressure of the penetration, like a ring sliding slowly over taut skin, stretching it backward, slowly moving the whole length of my cock to settle at its base, just above the balls, and from there radiating all over, as far as the tip, now deep within the warm, velvety spacious cavities, too spacious, though it was always possible to return by a simple withdrawal, to the narrowness of the passage, and start all over again. The sensations of pleasure alternated in dazed and self-perpetuating delirium. For delirium it was, but calm and mastered. No threat of an involuntary orgasm.

The other two seemed to be in a similar state of beatitude. When I penetrated his ass, the Invisible Man raised his torso and hollowed his hips. Then he went on kissing Tony, and I was kissing both of them. With my right hand, I was caressing his chest and belly, marvelling at their solidity, at the roughness of their muscles, and with my left I was playing with Tony's cock,

237

which had so often been in my ass and which, in my mind, at least, and in my memory, closed the circle of my sensations.

I have spoken of pleasure, but I don't see what economy would keep me from calling such moments happiness, and precisely because they are so precarious. We assume, experiencing them, that their perfection is a conclusion, that there is nothing else to be sought, that it is *this* which had to be known. But they merely send us *back* to the search, for how can we not desire, afterward, to encounter similar moments once again, even if only once more?

There was a pause for a final exchange of poppers, and a few *ritardandos*, to make sure of the perfect concordance of rhythms. And then all three of us came at the same time, with gasps which echoed in the irregular corners of the mirrored maze.

We remained lying there a moment, stretched out almost unconscious. The Invisible Man got up first. He made a strange noise with his mouth, a kind of two-speed whistle, a funny sound which seemed to mean something like *that was really something!* He gave us each a tap on the shoulder, then went away without saying a word. I glimpsed his face as he passed for a second through a zone of light. He seemed to be very handsome.

Tony and I stayed a long time at 8709 that night, and we went back to it three days in a row, in the hope of renewing this experience. There were other pleasures, but none that were comparable.

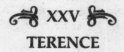

XXV

TERENCE

Monday, August 28, 1978

It was our first night in Washington on this trip. I don't remember where we had had dinner. Perhaps at Nora's, with whom we were staying in Arlington, or maybe in some restaurant in Georgetown.

Nor do I even remember if I had already been to *Mr. P.,* a bar on P Street. It's true that there is nothing very memorable about it. After the bars in New York and especially those of the West Coast, it seemed provincial and even a little Parisian. Nothing here of the triumphant serenity of the Californian fags, one community among others, and less of a minority than some. Here, once again, we were among the furtive, the repressed, and the barely tolerated.

Moreover, at first glance there was no one who interested me physically; whence, perhaps, the preceding bit of pessimistic theorizing.

From the street you walk into a first rather narrow and long room, in which boys are standing, quite densely packed in. To the left, about halfway down the wall, a passageway leads into a second room of about the same dimensions. The bar is to the right. There's a tiny floor opposite it for dancing, and to the left a window opens onto the street.

Tony and Nora headed for the bar but I didn't want anything to drink. There were no more than twenty people dancing, among them, a rather delicate Parisian flanked by a colossal black man. I had already seen the Parisian in New York last July, and then too he was with a black man, also built like a brick shithouse, as the phrase goes.

In the second room, the corner near the window has the feeling of a refuge. This was the only place that wasn't crowded that night. A few couples were there, kissing, some exhausted dancers catching their breath, one or two others. Among them, a black who immediately struck me as by far the handsomest boy in the place.

He had nothing in common with the Parisian's two friends. Moreover, if two examples are enough to construct a typology of tastes, the Parisian wouldn't have paid the slightest attention to him. He was in fact standing quite close to him and did not even look at him. Anyone particularly attracted by blacks in general

239

would not have been especially turned on by this one, since except for his very dark skin and rather kinky hair, he possessed none of the features traditionally attributed to his race. He had an aquiline nose, thin lips, very fine features, and a very thick moustache.

He was rather tall and broad-shouldered, but not at all massively built. His hands were long and delicate. He had a striking physical elegance, and he was dressed accordingly: jeans and a white shirt.

There was a banquette under the window and a table in front of it, on which he was sitting. I sat on the banquette. It seemed to me that he had noticed me, was looking at me now and then. We even exchanged a smile. Two boys came over and sat down to my right; I decided they needed room, so I moved and sat down on the table, beside the black boy. Then it was he who made the next step, but I don't remember what it was. No doubt we smiled at each other again. Maybe he put his left hand on my right thigh, and turned toward me:

"Hi! My name's Terence."

"Hello. Mine is Renaud."

Etc.: Wono, Frenchman, on vacation, how long have you been in Washington? He went away, offering to bring me something from the bar, but was soon back and sat down beside me again. I had to leave him myself, to see what had become of Nora and Tony. They had danced a little, but they were bored and wanted to leave. Moreover, they had noticed my connection with Terence, whom Tony found very handsome:

"Ask him if he'd like to go somewhere else with us, or if he knows another bar that's more fun."

Here various complications emerged: Terence didn't live in Washington, but in Annapolis. He had come in a friend's car, and so he would have to go home with him. "Unless," he added very timidly, and after some hesitation, "unless I could sleep at your place." On the one hand, I was also with a friend, and on the other we were staying with the girl he saw over there, Nora. Nora had a tiny apartment in Arlington. She had given Tony and me her room and her double bed, and was planning to sleep on the couch

240

in the living room. First of all, I had to propose to Terence that he sleep in the same bed with Tony and me, which did not offer difficulties, and then ask Nora if we could ask Terence back with us, a much more delicate question. Nora, as a matter of fact, was first of all a friend of Tony's, a childhood friend, and so I myself was in her house only by extension, so to speak. Even if she had long since had her ideas about the nature of the relationship between Tony and me, and about our sexual tastes, there had never been any explicit discussion of the matter between us, except very recently. She had taken it all very calmly, and even manifested an indubitable curiosity about this kind of life. It was she, after all, who had wanted to go to *Mr P.*, where there were only two or three girls, whereas we could easily have taken her to any straight bar. But to invite a third person with us, and on the first night? And there was a final point, which rather amused me. Nora belonged to an old Southern family; her parents had a plantation in Georgia. She was adjusting very easily to the notion that we had homosexual relations, but interracial? Her mother would have died of apoplexy if she had brought home a black friend, let alone a black fiancé. Such a thing was inconceivable.

Discreetly I plied back and forth through the crowd, between Terence on the one side and Tony and Nora on the other. Nora was splendid: she saw no problem of any kind whatever. On the contrary, he looks very sweet, he's very handsome, and I'm sure he can take us to some place much more fun than here. It was actually Terence who hesitated. But this was timidity and discretion, I think, and extreme *politesse*. Finally he agreed, if I was sure, but absolutely sure that he wouldn't be in anyone's way.

Tony came to look for us as we were interrupting our deliberations with a kiss. He was laughing:

"Come on, make up your minds, you two."

I introduced them all to each other. Terence said good-bye to his friend, a very macho short black boy, an entirely different type, and the four of us left, all in Nora's car. We passed joints back and forth. Yes, Terence knew another bar, one called *Exile*, and he was sure we would enjoy it more.

It was a Monday night, it was probably quite late, and there weren't many people at *Exile,* many fewer than at *Mr. P.* But the rooms were more spacious, and the boys better looking. There was one, in particular, playing pool, shirtless, who turned me on a great deal. But the arrangements for the night had been made.

I danced with Terence, he danced with Tony, with Nora; we danced together, all four of us. At the end, we were practically the only ones on the floor. I was the first to suggest that we leave. I was exhausted.

In the car heading toward Arlington, I sat in back with Terence, my head against his shoulder. He was wide awake, though a little stoned. He was talking about the various bars in town.

At Nora's, she suggested we have a nightcap. We were all four around a low table. The whole thing seemed to evolve into a cocktail party. I think Nora was delighted with the way things had turned out; she radiated kindness and hospitality, to which Terence responded with the same warmth. They made it a point of honor, as did Tony, to surmount everything that might separate them, which is to say almost everything. And they succeeded splendidly, thanks to their individual characters, courteous and expansive, to the natural friendliness of Americans—and certainly to the joints. More than once, though, it seemed to me that the conversation touched on very dangerous ground. Nora was talking quite freely about the blacks who worked for her father. With perfect imitations of each voice, she told about them, about the racist whites of the town, and about her family, stories which made the three of them scream with laughter, while I would usually miss the point altogether. Tony had his stories to tell, as well, and Terence wasn't to be left out. His parents had come from Carolina. The close Southern family feeling that had so quickly established itself among them seemed to me ideologically precarious, but I attributed my nervousness about it to my own anxious nature. In any event, it must have been three or four in the morning, and I was eager to get to bed.

This was a little difficult, under the circumstances. But, since the three of them were now so intimate, I allowed myself to withdraw in the direction of the bathroom. When I got to the bedroom which had been assigned to us, Terence came to join me there, followed by Tony:

"The two of you go to bed. I should stay with Nora a while longer; it's only fair especially since she's very high. She's telling a lot of funny stories."

Terence and I went in to say goodnight to Nora, then we undressed and went to bed. Tony remained with her awhile. We could hear them both laughing like mad.

Terence's body was an anatomy lesson. His skin was very fine. Under it you could see each of his muscles, clearly articulated, admirably distinct. None save those of his buttocks and his thighs was particularly developed and prominent, but all were readily observable and incredibly hard. His stomach was especially remarkable. It displayed a rigorous grid, very detailed, which was divided by a line of very soft hairs that rose toward his chest, spreading out there in a palm leaf design. The buttocks and thighs were those of a dancer, powerful and bulging.

It was obvious from the start that we would get along extremely well. For him as for me, the intensity of contact was much more important than any specific sexual position or practice. Our mouths remained endlessly glued together, our tongues mingling, our hands were clasped behind each other's necks. Our legs intertwined to keep us riveted together. We were rolling across the bed over and over each other. His cock was very large as were his balls. I sucked him, he sucked me; I licked his ass, he licked mine; we fucked each other, but I didn't want to come before Tony joined us. When he did, we were lying together, sweating and still kissing each other.

Tony undressed, knelt at the foot of the bed and took Terence's cock in his mouth. Terence leaned down to take Tony's cock in

243

his mouth at the same time. I kissed Tony over Terence's cock, which we passed to each other, back and forth.

As for what followed, the details escape me. Oh! I know that Tony fucked Terence, that he came very quickly, and that he was furious with himself for doing so. He must have been completely exhausted, because he fell asleep immediately afterward. In turn, I fucked Terence, but at much greater length, and waited to come until he came too, playing with himself as he lay on his back, legs in the air. I was still so turned on afterward that I licked up the white sperm that had spread over the beautiful grid of his stomach.

Nora had fallen asleep, leaving the music on at top volume. I went in to turn off the machine. In the morning, between eight and nine, she came in our room, which is to say, her room, to get some clothes out of the closet. It was very warm, we had pushed off all the sheets, our bodies were incredibly tangled. I remember opening one eye. She walked through quite calmly. And we slept until two in the afternoon.

Tony, Nora, and I had in fact had a fine dinner at Nora's the night before, so when we got up we were able to put together a very passable brunch out of leftovers. Terence ate virtually nothing—it is probably on such a diet that one acquires and preserves the kind of body he had. I no longer remember how old he was. Twenty-five, perhaps. I think I was surprised by his youth.

Tony wanted to go see some seventeenth-century French paintings in Georgetown at the house of a collector who was also something of a dealer. Terence and I accompanied him in the car we had rented at the airport. The collector wasn't at home, but had left instructions that we be shown the paintings.

I was afraid that Terence would have only the vaguest interest in canvases by Patel, Lemaire, Mellin, or some pseudo-Poussin or other. But he seemed full of curiosity and examined them all, one by one, with great care and much enthusiasm. Nonetheless, when Tony went on to the engravings, I decided it would be better to do something else for a while. Besides, I wanted to walk around

Georgetown, which I like a lot. We told Tony we would come back for him in a half or three-quarters of an hour, and we left the building.

It was stifling outside, a tropical day. Not a breath of air. Yet we walked from the main street of Georgetown, whose name escapes me again (it's the name of a state), all the way down P Street to a rather steep incline which marks the limit of the district. We walked side by side between the old brick houses, much more evocative of Henry James than the unfortunate witnesses of the period remaining in New York, if not in Boston. And then we had a long conversation. I remember the tone, the sentiments of trust and affection which were growing between us, Terence's sweetness and timidity, his desire to adopt immediately whatever opinions I was expressing, even to emphasize them, but I don't remember at all what we were talking about, except for the houses. I was wondering if each one was inhabited by a single family, even today, or if they were divided up into apartments. He didn't know. From time to time he pointed out one or two that he wanted me to notice particularly. These were usually not the oldest, nor the prettiest, but the most elaborate. He had the greatest respect for the people who lived in them. They were all, he said, people of the best families.

We reached a park. It was here that he told me a little about himself. He said that he was the night manager of an ice cream parlor in Annapolis. He was on vacation this week, but usually he couldn't go out evenings. He came to Washington only on weekends, always with the same friend, the one we had seen the night before. He shared an apartment with another friend, an ex-lover, but there was nothing between them any longer. He was hoping to be able to move soon.

In the middle of the green lawn in front of us, a white man about thirty, maybe a little older, bare-chested and in shorts, was doing exercises. His whole body was streaming with sweat. He had enormous muscles all over. Terence stared at him with a dreamy expression:

"That's how I'd like to be . . ."

245

"No, you're crazy. Besides, if you were like that, you'd be much too intimidating. I find you intimidating enough as it is."

"You're the one who's intimidating."

To tell the truth, I confess to having a little theory about Terence. He was the most ardently integrationist black I met in America. Although he could have gone to the exclusively black and gay bars that exist in Washington, he preferred *Mr. P.* or *Exile*, which are almost exclusively white. But among whites he had his preferences. Tony and Nora, liberal upper-middle-class types, had immediately attracted him. As for me, I offered a still greater advantage; I was a foreigner, a Frenchman, and I escaped—and he with me, and our relations as well—all the racial codes he knew. Of course, he wouldn't have put it this way, and no doubt he wasn't conscious of the procedure I am attributing to him: but what he wanted, as I saw it, was to get out of a certain discourse, and of the part it assigned to him.

This attitude of Terence's was questionable, perhaps, from a political or racial point of view. But it was not inspired by anything like calculation or ambition or even snobbery. He merely desired a better life for himself, a richer, more exotic, more interesting, less predetermined life. He was tired of being a black the same way one can be tired of being a homosexual: neither whites nor straights ever dream of defining themselves as such.

From the park, we set out in another direction, this time down N Street. On two occasions Terence was accosted by blacks; one was handing out leaflets and the other was a kind of crazed beggar who called him "brother." Terence seemed to apologize for these episodes and to ignore why it was that these men addressed themselves to him rather than to me.

We returned to Tony, who was very worn out by the heat, as were we. I had thought of driving around in the car to see the monuments, since we were leaving the next day, but I gave it up. We decided to go back to Nora's. We didn't sleep or make love, but we stayed there for two hours, exhausted, drinking, looking through magazines, listening to records.

246

Tony and I were to have dinner that night with two French friends. One was a young diplomat who had just been appointed to Washington, some branch of an international organization, and the other boy, with whom he had lived in Paris, was a young doctor who had come to Washington to spend his vacation with his friend. It was already agreed that Nora would join us, and we invited Terence to do the same. But again he was afraid of imposing, of getting in the way, and we had to insist a great deal before he would accept. Also he was afraid of not being appropriately dressed. Plus his shirt was dirty, he said. That didn't matter, we could lend him one. But later he would have to find his friend from the night before so he could get back to Annapolis. The friend would be at *Exile* later. We could stop by there after dinner.

So all of us went to François' place. He had been assigned an official apartment in a sumptuous building with an imposing door-man, which amused me a good deal when I recalled his former existence in less opulent circumstances. Terence was quite awed.

The apartment itself was almost empty. We had a drink there, talking about François' new life, and about the various restaurants we might go to. François knew one, quite close by, which was set up in the house of Ulysses S. Grant, a notion I found quite appealing. This was the restaurant we decided on, and all six of us walked to it.

François and Jean-Paul had informed me by various signs, and a few words in French, that they were quite curious about Terence, whom they found very much to their tastes. Nora was entirely at ease with these five men, and seemed to be having a splendid time.

The restaurant was in a huge townhouse more or less contemporary with Grant's presidency, but bearing otherwise little relation to him. There had been some confusion somewhere, unless François, absolutely determined to eat there and knowing my taste for historical associations, had invented this story to convince me. There were a lot of people and we had to wait, which we did while drinking some white California wine. The dining room was very high ceilinged, and of a formal character rarely linked, in the minds of foreigners, with the United States. I've entirely forgotten what we talked about, except that François, Jean-Paul, and I kept giggling hysterically at having, on account of Terence, to talk English to each other, which had never happened before. Terence didn't say much, but seemed quite happy.

Then François took us to a bar he was very enthusiastic about, near the docks. This was a neighborhood of very picturesque, abandoned, half-ruined streets full of clumps of weeds. The enormous illuminated mass of the Capital, looming overhead, gave it a still more fanciful, artificial quality, a Hitchcockian aspect. But the bar itself wasn't very interesting. Tuesday, Francois remarked, wasn't a good day. We soon decided to return to *Exile*.

We had come in two cars. To go back, the arrangements were changed: I ended up alone with Jean-Paul, who didn't know Washington much better than I. Both of us were quite stoned, we didn't have the address of *Exile*, to which I had been driven the night before without paying much attention to the way, and the others had not waited for us. We wandered around for about an hour along endless avenues, all just alike, which we passed in alphabetical order. And, we had just about abandoned hope when we happened to find ourselves in front of the door of *Exile*. Tony, Nora, and François, however, hadn't given us a thought. They were dancing. Only Terence was standing near the door, with a worried look on his face. But when he was reassured about our fate, he became radiantly energetic. The night before he had danced with me, suiting his movements to my manner, which is to say he danced badly. This time he let himself go. Only Nora could claim to follow him. So they danced together most of the time, with a mastery which became something of a demonstration. Everyone formed an admiring circle around them.

Terence's friend was there, and seemed amused by his friend's new acquaintances. Anyway, he had some engine trouble and he couldn't take the car back to Annapolis—he would be spending the night in Washington with friends. These friends could also put Terence up, but probably he would prefer to stay with us?

Terence seemed embarrassed by this question, but Nora, Tony, and I again urged him to spend the night with us.

"But you're leaving tomorrow, I'll just be in your way."

"No, I think we'll stay an extra day. We still haven't seen the new wing of the National Gallery, and after all, that was why we came—theoretically, at least."

"You're sure I won't be in your way?"

"We're dying to have you! Besides, you left your shirt at Nora's."

"Oh yes, and I have to give you this one back . . . All right, if you're sure."

So the four of us found ourselves together once again in the Arlington apartment. But this time it was much later still, Nora was dying of exhaustion, and Tony wanted to get up early enough to go to the Library of Congress. So we went right to bed. Tony, Terence, and I made love, but I have only two recollections of the occasion. When I was fucking Terence he kept saying "baby, oh baby, baby . . ." and he fucked me while Tony was fucking him. I don't know if it was in this arrangement that we all came.

Terence and I slept till one in the afternoon. We were awakened by the friend from Annapolis, to whom we had given Nora's number, and who announced that the car was now fixed: it was at Terence's disposal if he wanted to go home now. We made love once more, very slowly, very tenderly, face to face, without penetration, and came at the same time, our cocks against each other. Then while we were eating a little breakfast on the floor, completely naked, an old black man came into the apartment. This was the super of the building. He had a key, and he had come to regulate the air conditioner. I was quite ruffled, but he was very calm and explained his business in a jargon so incomprehensible to me that Terence had to handle the conversation. He rose to accompany the super to the machine. It was only when he came back that he put a towel around his hips.

I drove Terence to the address his friend had given him. The hood of their car was up, and the friend was still rummaging in the engine, but according to him everything was now in working order. They would drive back to Annapolis together. Terence kissed me several times. He seemed very moved.

[*Subsequently received two long telephone calls from him, one at three in the morning because he hadn't figured out the time difference properly. He would like to come to Paris, but doesn't have the money. I wrote him. He is waiting for my next visit.*]

TRANSLATOR'S NOTE

Over twenty years ago, I wrote: "It is more difficult to translate French texts dealing with pornographic subjects and low life than anything else. The French have developed a middle language somewhere between the smell of the sewer and the smell of the lamp, which in English is mostly unavailable. We have either the coarse or the very clinical, and I do not see how we can produce an English version of a masterpiece like *Histoire d'O* until we work up a language as pure and precise—though as suggestive and colorful—as that of Pauline Réage, whose French, for all the scabrous horror of her subject, is among the finest of the century." Only a very young or a very naive young man could have supposed it was possible so rapidly to "work up a language"—as if a language were no more than an emotion or an erection—and indeed the subsequent translation of *Story of O* in the following decade rather proved his point *a contrario:* direct dealings with high pornography tend—I am referring to *linguistic* transactions—to lower the tone, to reduce the patina, to falsify the tempo.

Why should this be so? Perhaps the American version of *Tricks* (so-called in the original—the French do not have it all their own way) will suggest an answer. Not that I want to apologize for my text, which must stand on its own merits and fall on its defects, nor do I wish to intervene between the reader and Renaud Camus, who sounds, I am certain, a sufficiently idiosyncratic note to obviate any explanatory hocus-pocus on the part of his hard-driven translator. But these twenty-five *relations* do give us an indication of the problems all good writing about sex must contend with, in translation. The French words for sexual parts—and this is what I think I was trying to say, back in the censorable fifties—are not metaphorical, or at least they are *immediate metaphors:* to call the penis a *verge* (rod, staff, as in our word *verger*, who carries the rod or wand of office) is still within easy reach of the most modest associative capacity. But to call it a *cock* is to invoke an entire range of imagery outside the immediate concern (unless we are talking about chickens). Almost every English word at the colloquial level for the sexual parts, male and female, is thus extravagantly metaphorical, even—am I stretching it?—poetic. I believe that our Anglo-American uneasiness, in the upper-middle class, about the words for sexual parts, and even for the unexposed corners of the body likely to become the focus or the fetish of sexual attention, is entirely characteristic of a certain social problematic. Perhaps the jitters are always responsible for metaphorical treatment; perhaps we always use *other words* when we are afraid. This differentiates us from French literary culture, which has here—and indeed traditionally so—the advantage. "They order these things better in France," Sterne claimed, and is this not how they ordered them? Called a spade a spade, and a penis a penis, when we who use English are "happy to say," like Cecily in Wilde's play, "that we have never seen a spade: it is obvious that our social spheres have been widely different."

And there are minor difficulties (though it is always minor points which constitute the major claims of writing to be literature). English has not separate names for the hair growing on the head and the hair growing elsewhere on the body. Of course we supply the lack by adjectives, but the simplicity of that *poil / cheveu* opposition escapes us. To conceal such discrepancies is any translator's business, and I am not offering excuses, I think, when I note that writing about sex explores the genius of a language in its most intimate recesses, its most subtle emergencies. All that is not mere sociology, all that is not mere exploitive eroticism, is what tends to fall between the medical and the foul-mouthed. And surely it is not just wringing one's hands in public (though considering what is done these days in public . . .) to point out that we have not, in English, even a simple verb for "getting an erection" unless we resort, again, to metaphorical equivalents of dubious charm.

No matter: the translation attempts to offer a clear view into Renaud Camus's drastic world, and though I no longer believe we can work our way up to the proper expression straightaway, perhaps this book affords one more occasion to make the effort, to round the corner, to fill the gap—if you see what I mean.

Richard Howard

252